Haunting Refrain

Ellis Vidler

SILVER DAGGER

M Y S T E R I E S

An Imprint of
The Overmountain Press
JOHNSON CITY, TENNESSEE

To Helen Duke Johnston
—I love you, Mother

Acknowledgments

First, I want to thank Scott Regan—the most encouraging, inspiring, and giving of creative writing teachers. Without him, I would never have done this.

A special thanks to Cindy Hudson, for all her help and ideas.

And next, I must thank everyone who gave me the technical advice I asked for: the multitalented John Martin, musician, computer guru, and photographer; Detective Terry Christie of the Greenville Police Department; Shane Rogers of Scuba World; Ashley Martin, for her grace, beauty, and patience; Tim Jarrett of Wolf Camera; and my grandmother, Violet Duke, the real clairvoyant in my family. The mistakes in this book are entirely mine, whether through not asking the right questions or misunderstanding the answers; these kind people are in no way responsible.

To the wonderful crew at Silver Dagger Mysteries: Beth Wright, Sherry Lewis, Karin O'Brien, and all the others—thank you!

And always, Michael.

Chapter 1

IF SHE HAD KNOWN what it held, she would never have touched it the first time. Now it was too late. The simple sweatband, deceptively harmless, lay like a white asp on the desktop in front of her. Kate McGuire regarded it with loathing. When she had touched it, its secret sprang forth like some evil genie, overwhelming her with its force.

Coward. Do it. Pick it up again. The band was such a small thing, she told herself. Nothing.

She took a breath, stretched out her shaking hand, and grasped it. The vision slammed into her, instantly.

Hands, cold and hard, tightened around her throat, choking her. Long fingers encircled her neck, and fingernails cut into her flesh. Strong thumbs pressed into her windpipe, forced her head back. She clawed at them, tried to free herself. Blinded by the rain and the curtain of hair that covered her eyes, she couldn't see the face above her. She fought, desperate for air. Those powerful fingers squeezed harder. The world around her dimmed. She was dying. "Bitch, bitch!" The voice rang through her head, then faded.

Kate drifted out of the terror and into a deep sadness. Only the silence and the rain remained. Then, from a distance, she heard new voices calling her name. She became aware of hands, warm this time, tugging at her arm. She gasped, choking, struggling for air.

Professor Martin Carver, abandoning his role as an observer, pried the headband out of her locked hands, tossed it onto a chair. He grabbed her shoulders and shook her. "Kate! Kate!"

From a long way off she saw him, felt his hands. Her friend, Venice Ashburton, knelt on the other side of the desk, clasping Kate's arm and fanning her with a lacy handkerchief. "It's all right, dear. Let it go. It's over."

Through a white mist, Kate struggled slowly back to the present. The classroom swam into view, its familiar walls somehow comforting. She drew air in ragged gulps, fought to quell the queasy waves in her midsection. She blinked at the two elderly figures hovering over her. "I'm okay." The words came out in a hoarse whisper. She shuddered and touched her throat, still feeling the need for air. What had happened to her?

Martin patted Kate's shoulder. "Venice, would you get her a Coke?"

Venice started for the door, only to be brought up short by her purse. Martin automatically leaned over and unhooked the shoulder strap from the desk she'd been sitting in.

Kate sank into Martin's big chair. Her hat tumbled to the floor, loosing a mass of red hair. "You have to tell me who owns that headband."

"First you need to tell me what happened," Martin said, pushing the hair back from her pallid face. "I don't want anything to influence you before you describe what you saw. I'll tell you after that, I promise. That's why I couldn't tell you during the meeting. Wait for Venice."

He moved away and took a white index card from his pocket while Kate collected herself. Exhausted, she slumped in the chair, silently acknowledging the wisdom of his statement. She was glad he'd asked her to repeat the experiment after the others had gone.

Kate could tell from his hunched posture and the way he stared at the card that what he had to say wasn't good. She knew the card contained the data about the sweatband: the owner's name and physical description, any other pertinent information. As she watched, heaviness fell like a mantle over the professor, and he looked every one of his sixty-nine years. A knot formed in her stomach. What was on that card? Who did that damned thing belong to? Deep inside her, fear grew.

She drew inward, reaching for her inner calm, focused on putting this . . . this nightmare in perspective. The experiments had begun innocently enough. Venice had urged her to join Professor Carver's parapsychology group, urging her to get out and mix with other people. Kate found them nice enough—a few airheads, some with real psychic ability, though none matched Venice. Kate herself had always had little flashes of knowledge—nothing significant, just brief glimpses that passed through her mind. Intuition, she had claimed when she found her friends' car keys, her mother's earring. Or Venice's purse—although, she'd had a lot of practice at that.

Until an hour ago, Kate had considered herself a relatively normal woman—not much money, no love life, but her own person, pursuing her own goals. Generally pretty happy. But normal people did not have visions of murder. Neither did she, she insisted, at least not until tonight, when she'd picked up the headband.

Venice returned with a paper cup.

Martin took the Coke and held it to Kate's lips. "Come on, Kate. Drink this."

She took the sweet liquid with shaking hands, forced herself to sip. "Thank you, Venice."

When she felt able, Kate began recounting what she had experienced, making an effort to remove herself from the vision and be objective. "It was the same as before, only worse. Someone tried to strangle me. I felt these hands closing around my throat. Just squeezing tighter and tighter. He killed me—her."

"I'm sorry, Kate." Martin patted her hand. "I hoped it would be different this time. Can you describe it? What did you see?"

"Just . . . just hands around my throat. Choking me. Something covered my eyes, maybe hair." What else had she seen? What clouded her vision? Water? Tears? All she could think of was the terrible need for air.

"You didn't see anything at all?" Martin asked. "No one else?"

"It was the same as before. I *was* that girl. It was happening to me. The face above me was dark, blurred. I was only aware of the hands—I couldn't breathe. I have a terrible feeling of finality." She shivered, whispering, "I know she's dead, whoever she is."

Martin looked sick. "Do you have any feeling about the person who was strangling her? Was it someone she knows?"

"I think it was a man. I couldn't see, but I have an impression of size and strength that suggests a man. That's all. Please tell me what this is about."

"Only one more question. Could you tell what time of day it was?"

"What does that matter?" she asked. "It was dark. Night. Now, whose is it?"

He took a deep breath and held out the card. "The sweatband belongs to Kelly Landrum."

Kate reached for the card, trying to think where she had heard the name. "Kelly Landrum? Who's—"

"She's the girl who's missing!" Venice cried, catching the cup as it slipped from Kate's hands. She took a quick sip and choked.

Kate snatched the card, needed to see it for herself. She read the name. *Kelly Landrum.* A spot like a teardrop blurred the blue ink. *An omen? Please, don't let it be true.*

"Yes, she's the student who's been missing for four days." Martin kept his eyes on Kate's drawn face. "Her face is on every newspaper and television screen in South Carolina. Someone found her car here on the campus. The police have been all over the place since then. We should call them, Kate."

"No! I haven't seen anything that could help them, and I'm not touching that thing again." She retreated into the chair, pulled her knees up under her chin, and wrapped her skirt around her legs, holding herself tightly. If she didn't, she might fall apart—the image was so strong, so *immediate*. She touched her throat. And if it was true. . . .

Venice leaned forward and reached out, patting Kate's arm. "It's all right. Remember, whatever you see, it isn't happening to you." She turned to the professor. "Martin, you'll have to let me try." Venice's face was almost as white as Kate's, but her voice was calm. She looked at the crumpled band.

"All right, Venice, if you're sure." Martin looked back at Kate.

Torn, Kate watched her friend. Did she want Venice to go through it? Although Venice's theatrics often clouded the picture, Kate considered her truly clairvoyant. Venice might see something herself, or she might pick up Kate's vision, but either way, Kate would consider it a confirmation. She felt the hands tighten on her neck again, sucked in air.

"No, Venice. Don't do it." Kate blinked back tears. "It's terrible."

"I'm all right, Kate. I may not see anything at all." Venice sat down in a student desk and held out her hand. Martin handed her the band.

Venice closed her eyes and pressed the band to her forehead, rocking slightly in the chair. "The night is dark and quiet. I see patterns of light, perhaps reflections in a pool. Trees." She shivered. "I feel fear, a woman terribly afraid. The air is filled with menace— a presence, dark, angry, raging!"

Abruptly she straightened. The remaining color drained from her face. Her eyes widened, then rolled upward as she swayed like a reed in the wind.

Martin threw his arm around the stricken woman and snatched the headband from her hands, tossing it onto his desk.

Kate leapt from the chair and caught Venice's icy hands in her own. The three of them clung together for a minute until Venice took a deep breath and drew herself up. "It's all right—it's gone now. Is there any more of that drink?"

"I can't believe this is happening." Stifling a burst of hysterical laughter, Kate gave herself a mental shake and put the remaining Coca-Cola in Martin's outstretched hand.

Martin, none too steady himself, held the drink for Venice. "What did you see?"

"A lovely young woman with brown hair. Hands closing tightly around her throat." Venice shivered, touching the gold band at her neck. "'Bitch. Lying bitch.'" Frowning, she added, "I'm sure I heard the words over the roaring in my ears—a deep, grinding voice."

Kate rubbed her eyes. Why? Why was this happening to her? She wasn't psychic, just had a modest little ability to see things in her mind when she touched something—and even that wasn't reliable. And now this terrible vision. She felt as if she were the woman being strangled. "Venice is seeing it from the outside. I see it as if it's happening to me," she said.

"That's an interesting point. I'll have to record that in my journal." Martin brightened as he considered the new information and returned to the intellectual implications of the experiment.

Why this sudden, clear vision of murder? Kate wondered while the professor scribbled happily in his black notebook, the women momentarily forgotten. She had no connection to the missing girl. Nor had she ever had such a vivid experience. Nothing on this level.

"I wonder how Kate is receiving such a personal picture," Martin said, fingering the card in his pocket.

"Perhaps Kelly was in this classroom, or sat in this desk," Venice offered. "Maybe there's a stronger link than you're aware of, Kate."

Was I thinking out loud? Kate looked at the pair of them, startled to have them both reading her mind, although she should be used to it with Venice. Kate forced a smile, knowing Venice meant well in spite of her insatiable curiosity. The plump older woman always seemed to be slightly out of focus to Kate. She had a scarf or shawl trailing down her arm, bracelets tangled in her clothes, her hair askew—always something. But she had a good heart, and Kate could count on her.

They had been acquainted for ages but had only become friends during the last couple of years. Then last fall, Venice had become her first commission for a portrait in her new photography business. The picture had been outstanding, a great advertisement. Kate hadn't wanted to charge her, but Venice insisted on paying, making it official.

Looking at her now, Kate wondered how she had ever achieved such a haunting effect. Daffy, dear, kind—those were the words that came to mind, but Venice had been so pleased with the darkly enigmatic study. Noticing the older woman's struggle, Kate reached over to release Venice's bracelet from her shawl. Smiling briefly, Kate thought that with the portrait, she might have committed fraud instead of capturing the essence of the woman's soul, as Venice believed.

Kate leaned against the desk and thought about the portrait. It had gotten her into Martin Carver's parapsychology experiments.

The mysterious picture had somehow convinced Venice that Kate had psychic ability, and she had drawn the young woman into the professor's group. It had been fun until tonight.

"This is too much," Martin said, interrupting her thoughts. "We have to call the police. I don't know what any of this means, but that sweatband belongs to someone who's been missing for four days, and you're seeing something that could be important."

"No, please don't," Kate said. "I'm not a real psychic, and I don't want any part of this. They won't believe us anyway." She fished her hat out from under the desk where it had rolled, and brushed it off. Looking up, she dared them to contradict her. "I'm not touching that headband again. Not for anything!"

"But, dear," Venice said. "If we could help the police through our gifts—"

"You can help them with *your* gift, Venice, but leave me out of it. I am *not* psychic! Besides, how could this possibly help? The police already suspect something has happened to her." She jammed the hat on her head, glaring at the pair of them. "And no one had better mention my name in this. I'd probably lose my only serious clients—they'll think I'm crazy. Or worse. Don't forget, a significant portion of the people here in the Bible Belt do not look kindly on this sort of thing."

"There is nothing wrong with what we do." Venice tried to step away from the desk but was secured by the tangled fringe of her shawl. Tugging at the length of silk, she said, "Besides, we could use *my* name. I do give readings for people."

"Well, I don't. Leave me out of it." Kate crossed her arms over her chest, hunching her shoulders. The memory of cold fingers brushed across her neck. She didn't want any part of this.

Martin reached over and extricated Venice. "I can't help but feel you're right about Kelly. I hope I'm wrong." He turned to Kate. "Come on. I'll walk you and Venice to your cars."

"Thanks." Kate wanted to get home, but she was still shaken and didn't relish the idea of being responsible for Venice in the darkened parking lot. "The car—Kelly Landrum's. Where was it found?"

"Behind the library," Martin said, "where she was last seen on Friday night. The keys were still in the door."

"It would have been dark. That's why you wanted to know the time of day—to see if it fit," Kate said, digging out her car keys.

"Yes." Venice waved her hand skyward. "It was night, and the library is just over there, through those trees. That's what I saw— the trees at the back of the parking lot."

"I'll wait until tomorrow and think about it," Martin said, "but

I'm convinced we should report what you've seen. Meanwhile, don't say a word about this to anyone. Is that clear?" He looked pointedly at Venice, who rounded her eyes innocently.

"Yes, Martin."

Venice sounded unusually meek to Kate. "Venice," she said, "you won't call them, will you?"

The older woman turned to Kate. "I won't call the police. I promise. But you do realize there's a murderer out there, don't you, Kate?"

Kate accepted her promise but remained skeptical. Venice always managed to do things her way.

Chapter 2

JOHN GERRARD SCROLLED THROUGH a short article on his word processor and frowned as he prepared for the Sunday edition of the *Times Herald*. The Kelly Landrum case had dried up—the police hadn't come up with anything since finding the car. At least, nothing they were willing to talk about. And having just come from the police station where he had talked to Lynne Waite, the detective in charge, he didn't think they were keeping anything back. Waite was a good cop, fair, and while he knew she would withhold anything she thought necessary, he was sure she was being straight with him this morning. She needed a lead as much as he did. He considered checking the morgue—the reference files of old news stories—for any unsolved murders. And he wanted to review one in particular that he'd covered a year or so ago. As he rolled his chair back to get up, the phone rang.

"News room. Gerrard."

"Are you the reporter covering the missing student? Kelly Landrum?" came the female voice.

Grabbing a pencil, he answered, "Yes, I'm the one."

"I have some information about what happened to her. I thought we could meet somewhere and discuss it. Are you interested?"

The voice sounded older, well educated—there was something old-fashioned about it, John thought, cupping the phone under his chin.

"Yes, but who is this? Do you know her?"

"My name is Venice Thurn Ashburton."

She sounded as if the name should mean something. Thurn was a big name around here, but there were hundreds of them. John scribbled it on a pad and pushed it across to the desk that backed up to his, signaling another reporter to check the name for him. "Right. How do you know Miss Landrum?"

"I don't know her directly, but. . . . It's a little difficult to explain. Do you know the Black Forest Cafe, the restaurant on Poinsett Street? Perhaps we could meet this morning for coffee. I'd like to bring a friend who has also had contact with Miss Landrum."

"Contact? You mean someone who's spoken to her?"

"Not exactly spoken. Been in touch is more accurate. Can we meet at eleven?"

"Who's your friend, Ms. Ashburton? I don't know what you mean by 'been in touch.'" John nodded his thanks as Mike, waving his finger at his temple in a circular motion, returned the pad with *Thurn* underlined. The cryptic note read *Vincent Thurn—old money—daughter tells fortunes!* John shook his head, wondering if the moon was full tonight.

The woman interrupted his thoughts. "It's Mrs., not Ms., although I'm a widow. She's a charming woman named Kate McGuire, a portrait photographer. I'm sure you'll find what we have to say interesting, Mr. Gerrard. The pastries at the Black Forest are wonderful. Shall we see you at eleven?"

The line went dead. He replaced the receiver. *Was her rapid change of subject deliberate?* The Thurn name was intriguing—Vincent Thurn had owned several textile mills and had given generously of his wealth to the community and the local college. But his daughter a fortune-teller? Mike was right—it sounded crazy. Maybe the other one, McGuire, was nuts, too.

He retrieved a phone book from a desk drawer and turned the yellow pages to PHOTOGRAPHERS, PORTRAIT. An inconspicuous little ad for K. McGuire, specializing in creative and period-costume portraits, was barely noticeable among the larger, bolder listings. No frills. He recognized the address. It was the same as that of the Principal Players. He couldn't remember seeing anything else in the vast warehouse where the Players had their theater. Probably senile, he decided, thinking about the women. Still, breakfast had been a long time ago, and he didn't have any other leads on Kelly Landrum.

John circled the block, checking out the area. The cafe was in one of Greenville's older neighborhoods, where small businesses could afford the rent. A parking lot lay between the Black Forest and its neighbors. He circled through it, looking for an empty space, and noted a dusty white Land Rover in the shade behind the restaurant. He left the filled lot and found a metered spot on the street.

A bell tinkled when John opened the door of the tiny restaurant. Although a baritone hum drifted out from the kitchen, no one appeared, so he selected a corner table and looked around the room. The tables, each with a condiment basket dead center, were neatly arranged in rows. Several trays of pastries were displayed in a small glass case beside the cash register. On a blackboard behind it, someone had written the menu in precise script.

He had just decided to come back one night to try the schnitzel, when a woman laden with gold bracelets and trailing a red silk scarf waltzed in. He knew immediately that she was Ashburton.

Before he could stand and speak, a frowning redhead burst through the door behind her. McGuire? Maybe she wasn't senile, but there was definitely something peculiar about her. A faint, unpleasant odor wafted his way. If she would change her perfume and invest in a hairbrush, he speculated, she might not be too bad.

John studied her quietly while she fussed at Ashburton. Something about her seemed familiar, tweaked at his memory. Surely he'd remember someone so . . . vivid. He couldn't think of a better word. On top of her head, a precarious knot of hair appeared to be held in place by a single pencil. It wasn't very effective, judging by the amount of hair that had already escaped. As the women moved closer, he could see the broken point on the blue pencil. It matched the rest of her clothes—a man's blue work shirt that came almost to the knees of her faded jeans, and a pair of worn running shoes. He would be willing to bet that the counter where she worked came to just above her waist—evidenced by a horizontal streak of brownish stains across the front of the shirt.

She was still grousing. "Venice, why did we have to do this right now? I had to leave the darkroom to meet you here."

"My dear, do I detect the odor of rotten eggs? You really should be more careful in the kitchen."

"That's sepia toner, thank you very much. I was not cooking, I was working," she said, tucking a long tangle of hair behind her ear.

Thinking it a good time to intervene, John stepped forward. "Mrs. Ashburton? I'm John Gerrard."

Venice, ignoring Kate, touched his hand. "Please call me Venice. And this"—she indicated without looking at her companion—"is my friend Kate McGuire. Kate, this is the young man I told you about." She smiled and took the chair he held for her.

Kate, looking embarrassed, shook John's hand and dropped into a chair. "Sorry, I didn't realize you were here. I was just telling Venice I don't think this is a good idea. I don't see how we can possibly help you."

Venice interrupted before Kate could say more. "He understands, Kate. But he is trying to find out all he can about Kelly Landrum."

The sudden appearance of Helmut Kusch, the restaurant's burly owner, interrupted them. He carried a round aluminum tray. "I know that it is coffee for you, Kate." He placed two cups on the table, with the handles parallel to the edge. "I serve only coffee and tea, none of that pop. I brought coffee because the tea is not made. And also," he said to John, "you do not look like a tea drinker. Venice must wait."

"Coffee's fine, thanks." John looked up at the big flour-dusted man. He looked more like a Monday-night wrestler than a baker, but the mouthwatering scent of baking bread followed him from the kitchen, and John was hooked.

Venice nodded at the reference to her tea and asked for a slice of Sacher torte. "You needn't be afraid to eat in here. Helmut uses only real food—no artificial ingredients—and he does all the cooking himself."

"Mmm, Helmut, I want a big piece of apple strudel." Kate smiled at the man towering above her.

"That sounds good," John said without looking up. "Apple strudel for me, too." He watched the light shining on the nimbus of bright hair that framed Kate's face. Every time she moved her head, another strand slid out of the knot. He was fascinated, waiting for the pencil to fall.

Helmut took the orders in silence and went back to the kitchen. Venice turned to John. "Let me explain how we found Kelly. Kate saw her first."

"Venice!" Kate glared at the older woman, clearly disapproving. "We didn't *find* her. And I did not *see* her. I'm sorry to disappoint you, but I have no information about Kelly Landrum. I am not a psychic, Mr. Gerrard." Her smile had a fixed look.

"Please, call me John." *Psychic?* Inwardly, he groaned. "What sort of contact did you have with her?"

Venice answered him, dismissing Kate's threatening expression. "Before you get confused, I should tell you about the group. We participate in a parapsychology research group under Professor Martin Carver at the college. The professor has received a grant for his work with paranormal phenomena. Each person in the group is a volunteer, and we all tested above average in ability, although I must say, some of us are certainly more gifted than others. Kate is very gifted in a limited way."

Kate, her elbow on the table and her chin propped in her hand, sighed. "Believe me, Mister—John, there's nothing to tell. We can't help you."

Venice continued as if Kate hadn't spoken. "Last Tuesday we were doing a test, guessing about the owners of some unidentified items that people had donated to Martin's project."

Pleased to find that at least Venice could be informative when it suited her—John didn't hold out much hope for Kate—he asked,

"Did the professor know whose things they were?"

"No," Kate said. "One of his grad students logs them in, and after we've guessed, Martin compares the guesses with the log. Then, if necessary, he calls the owners for more information."

Helmut interrupted again by backing through the swinging doors with a large tray. He placed a china teapot in front of Venice, realigned Kate's cup, and freshened the coffees. As he served the torte and strudel, he grumbled, "Another waitress has quit. These young people of today are lazy good-for-nothings. So I must cook and serve as well until I can find another."

"You frighten them away," Venice said, fingering a gold ankh that hung from a chain around her neck. "You rant and rave about everything new—all the things they love."

"What do you know? And now you try to corrupt a sweet girl like Kate." Helmut glared at Venice and spoke to John. "Kate is a good girl. Don't let her listen to this gypsy foolishness from Venice."

"What gypsy foolishness?" John asked. Both combatants continued as if he hadn't spoken. He wondered if Kate would object to the *girl*, but she didn't seem to notice.

"It is better to say nothing when you don't know what you're talking about, Helmut." Venice jangled her bracelets and started on the rich layers of the Sacher torte.

"Who doesn't know? You are taking an innocent girl and making her crazy with all these visions and spirits." Helmut was obviously prepared to stay and pursue the matter.

"Come on, you two." Kate turned to John. "Sometimes I feel like I'm in the middle of the Mad Hatter's tea party. Don't pay any attention to them. They aren't happy if they don't have something to argue about."

Muttering to himself, Helmut returned to the kitchen, and Venice returned to her subject. "Don't mind Helmut. He thinks I dabble in the black arts, or some such thing. He dotes on Kate, so I haven't told him about Kate's gift."

"What gift?" John asked, envying Helmut his escape to the kitchen. "And why does he dote on Kate?" *Doting* wasn't the word he would have chosen for the look Helmut had given Kate. The guy wasn't as old as he'd first appeared, either. Probably not over forty.

Venice's voice broke into his speculation about Helmut's intentions, drawing his attention back to their fragmented conversation. "She took his picture. Kate is gifted in psychometry. Touch. So when she chose her article, it happened."

"What happened?" John's patience was disappearing, and he found Venice's explanations more than a little sparse. At least Kate had the grace to look embarrassed.

"Kate picked up a white headband. She saw a beautiful young woman being strangled."

"Venice!" Kate flicked her gaze in John's direction. Through gritted teeth, she said, "That's not exactly right, John. It's probably nothing at all."

So, she didn't know any more than Venice, but at least she admitted it. He figured he had just wasted the morning and ten bucks buying coffee and cakes for two ditzy women. Actually, it was kind of funny. He could see that McGuire wanted to kill Ashburton and was trying to hide it. With an effort, John maintained a solemn expression. "What, exactly, did you see?"

"It's difficult to describe. Usually it's just a flash of knowing, like I'm suddenly aware that Venice's purse is behind the sofa. It's more of a feeling, although I sometimes see things—maybe a glimpse of the sofa frame. It's sort of vague, the way you see something out of the corner of your eye."

"She does this when she touches something," Venice clarified.

"Yes, I understand. But what was this feeling you had?" John tried not to look at his watch. Next they'd be pulling rabbits out of Venice's scarf—or the rat's nest on McGuire's head.

"This may not even be about Kelly. It may not mean anything." Kate was obviously reluctant to tell him, but she continued. "The first time I picked up the sweatband, I felt terrible fear. Almost panic. Someone was very angry with her."

"We've done this twice, with the headband," Venice said. "Go ahead, dear. Tell him the rest."

"Venice, this is a bad idea. We don't know if it was real or my imagination. I'm so sorry," she said to John, standing to leave. "I really don't want to do this."

"Kate, sit down," Venice said. "Tell him what you saw, and let him decide. It may help."

"Yes, please go on."

"Someone was strangling her—but it may not have been Kelly— I don't know who it was." She shivered and touched her throat. "It was terrible."

Interested in spite of himself, John leaned forward. "And what did you see, Venice?"

"I saw a tall man in an aura of darkness. This lovely woman was terrified of him, and he was raging at her. They were in a parking lot. When she tried to run, he grabbed her around the neck and strangled her." She took the last bite of the torte and finished with a sip of tea.

Kate, who had abandoned her strudel halfway through, raised her eyebrows. "My, my, Venice. You did see a lot."

John asked, "Can you describe either the woman or the man? What makes you think it was Kelly? Did you say the man was dark?"

Kate answered, not giving Venice a chance. "I'm really not sure of anything. I thought she had dark hair and was tall . . . I could see . . . before he grabbed me. . . ." She stumbled and started over. "She was tall enough to look down on the roof of her car. I'm not even positive the other person was a man. It's just an impression I had."

"You saw the top of the car, though. Describe it."

"Oh." She looked blank for a second. "Dark. Maybe dark blue, and not new, not shiny. But wet," she added, sounding surprised. "It must have been raining."

"Wrinkles, dear. Wrinkles," Venice said, absently pouring herself another cup of tea.

Kate blinked at her. "Wrinkles?"

"Your forehead. Don't frown," Venice whispered for all to hear.

Kate rolled her eyes.

"A station wagon?" John asked, trying to keep her attention on the subject. "Big? Little?"

"No, just an average car." Her gaze focused on something he couldn't see. "The roof was fairly long. Maybe a four-door sedan."

John thought Kate was either a very good actress—a possibility, considering her association with the Principal Players—or she really believed she had seen this stuff. Landrum's car was old, a dark blue Chevrolet Impala, but that was easy enough to find out. Venice he wasn't sure about. She was calm and confident, but her visions sounded like something dreamed up by a roadside palmist. He asked Kate, "Where was she? Was she near a house, a shopping center? Did you have any other impressions?"

"That's all I saw. I'm sorry."

"I did." Venice patted her mouth with a napkin. "I saw trees swaying in the wind. She may have been at the edge of some woods, such as those at the library. The trees weren't overhead, but in front of her. There was such anger in the man. It overshadowed anything else I might have seen about him."

"I hope we haven't upset you," Kate said. "It may not even be your friend that we're seeing."

"Thanks for your concern, but I don't know her. This has been very interesting, but I'm afraid I have to get back to the office, or I won't make my deadline." He might mention them as a filler if nothing turned up, but there was no real information here. Maybe he would call the professor to find out more about their parapsychology group.

"You don't know her? And what do you mean, deadline?" Kate

asked. The frown was back, wrinkles or no.

"The deadline for tomorrow's edition. I have some more things to check before I write the article." He stood, wondering at Kate's reaction. What was the matter with her? Venice seemed to be deeply involved with the contents of her handbag.

"Tomorrow's edition? Are you a reporter?" Kate sprang to her feet, enraged. To him, she looked like a bomb about to go off.

"Of course I'm a reporter. What did you think I was?" Maybe she was crazy after all. He looked at Venice, who continued to fumble in her purse.

"You can't use this! You can't take advantage of people this way. How could you pretend to be a friend of hers? Who do you work for—one of those supermarket rags? Don't ethics mean anything to you?" Kate looked at him as if he were scum.

"Look, lady. Your friend here called me. I didn't call her."

Kate's eyes widened. She turned to Venice. "You said he was a friend of hers! Venice, how could you?"

Venice was silent.

"I never said—" John found himself speaking to Kate's back as she stormed out of the restaurant. Who was she to question his ethics? He prided himself on his integrity—it was the code he lived by. She didn't know the first thing about him. Put out by her unwarranted criticism, he turned to Venice. "What, exactly, did you tell her?"

Venice's faded blue eyes rounded. She snapped her purse shut and smiled. "Wasn't the pastry good."

Disgusted with them both, John was reaching for his wallet when Kate marched back in with her lips compressed into a thin line. She glared at them and slapped three crumpled bills on the table, then turned on her heel and left. The sudden spin dislodged the pencil, and her hair spilled down over her shoulders.

"I'm glad she's your friend and not mine." John picked up the pencil, turning it over in his hand. NON-REPRO BLUE, it read. He shrugged and tucked it into his pocket.

"I must admit, she's not at her best today." Venice gathered her belongings, untangled her scarf from the arm of the chair, and started out. At the door she turned and said, "She's not very fond of the press, you know."

No, he didn't know. And what was that supposed to mean?

Chapter 3

HE WAKENED BEFORE DAYLIGHT, anxious to see the newspaper. When a soft *thunk* announced its arrival, he wondered briefly whether excitement or fear caused the tightness that gripped his stomach. He ran across the lawn and snatched up the plastic bag holding the thick Sunday paper, opening it on the way back to the house.

The story had dropped to the middle of the front page. Good. It meant nothing more had been discovered about the bitch.

Inside the house, he quickly read through the brief article, laughing at the lack of information. The story began with a description of Kelly Landrum and her activities prior to her disappearance, including quotes from her roommate and friends. Finding her car with the keys in the door was the only discovery the police had made since she had been reported missing.

Then he turned to the continuation on page three. The last paragraphs concerned a university-sponsored parapsychology test group. Two of the psychics, after handling an article belonging to the missing Landrum, claimed to have had visions of a woman being strangled.

Kate McGuire! he read. *Venice Ashburton!* He knew them both, had always thought Venice was nuts, but he'd had no idea Kate was a psychic. She seemed normal, had never mentioned anything. For an instant, he was overcome by panic.

What did they see? Could they describe him? Did they know who he was? Flinging the paper to the floor, he shoved his hand into the pocket of his robe, feeling for the worry stone he always carried. Stroking the smooth surface calmed him a bit, allowed him to think.

He snatched the phone book off the shelf. *Ashburton* was easy: *V. T.* was the only listing. He wrote the address in a small notebook and then flipped to *M* and searched for *McGuire.* There were several—two with the initial *K*, but one of those was a middle initial. It could be any one of them. Women did such funny things with their telephone listings—she might not even be in the book. But he knew she was a photographer. He switched to the yellow pages and quickly found what he was looking for. It would be better to wait until tomorrow, when she should be at work and he could be sure of finding her.

Still, he could drive by those addresses, but with his distinctive car, he would have to be very careful. He couldn't do anything about it today, but maybe tomorrow he could borrow the book-keeper's junker, tell her his car was in the shop. Or he could use Carson's old Dodge. The janitor was always willing to loan out the gas-guzzling pickup for a tank of fuel and a six-pack.

He poured a glass of tomato juice and began thinking of ways to get to the women. First he would watch them, learn their habits. He wouldn't mind watching Kate. She had a tight, sexy little body that had always appealed to him. And that hair—he bet she was a tiger.

That was it—he'd watch her and then decide what to do. He couldn't afford to do anything unnecessary. It would only add to the risk. But he really wanted to get started. Waiting was risky, too, he told himself. He could always rent a car for one day.

Distant bells signaling the start of early church services woke Kate. Monsters and murderers had pursued her through the night. She dreamed of Kelly Landrum. She decided a brisk run was the simplest way to clear her head. Dressing quickly in shorts and her favorite T-shirt, she stopped at the mirror to put her hair in a pony-tail. She smiled at the picture on her shirt. Under a fat, warty bull-frog, it read MY HANDSOME PRINCE TURNED INTO A FROG. Hers certainly had. Never trust a handsome man, she reminded herself.

The smile disappeared when she placed a terry-cloth band over her forehead. Kelly Landrum. Kate pictured the girl with wet hair clinging to her face. She shivered, dispelling the image from her mind, and reached for her worn Nikes. *Talk about auras,* she thought, *I wonder what kind of images one could pick up from old shoes.*

After minimal ablutions in the bathroom, she put on a pot of cof-fee to be ready when she got back. On the porch, she locked her front door and dropped the key into the pocket of her shorts. Then, after stretching a few times, she took off on her three-mile route.

As she started down the street, the rear end of a red Taurus van-ished around the corner. A sudden coldness enveloped her. Some-how, that car didn't belong, wasn't right. She felt a mindless urge to run back to her house and lock herself in. Instead, she searched for a rational explanation for the feeling. In this neighborhood, her own Mazda RX-7, old as it was, was dangerously ostentatious. She told herself the car probably belonged to an investor out cruising for property, but the uneasiness stayed with her for several minutes after the car had gone.

Jogging past the rickety boarding house on the corner, she carefully wound her way through the sprawl of rusty, battered vehicles. They littered the yard and spilled over onto the sidewalk—she was glad it was too early for the inhabitants, whom she had dubbed the "motley crew," to be up and about. She ran on and crossed the street, sidestepping the potholes, reveling in the cool of the late-September morning.

Gradually, her muscles loosened and the tension slipped away. At a long, uninterrupted stretch of road, she opened up, running flat out until she reached the main intersection. She loved the exhilarating burst of speed, the feeling of flying.

Slowing to an easy lope for the last mile, she completed her loop in good time. Two blocks from home, as she dropped to a cooling walk, she saw Venice's Cadillac idling on the street in front of the house.

Venice stepped out of the car and, like a scarlet macaw surveying sparrows' nests, stood for a moment gazing at the drab street and decaying houses. She gave a faint shake of her head before waving a bakery bag as she joined Kate on the front steps. "I wish you would move to a nicer area, Kate. I'm afraid to get out of my car until I see you."

"It's cheap. When I get rich, I'll move." Kate eyed Venice's bag. It did smell good. A peace offering, probably. Kate hadn't completely forgiven her for calling that reporter. "Why are you here at this hour?"

Venice, ignoring the question, studied her through narrowed eyes. "You haven't been sleeping much, have you?"

"So-so." As Kate unlocked the door, she glared suspiciously over her shoulder at Venice. There had to be a reason for the woman to be here this early. "What do you want, Venice?"

"Have you seen the morning paper?" Venice asked as she followed her into the house.

"No." Kate spun around and stared at Venice. A chill ran down her back. "Why?"

"Well," Venice said, taking a folded newspaper from her bag. "John has an article on Kelly Landrum this morning."

"How bad is it? Did he use my name?"

"It wasn't a very interesting article. I doubt if anyone will read it."

"Venice!"

"Yes, he did," she admitted. "But only at the very end." A gray wisp, still threaded with brown, peeked out from under the auburn curls. "If you had been a little nicer, I'm sure he would have written more about us."

"If you had told me he worked for the newspaper, I would never have spoken to him at all," Kate retorted. "He could have at least mentioned it, the swine."

Venice refused to see him in the same light. "It wasn't his fault." Looking away from Kate, she touched the back of her hand to her left eyebrow.

"Venice, you can drop the drama. I'm not mad anymore. Let's see the article. If I'm going to be burned at the stake, I want to be prepared."

"Don't be silly. Ever since you married that nitwit, you've been paranoid about the press." She held out the paper to Kate. "Here. Read it yourself."

"They made my life miserable," Kate said.

"Don't whine, Kate. It's unbecoming. J. B. made your life miserable. He was the one who thought the press found him irresistible and watched his every move—and yours."

"Well, it's over now. I just want it to stay that way. I don't want any involvement with the news media in any shape or form." She folded back the paper to read. The headline caught her eye immediately: COED STILL MISSING, NO LEADS. Guilt made her wince. Martin had been after her to call the police. Still, what could she have told them?

Kate put the paper down long enough to pour coffee and bring napkins for the pastries. Then she settled on the sofa beside Venice. Finishing the sweet roll and the article at the same time, she said, "There's nothing new here. Maybe no one will read it."

"That's just what I said—no one will read it." Venice still sounded disappointed.

Refolding the paper, Kate dropped it on the coffee table, thinking about Kelly Landrum. She couldn't imagine what caused her reaction to the sweatband. Why? Was it because, by perspiring into the band, the girl's aura inhabited it so strongly? Could they possibly help find her? And how?

"Yes, dear. I believe we can help her."

"Dammit, Venice! I hate it when you do that. At least pretend you can't read my mind!"

Venice laughed. "Your face is so expressive that I don't have to. Your thoughts are very clear."

The phone interrupted them. Kate licked the sticky pastry filling off her fingers and answered while Venice continued to eat.

"Kate, this is Martin Carver. Sorry to bother you, but I've just read the article by John Gerrard. He came to see me yesterday and told me about your meeting. I wish Venice hadn't called him, but it's too late now."

"It's not as bad as I thought it would be. We just need to gag Venice if anything else comes up," Kate said.

"That's partly why I'm calling. I happened to be talking to Detective Waite yesterday, and I mentioned your visions. As you thought, the police weren't very interested."

"You *just happened* to be talking to the police? You sound like Venice."

"I thought it was important." He cleared his throat and added, "But after reading Gerrard's article this morning, I called her again. This is too serious to ignore, Kate. I'm convinced you saw Kelly Landrum."

"Martin, I know you believe in us, but no one else is going to get excited about a few visions—most people consider us closer to psychotic than psychic. Please, just drop it."

"No, I can't do that," he argued. "I told Waite the university was concerned that the police weren't taking you seriously, especially as the missing girl was one of our students."

Kate lowered her face into her hand. Sighing, she asked, "So what are they going to do? Give us a lie detector test?"

"If Kelly Landrum is still missing Tuesday night, Detective Waite wants to send someone to the para group meeting."

"*Wants?* I'll bet. She's probably disparaging your ancestry right now." Kate could hear the professor's indignant sniff. "I'm sorry. I know you're doing what you think is right. I just don't think I can help. I may never see anything else. Maybe Venice can do something—if you can get her to stop showing off long enough for anyone to believe her."

"I want you to go first at the session for just that reason. Venice makes such a bad impression sometimes."

"Go first?" Her voice dropped an octave.

"I insisted Detective Waite bring something of Kelly's for you to test. You might have some valuable insights to offer."

After she hung up, Kate turned to Venice. "I don't know why I thought no one would read that stupid article. Martin Carver was so impressed he called the police about it." She told Venice about the plans for the next meeting.

Venice left in a frenzy of excitement, hardly able to wait until Tuesday.

Thinking of her recent—and probably short-lived—commission to photograph a group of bank officers, Kate was so depressed she cleaned out the refrigerator. When the phone rang again, she was down to a plastic dish of something green and slimy that appeared to be growing. She dropped the whole thing in the garbage and let the answering machine get the phone.

The voice belonged to Betsy, one of the students from the para group. "Hi, Kate, are you there? I saw the article in the paper today. Why didn't the professor tell us that sweatband belonged to Kelly Landrum? Now that I know, your vision is really creepy.

"But you know," her tinny voice continued through the machine, "this story sounds like you saw the whole thing. At the meeting, you said that poor girl had been strangled. Her family's going to be really upset. And if she was strangled, what will the murderer think?"

Kate groaned. *My thoughts exactly.*

By Tuesday, Kate had heard nothing new about Kelly Landrum. She sat at a table in Gene's Restaurant, idly poking at her mashed potatoes. The nagging feeling of unease that had followed her home Monday night had almost disappeared. She thought about calling John to see if he knew anything—after all, she reasoned, Venice had called him, and the article wasn't that bad.

"Hello, Kate. Mind if I join you?"

She looked up, startled to find Thomas Andrews staring down at her. Yes, she did mind, but she couldn't say so to the overly handsome man. "Of course not. What are you doing here, Thomas? This doesn't seem like your kind of place."

He gestured at the crowded tables and smiled. "How's your photography business? Anything interesting in your life right now?" He brushed off the seat of the chair opposite her and sat. "I remembered your mentioning this place when we were in marketing class last fall. When you were too busy to go out with me."

Trust him to remember something like that, she thought. He had asked her out several times, but she had demurred, blaming it on the demands of her new studio. "Nothing new." *Unless you count a sudden descent into murder and the supernatural.* "Still working, trying to get it off the ground."

He picked up the menu, a little distastefully, she thought. "Didn't I see your name in the paper the other day?" he asked. "I didn't know you had other talents."

I hate John Gerrard. "I don't. It was a fluke. Just a dumb experiment that went wrong." And she had thought no one would read it! Was there anyone who hadn't?

"It sounds interesting. I had no idea there was such a group in Greenville. How does it work?" He leaned forward, resting on his elbows, and folded his hands together.

She gave him the barest possible explanation, searching desperately for a distraction. "Are you still taking night classes? Weren't you working on a graduate degree?"

"Yes. I should get my MBA in the spring. I'm considering starting my own firm. Maybe I'll need some photographs, for brochures and advertising, you know?"

"Good luck." She wouldn't take the bait, didn't want to give him an opening for further conversation. Had he come here to ask her out again? She hoped not. She couldn't think why the obviously successful, immaculately dressed man would be interested in her. However unfairly, he reminded her of J. B., and she would never accept an invitation from him. She crossed her knife and fork over her half-eaten lunch and swallowed the last of her iced tea. "I have to get back. I have a client due soon."

"Good-bye, Kate. Good to see you again."

She left quickly. Where were the average guys? The ones she might like to spend time with? John Gerrard flashed into her mind, but she refused to allow the thought. Once more she considered calling about news of Kelly Landrum. In the end she couldn't do it. Anyway, she could always ask the police at tonight's meeting. How had she gotten to such a state?

Pushing everything else from her mind, she returned to her work, but she ruined two sepia prints before she was able to concentrate on a portrait of a mother and child in Victorian dress. A shaft of light, artfully provided by Kate, lent a luminous quality to the mother's somewhat plain face. Kate was pleased with the results of the third print, and her enthusiasm returned.

The work was going so well she hated to quit and change clothes for the para group meeting, but since the police were going to be there, she wanted to look like a sober, responsible member of society and not some glue-sniffing, new-age hippie.

She locked the studio and pushed the button for the ancient freight elevator. Two paneled models had been installed to take patrons from the lobby to the theater on the third floor, but only the old freight elevator in the back of the building came to Kate's studio on the fourth floor.

Stepping in, she thought about a morning some months ago when, with her camera, she had captured the figure of a sleeping drunk sprawled in the shadowed cage. She had thought the stark portrait would be an interesting contrast to the beautiful people on her walls—a little reality to contrast with the illusions. The gritty black and white in which she had printed the photo enhanced its desolate character. She was preparing to hang it when Venice had come in and recognized him—a local businessman with a family.

The sight of the photo, which Kate, after much soul-searching, had given him, had first shocked him and then sent him into a rage of denial. Kate left, sorry she had tried to help. A month ago she received a bouquet of roses and a letter saying the picture had finally sent him to Alcoholics Anonymous. He told her he had just reached the end of his third sober month and that he kept the photograph in a drawer, to look at when he had a bad moment.

She thought about him on the drive home. Even as her thoughts drifted, Kate checked her speedometer and then, guiltily, her rear-view mirror for police cars. A beat-up blue pickup a car or two behind her caught her eye. She had seen the same truck last night when she left the studio. She recognized it by the dented front bumper. A new neighbor? Somehow, she didn't think so. The uneasy feeling she had experienced last night returned.

Before she got a look at the driver, her attention was diverted by a couple of men walking unsteadily along the street. Swerving to give them plenty of room as she passed, she thought maybe Venice was right about the neighborhood.

Easing the car onto the broken concrete strips that formed her drive, she stopped, resting her forehead on the steering wheel. What was she doing, she wondered, living on peanut butter and calling herself a photographer? She could have found a job at a reasonable salary in the business world, but she loved working with a camera. And the business was getting better—if John Gerrard didn't frighten off her hard-won clients.

As soon as she got inside the house, the momentary weakness passed. It was her life, and she was enjoying it. "At least, most of it," she muttered, recalling the police presence planned for tonight's meeting.

Unbuttoning her shirt as she ran upstairs, Kate hurriedly shed her clothes and hopped into the shower. Venice's remark about the smell of rotten eggs the other morning had hit home. She hoped her hair didn't smell; she didn't have time to wash it. Checking her closet, she selected a neat gray suit and a white silk shirt, leftovers from her former life as a marketing account rep and Teflon wife.

She brushed the mass of red hair and pulled it back into a soft chignon at the nape of her neck, spraying it into submission. In the mirror, she checked her makeup carefully, then added discreet gold earrings and low black heels. She took a pair of clear glasses from the nightstand to complete the effect. Ignoring a spreading ripple in her reflection about hip-high—the mirror had cost two dollars at a rummage sale—she inspected herself and laughed. She had wanted to appear sober, conservative, sensible; she figured she could pass for a Young Republican. She sent up a silent prayer for Venice to hold it down, but didn't have much hope. Ready. After retracing her steps in a frantic search for her car keys, she left.

Kate waited until a beat-up Toyota passed, and then backed out of her crumbling driveway. Using her rearview mirror, she maneuvered around a van angled into the curb across the street and shifted quickly into first gear as a blue pickup pulled away from the curb down the block. A gray Buick—the one she'd seen at lunch?—eased into the street behind her. The gray car turned left at the corner, and she saw that it wasn't the one that had been behind her at lunch. She sighed and relaxed. She wasn't usually so jumpy—it must be this business with Kelly Landrum.

Glancing at her watch, she turned off the traffic-clogged main road and took a right up Paris Mountain, a 2,000-foot peak wedged into the north side of Greenville. The way ahead was clear, and she increased her speed, holding the tight curves easily. She came to an open stretch where she could see the road behind her and checked it automatically. No police cars, just a red convertible with two passengers, and a glimpse of something blue—she wasn't sure what, but it definitely wasn't a patrol car.

She was more cautious than she used to be. The urban developers were gradually devouring the wooded mountain, and crossroads and driveways intersected the twisting two-lane more and more frequently. This way might no longer be faster, but it was still more fun.

She got to the meeting a couple of minutes early and saw that the entire group was present tonight. She guessed the word had spread. Choosing a desk in the semicircular arrangement, she took a small notepad from her purse, determined to be calm and dignified.

An awkward young man in a blue uniform represented the police. Detective Waite wasn't wasting her time with the lunatic fringe, Kate thought. She knew the only reason the police sent even this man was because Martin insisted that the university was upset.

Martin, taking in Kate's appearance with a raised eyebrow, introduced Officer Paul Wolynski to her.

"You're not quite what I expected, Ms. McGuire," Wolynski said.

Kate, hoping none of the students would comment on her unusual attire, remained seated and offered her hand. The officer shook it politely. "Please," she said. "Call me Kate."

All conversation came to an abrupt halt with the entrance of Venice. It could only be called an entrance. Kate covered her eyes and groaned. A full-length, wine-colored cape swirled over her flowing skirt. Tinkling bracelets lined her arms, and a cascade of gold hoops fell from her ears to her shoulders; but it was the gold lamé turban, hiding all but a few hennaed curls, that held everyone's attention. She sailed into the room like a gypsy queen, fixing them all with a dark stare. Kate wondered at that until Venice got closer, and she realized that a thick layer of false eyelashes kept the woman's eyes half closed. She resolved to kill Venice after the meeting.

The group, still silent, focused on Venice as she extended her hand, heavy with jeweled rings, to the policeman. He looked as if he didn't know whether to shake it or fall on his knees and kiss it. Martin blinked several times as if clearing his vision.

Kate, taking pity on the speechless men, stood and made the introductions. "Venice, this is Paul Wolynski, obviously from the police force. Paul, this is Venice Ashburton, a harmless lunatic we've taken in." Smiling at Venice's indignant glare, Kate added, "She's also a gifted psychic."

It wasn't until Kate turned to sit back down that she saw John sitting quietly in a corner. He smiled and shrugged toward Venice, who had taken the seat beside Kate.

So that's what this show is about, Kate thought. *That old witch let the reporter slip in without being noticed. She's probably hoping he'll put her picture in with his next article.*

Kate nodded curtly in his direction but didn't denounce him. Instead she turned her back and concentrated on what Martin was saying:

"By now you've all read or heard about Kelly Landrum and know that the white sweatband belongs to her. Officer Wolynski is here on behalf of the police to observe our tests. But under the circumstances, I don't think we would get very far with our usual experiments, so I'll let him explain what he wants first." He nodded to the policeman and then sat down.

The young officer coughed, cleared his throat, and said, "Uh, I brought some things that belong to Kelly Landrum, and I would like for the two, that is, for Ms. Ashburton and Ms. McGuire to take a look at them and see if they, uh, can tell us anything."

Venice immediately rose in a swirl of color and stepped up to the table beside him. "Certainly. What did you bring?"

Wolynski looked helplessly at the professor, who said, "Venice, if you don't mind, I would like for Kate to go first. You will have a different article, and we'll see what happens."

Venice, miffed, swept her skirt around and returned to her seat.

Kate, resigned to her role in the fiasco, said nothing and stayed at her desk. She held out her open hand to the officer.

He opened a plastic bag on the table, pulled out a small scarf patterned with coins, and laid it carefully across her palm.

Like crossing it with silver, she thought. But her hand trembled as her fingers tightened around the wisp of silk. She closed her eyes. No one made a sound. After a couple of seconds she let out a relieved sigh and looked up at Wolynski, puzzled. "I sense someone happy, laughing. A very young girl, I think. Sorry, it's not the same girl as before. I don't know why."

Wolynski took the scarf back and held out the bag to her. "Would you try something else?"

She reached in and pulled out a comb. Lulled by the scarf, she was off guard. Like a stone, she sank straight into the dream. "Water," she gasped. "A lot of water. Dark, cold. I'm—she's standing in water. No, under the water." Kate, unaware of her actions, raised her arms, palms down, in a high, loose gesture, her eyes wide and staring. "Her hair's floating around her face." She paused, then whispered, "She's dead."

This time she was shivering, but not terrified as before. She dropped the comb on the desk, curbing a desire to wipe off her hand. "Take it," she whispered.

Martin asked, "Are you sure she's dead? Describe everything very carefully."

Wolynski returned the comb to the bag; Kate's shoulders sagged. She had been holding herself stiffly, watching the comb. She breathed more easily when the officer took it away. "Mostly water— a lake, I think. There were trees around her, sort of shimmering. Maybe I was seeing their reflection. That's all. Just her, staring, dead. I'm sorry, I can't help you any more."

"Could you see what she's wearing?" Wolynski asked.

"It's too dark. But maybe her clothes are dark, too, because I can see her face and hands." Kate slumped in the desk, her face in her hands. Then she added, "And more trees. Dead, lifeless. Different."

"Different? Dead? Like in the winter?" Martin asked.

"No, just dead trees around her. The impression is vague, but the feeling of death is very strong." The feeling of sadness was also very strong; Kate felt like crying. She realized then that she had accepted that the dead woman was Kelly Landrum.

"Thank you, Ms—Kate." Wolynski looked uncertainly at her, fumbled awkwardly in the bag for something, and then turned to Venice. "Now, would you try something, Ms. Ashburton?"

"*Mrs.* Ashburton. But you may call me Venice, young man." She shielded her eyes with one gracefully arched hand and delicately lifted a red ribbon from his outstretched hand with the other. Abruptly, she uncovered her eyes and glared. "Paul! This belongs to a child. If this is a test, *you* have failed it. This ribbon does not belong to Miss Landrum."

The ribbon slid from her extended hand and drifted to the floor.

The blushing officer picked it up and stuffed it into his pocket. "Please, take something else and try one more time."

Venice looked down her nose at him for a second, then smiled and nodded at him, a queen bestowing forgiveness. "I'm sure you are acting on your instructions. Give me the bag."

She took a small makeup brush this time, closing her eyes as before. "I feel the dark, cold water. Night surrounds a pale face. Hair. Dark, floating hair. Her eyes stare blindly at the moon. Dead, all dead. . . ."

Kate, still shaken from her own vision, couldn't tell whether Venice was seeing through her own eyes or through Kate's. She knew Venice was very suggestible. It probably didn't matter—if the police had been serious about testing them, they would have seen the two of them separately. Watching the policeman's face, Kate could tell he was skeptical. Even if he had been inclined to believe them, Venice's dramatics would have made him think they were either crazy or desperate for attention.

"That is all," Venice intoned, spreading her arms wide.

"Well, um, thank you all for your time." Wolynski dropped the comb and makeup brush into the bag, sealing it on his way to the door. Clearly anxious to get away, he said as he passed, "Thank you, Professor Carver. I'll leave you to your experiments while I make my report. We'll be in touch if we need more information."

Martin took a few steps after him, then gave up when the young man disappeared from view. The professor shrugged, his disappointment evident, and turned back toward the front of the classroom.

Kate, watching the policeman's exit, was startled to see John slip out after Wolynski. *Damn!* After she had touched the comb, she'd forgotten he was there. She hoped he had enjoyed the show.

Putting away the recorder, Martin said, "I think we've had enough for tonight. We'll go on with the regular experiments next week."

The other students gathered around the professor and walked him out the door, talking quietly among themselves. They avoided the area where Kate and Venice still sat.

Kate stood slowly and returned her notebook and glasses to their place in her purse, then said to Venice. "He didn't believe us. None of them do except Martin."

"Most people don't really believe, my dear. They're only interested in tall, dark strangers and wealth that's just around the corner."

"That's unusually prosaic for you, Venice," Kate said. "But if the police don't believe us, they're probably looking for Kelly in the wrong places."

"There's not much we can do about that. Eventually we'll be proven right. And next time the police will be calling us."

"I don't want there to be a next time. This one is driving me crazy." Kate pulled out her hairpins to let her hair fall free, and ruffled it to break up the stiff spray. "Oh, that feels better.

"I can't stop thinking about her. I know she was murdered." Kate swallowed hard, recalling the powerful feeling of cold and death. "I'm going to see what I can find out. Will you help me?"

"Of course I will." Venice patted her shoulder. "But what can we do?"

"We know she's in a lake somewhere. How many can there be around here? Maybe we'll get some more images if we can find the right one. Venice, you realize there's a murderer walking around loose?"

"Yes, I do. That's the part that frightens me. Not the visions." Venice tapped a long red fingernail against her purse.

Kate noticed that the glue showed around the edges and the nail wasn't on straight. Dear Venice.

Then the older woman brightened. "I suppose I could talk to Ramses. Perhaps he can help."

Kate was never sure whether Venice was serious about the spirit who inhabited her crystal ball. She swore that he was there and spoke to her, but Kate had caught an irreverent twinkle in her eyes more than once. "Ramses? I thought he only communed with the—"

"The dead. He does, although he isn't limited to those on the other side. However, in this case it might be most helpful. Don't you agree?" Venice lifted her turban off and twisted it in her hands. "Don't you love the way the gold catches the light?"

"Lovely," Kate muttered. "Well, while you and Ramses commune, I think I'll start investigating on my own."

Preoccupied with Kelly Landrum, Kate didn't notice the blue Dodge pickup that eased out of the parking lot behind her. As usual, she turned off the highway to take the winding road over Paris Mountain. The pickup took the same turn.

Chapter 4

JOHN DIDN'T CATCH UP with Wolynski until he got to the police station, probably because he was trying to reconcile the cool, professional Kate at the meeting tonight with the firebrand who'd left the Black Forest spitting nails. They might have been two different people. When she did that bit with the comb. . . . It was chilling. He didn't know what to think of her, but she interested him. She had an elusive familiarity that puzzled him, but he couldn't place her. Venice he considered an eccentric old woman who took her leads from Kate, but he would check further into her background before he wrote her off. He knew too well the price of dismissing someone because of an unlikely story.

He introduced himself to Wolynski.

Alarm flashed across the officer's face. "The police are not working with these people—we just went as a courtesy to the university." He looked around the room as if seeking help.

"It's okay," John hastened to tell him. *Poor guy, he probably envisioned headlines such as "Stumped Police Consult Psychics" and his career blown away like yesterday's news.* "I understand. I'm really interested in the items you had with you. I just want to know if the women were on the mark about where the stuff came from."

"I'm not sure I should be talking about this with you." He glanced at a picture on his desk. "You ought to talk to Detective Waite."

John followed his gaze and saw a small dark-haired child sitting on a pink tricycle, a hairy creature with his tongue hanging out lolling beside her. He would bet he knew where some of the articles came from. "Cute little girl. I guess that's her dog beside her. I've never seen one quite like it."

"Yeah, that's my little girl, Lisa," he said, a fond look on his face. "The dog's Chips—poodle and Heinz."

"Lisa's ribbon and scarf, I guess," John said. "Those women may be nuts, but they seemed pretty certain. Spooky, huh."

"Yeah, they are."

The awe in the young man's voice told John all he needed to

know. Shifting awkwardly on the distorted chair angled against the gray metal desk, the reporter said, "Ashburton I don't know about, but McGuire was pretty impressive." They didn't encourage visiting here.

"Yeah, she was scary with that stuff about the water. Don't know what it means, though." Wolynski locked his hands behind his head and leaned back in his chair, more relaxed now.

"I guess Detective Waite told you to find some other things to mix in with Landrum's." John propped his ankle on his knee. He'd had about all he could take of the chair.

"Yeah, so I brought some of my little girl's stuff." Wolynski shook his head in wonder. "She knew. Somehow, they both knew."

"Thanks, Wolynski." John stood, grateful to be out of the chair, and held out his hand. At the younger man's worried look, he added, "It's okay, you can ask Waite about me—I'm not out to make you guys look stupid. I'm trying to figure out those women."

Traffic over the winding mountain road was usually negligible this time of evening, and Kate shrugged her shoulders, trying to loosen up and enjoy the drive. She noticed the headlights coming up behind her and reduced her speed automatically. She absolutely could not afford a ticket, and she knew from experience that the RX-7 attracted an excessive amount of official attention.

Few homes graced the back side of the mountain, and the temptation to accelerate rode with her. Ignoring it, she concentrated on staying within the speed limit, especially since the trailing vehicle now maintained a steady distance behind her.

As the road rose and the curves tightened, the headlights shifted to high beam and the gap between the two cars closed. The bright lights loomed high in her rearview and side mirrors. The fool was right on her tail, blinding her. Gripping the wheel firmly in her left hand, she adjusted the angle of the rearview mirror, but the reflection in the side mirror still glared in her eyes.

The road straightened momentarily. With growing unease, she slowed and pulled as far to the right as she dared on the mountain road, hoping if the person was in a hurry, he would get on with it and pass. Instantly the driver pulled up beside her, crowding her dangerously close to the edge. She glanced over. A truck. She couldn't see the driver. *Whoever it is, he must be drunk*, she thought, gritting her teeth. *Probably some kid, wanting to prove he's king of the hill.*

In a few hundred yards, she would be on the outside of a series of sharp curves. If the truck stayed beside her, he would be on the inside.

She slowed further. He slowed with her, edging closer. Was he crazy?

They entered the first curve. He was going to push her off! Holding the wheel in a death grip, Kate dropped her right wheels onto the narrow shoulder. The RX-7 lurched on the uneven surface. She stepped hard on the accelerator and shot out in front of the truck, spitting gravel.

She could feel the pull on the back end as the car leaned into the curve, but it held the road. She fled up the mountain, leaving the lunatic in her wake.

Still shaking when she pulled into her garage, Kate considered reporting the incident to the police. She pulled the doors closed behind the car and dropped the latch in place, picturing the steep drop. If she had been in an ordinary car, she would most likely have gone over. Flicking off the light, she scooted out through the door into the backyard, still thinking about reporting the near accident.

But what would she say? "Someone, either drunk or crazy, in a dark-colored truck, tried to run me off Paris Mountain. No, officer, I didn't get the license number. No, officer, I can't describe the driver. No, officer, I don't know what kind of truck. Yes, officer, I'm the psychic who thinks she's seen Kelly Landrum floating in a lake." That should go over well. They would probably lock *her* up.

Kate decided to forget the whole thing, put it out of her mind. He was probably drunk, and there was nothing she could do anyway. The police weren't interested in anything she had to say, although she had to admit she hadn't given them much to go on so far. A lake. Kelly Landrum had been strangled and was in a lake. That was about it. Upstairs in her room, she ditched the suit and sank gratefully into bed.

When a car backfired early the next morning, Kate groaned and sat up, knowing she would never get back to sleep. She shook off the cobwebs and groped her way down the steps. *I'm going to have to find Kelly myself,* she thought, measuring coffee into the filter. *But how?*

"No leads." The headline from John's last story ran through her head like the message on a computerized sign. She decided to make a list of everything she knew about the girl. Searching through a drawer, she discarded two dried-up pens before finding one that worked, then she sat down at the kitchen table with a small notepad. Starting with the two articles John had written, she wrote whatever seemed pertinent. Her list wasn't long. There had been other stories, but she didn't have the papers and couldn't remember anything specific. While the coffee gave a last gurgle in the machine, she dialed Venice's number. She was an early riser. After several rings, Venice answered breathlessly.

"Did I interrupt something? Were you and Ramses in conference?" Kate quickly poured herself a cup of coffee and returned to the table and her notepad, listening to Venice.

"I was outside looking for the paper."

Kate could hear the pages rattle. "I'm making a list of what we know about Kelly." She read the brief notes to her. "Can you add anything?"

"Only that she was mixed up with the wrong man. I think he said something about her lying. Do you know anything about the kind of person she was?"

"No, but that's an interesting thought. I see from one of John's articles that her roommate at Poinsett is Josephine Wardlaw. I wonder if she'd talk to me?"

"She's probably been questioned to the point of persecution by now. She may not be receptive."

"I think I'll try." Nibbling at the end of her pen, Kate thought about trying to recall the visions. "Do you think it's possible to die from a vision? If Professor Carver hadn't stopped it, would I have continued to choke?"

"I don't think so. I believe you would pass out first."

"That's comforting." She definitely wouldn't try that alone. "Can you think of anything else?"

"You said she was tall, that she could see the top of her car, so the killer must be quite tall. And very strong. Maybe her roommate could describe the men she went out with."

"What about the lake? And the ghostly trees? Could it be in an area near a forest fire?" Kate sipped her coffee, afraid to go too near the visions.

"Somehow, that doesn't seem right. Maybe if you look at a map, something will come to you." More paper shuffling. "I don't see anything in today's paper. Why don't you call John?"

"Thanks anyway, Venice. I'll call you later. Tell Ramses hello for me."

She went to the living room and sifted through a stack of papers on her desk, looking for a map, but found only Alabama and Virginia. Nothing on South Carolina or the Piedmont area.

Her stomach growled, reminding her that she had skipped supper last night. A survey of the cabinets turned up a box of Grape-Nuts, a jar of peanut butter, and some canned soup. She opted for the cereal and hoped she had milk. In the refrigerator she found a half-empty carton and a loaf of stale bread. The milk had a few suspicious swirls, but it smelled all right. She poured it over the cereal and carried it back to the table. As she ate, she planned what she would say to Josephine Wardlaw.

Maybe Jo? Jodie? Josie?

She scraped the mold off the corner of a slice of bread, toasted it, and smeared it with peanut butter, thinking about the image she would need to present to approach Kelly's roommate. The girl had surely been besieged—by the police, the press, friends, and the merely curious.

Kate finished the toast, rinsed the peanut butter and crumbs off her fingers, and ran upstairs to rummage through her closet. Pushing aside one hanger after the other, she rejected her clothing—too dressy, too sophisticated, too this, too that. The girl would have had enough of authority figures, but Kate supposed that she had also been overwhelmed by other students. Definitely no weirdos—she was likely to be frightened. Maybe someone conservative and solicitous, like a Sunday school teacher or a missionary type, could get in to see her.

A navy blue dress caught her eye. She usually wore it with a bold scarf and heavy gold jewelry, but if it had a white collar, it could look very sensible. A thorough search yielded only an old white blouse. Kate ruthlessly cut out the collar and yoke, then snipped off the cuffs a few inches from the elbow. She put the severed collar around her neck and pulled the cuffs on, then pulled the dress over her head. The effect was demure if boring, she decided. Too bad she hadn't thought of this outfit while she was married. J. B. would have loved it.

Maybe a little makeup—she wasn't aiming for dead. She looked longingly at her mascara. No, it would spoil the picture. She got out the glasses again.

Standing in front of the mirror, she twisted her hair into a tight knot on top of her head. "Wow. Miss Prim. All I need is a blackboard."

Thinking it didn't fit with her missionary image, Kate left the RX-7 at the far end of the parking lot and walked to Reed Hall, where she supposed Kelly's roommate still lived. She hoped the poor girl hadn't left college and gone home. In a suitably docile voice, she asked a young woman clad in red-and-white-striped tights and a star-studded blue T-shirt for directions to Josephine Wardlaw's room.

The flag-wearer looked at Kate strangely. "Upstairs, first door on the right."

"I'm from her church," Kate explained in what she hoped was a sweetly sincere manner, and ran up the stairs. She dismissed the laughter that followed her, thinking that visiting missionaries probably didn't run.

The door had no identification, but Kate, wondering if she should call the roommate Miss Wardlaw, knocked anyway.

It opened so quickly that Kate jumped. A large, muscular woman with chopped-off brown hair glared down at her. A baseball bat hung from her hand.

"Whatever it is, I'm not interested, and the answer is no," the amazon barked, slamming the door.

For a second, Kate stood speechless. She almost left, then decided she wouldn't be put off so easily. She knocked again.

"Are you deaf, dumb, or both?" Josephine yelled, jerking the door back and waving the bat.

"My name is—" Kate stopped short as the door swung toward her again. She needed to get Josephine's attention, fast. She flung her purse at the woman. "Listen, dammit. I need to talk to you."

Josephine, startled, let go of the door to catch the purse; and Kate, with one hand on the door and the other on the bat, shoved past her into the room. "Sit down, Jo."

"Who are you? You just go around throwing things at people, or what?"

Kate took the purse out of the woman's hand. "One thing at a time. I need to talk to you about your roommate."

"You and the rest of the world."

"I hope you can answer some questions for me." She softened her tone. "Please, I only want to help Kelly."

"Why? You a friend of hers?"

"No. I just can't explain right now. I need to know if Kelly went to a lake near here for any reason. Maybe to run? Walk?"

"Are you a cop?"

"No." Kate sighed. "Please, just tell me if there was a lake, or even a pond, where she often went."

"*Went?* I don't know what you're getting at, but you had better ask the police. Now get out." Josephine took Kate's arm and pushed her into the hall.

Kate heard the click of the lock. "Damn!" She thumped the door once with the side of her fist. "Now what?"

A chiming clock made her decision. "Nine-thirty! Mrs. Armstrong!" A couple of students watched curiously as she raced down the stairs and back to her car. She had visions of the bank president's wife—a nice commission—making the perilous journey in the freight elevator only to find the studio locked and empty. *Maybe she'll like my dress.*

When Kate left the parking lot, she saw that a crowd had spilled into the street in front of the building where Martin Carver had an office. The road was blocked by two police cars. Kate slowed and rolled down her window, waving to a police officer. "What's wrong? Can I get through here?"

"It's the prophet from the mountains, ma'am," he said as if she should know the name. "He's here because of the—"

"*The sinner shall die.*" A deep voice rolled over the officer's words. A tall figure in a long, dirty robe strode out of the crowd, came toward Kate. "*Thou shalt not hearken unto the dreamer of dreams: for the Lord your God will smite you with thunder and stones.*" He stopped a few feet from her car and raised a long wooden walking stick in the air. His dark eyes stared into hers, his face contorted in anger.

Kate quailed in the face of his fury. The man must be crazy!

"*And I shall not spare thee, sinner, neither will I have pity: thou shalt be punished in fire, according to thy false words and the evil in thy heart.*" He sliced the air with the stick.

"Sir, you're creating a disturbance here." The policeman stepped in front of him, motioning Kate to drive on.

She did, as quickly as she dared through the crowd of students. Those words had been meant for her, she knew. She vaguely remembered hearing or reading something about the man, but it wouldn't come to her. *Dreamer of dreams?* Did he know who she was? His deep-set eyes stayed with her. Probably the same look Charles Manson had. Her skin crawled.

She had to put him out of her mind. Later she'd figure it out, but right now she had to get back to the studio and Mrs. Armstrong.

The phone rang for the third time as John jumped off the ladder. He dropped the paint roller into the tray, silenced Pavarotti in mid aria with his left hand, and grabbed the receiver. "Yeah," he said, trapping the receiver between his chin and shoulder, trying to avoid transferring salmon-colored paint from his hands to the telephone.

"John, it's Susan. The police have found Kelly Landrum's body. She was in a lake called Joe Cassidy. If you want in on this, you'd better move." Susan, who monitored the police radio for the *Times Herald*, relayed pertinent information to the reporters.

"Where? Do you mean *Jocassee*, the one in Oconee County? That's a long way from home." He had to spell the name before she understood him. She had moved here from Iowa recently, and both the language and the geography of South Carolina were foreign to her.

"Yeah, that must be it. Where did they get a name like that?"

"Supposedly from a Cherokee princess who killed herself there.

It's a long story—I'll tell you sometime."

"Well, that's where the body is. Some fishermen found her at daybreak. The law from three counties is someplace called Devils Fork Landing."

"Thanks, Suse. I owe you one."

Ignoring the paint-laden roller and tray, he quickly washed his hands and arms in the kitchen sink. The story came first, always; the house might never be finished. What had possessed him to buy a place that needed this much remodeling? Instead of being a hobby, it had taken over a large portion of his life.

But by the time he reached the car, he had focused entirely on Kelly Landrum. On the drive out, he thought about the lake where she had been found, a large, man-made lake high in the foothills. The water covered hills and valleys, the convergence of three rivers. Trees, cemeteries, even churches and small rural houses had been flooded to make the lake—most still stood in the deep blue depths. He was amazed that she had been found.

When he reached Devils Fork, an ambulance was backing slowly down the boat ramp toward the water. Suse was right—cars and vans bearing law enforcement decals from three counties had the parking lot so crowded it looked like a midsummer Saturday afternoon. He parked between two black and whites, one from Greenville County and one from Pickens. Stepping over the yellow-tape barrier, he eased toward the crime-scene crew, trying to stay behind Lynne Waite, out of her view.

She and a large, heavyset man with an Oconee County patch on his sleeve were listening to a man in a plaid shirt and khakis, nodding together as he talked. Guessing he was the coroner, John edged up within hearing distance.

Waite, with the sixth sense he was convinced she had, turned to face him. "Beat it, Gerrard. We'll have something for you later," she said, pointing to the barrier. "Out."

"Just one question, Waite. How did she die? Can you tell?" He smiled at her. "I might have something new for you tomorrow."

"Not good enough. You've used that one too many times. Do you need an escort to find your way out?"

"I can make it on my own, but thanks for the offer." He held out his hands in mock surrender and grinned, knowing she wasn't bluffing. "See you, Detective."

Out of the corner of his eye, John saw one of the divers sitting on a rock at the shore. He thought the van containing the diving equipment was parked close enough to block Waite's view.

John approached cautiously, keeping out of the detective's line of sight. The young diver, holding his head in his hands, huddled between the big orange oxygen tanks that lay on the ground beside his fins. He looked sick. John squatted down beside him. "Pretty bad down there, huh?"

"Yeah. Bad," the diver said without raising his head.

"Anything different about this one?"

"Don't know—my first time when the body's been down there for a while." He swallowed hard.

"Could you tell how she died? Maybe she fell out of a boat and drowned."

"Only if she wanted to kill herself. She had concrete blocks tied to her feet."

John's stomach flipped. "She *was* murdered." He suddenly remembered Kate's vision. "Was there any visible damage?"

"Are you kidding? She's been down there at least a week. They're bringing her up now, but I bet it will take an autopsy to tell what happened. She was just standing on those blocks in the trees."

"Trees? What trees?"

"That's how they found her. The rope on one of the blocks caught in the tops of some trees about fifteen feet down. Fisherman snagged her hair. If she had gone to the bottom, it would have been maybe seventy or eighty feet. Probably never been found."

"Can you show me what position she was in? Could you tell what she was wearing?"

The diver stood and said, "Kind of like this, with her arms stretched out, kind of floating, and her eyes were open." He raised his arms, palms down, exactly as Kate had done. "Dark clothes, so she was harder to see."

John stood too, felt the hair on the back of his neck stand up. "Anything else?"

"Man, you should have seen those eyes. Funny they were still there." He turned green and sank to his knees.

John jumped back a step, only to bump into Detective Waite. She glared at him, making a slicing motion across her throat, and dropped to one knee beside the shivering diver.

Knowing he had pushed Waite far enough for now, John left. He still had one source—if you could call Kate a source—that no one else did. Did he believe her story? He wasn't sure. But she had been certain last night that Kelly was in a lake. And her description of the scene matched the diver's account too accurately to be dismissed. Even the part about the trees.

Chapter 5

WHEN JOHN REACHED THE OUTSKIRTS OF GREENVILLE, he stopped at a pay phone, found Kate's studio number in his notebook, and punched it in. After several rings, an answering machine picked up. He didn't bother to leave a message—he didn't think he would merit a call back in her books. Consulting the notebook again, he entered a second number.

Venice answered on the second ring. "Yes, this is Madame Venice. How may I help you?" Her voice dripped with mystery.

"This is John Gerrard. I need to see Kate right away. Do you know where I can find her?"

"John, how wonderful to hear from you again. She's usually in the studio by now. I can give you the number, but perhaps you would rather see her in person." Her voice lowered conspiratorially. "Is it something about our case?"

"This is not *our* case. It's just that the police found something, and I'd like to ask Kate a few more questions for my story. But I already called her studio."

"If she's busy, she doesn't answer. We can just go on over."

"I'm in kind of a hurry. I had better go straight there."

"That's fine. Her studio is at the Principal Players Theater. I'll meet you at the back entrance in a little while."

There was a click and he heard the dial tone. He sighed and hung up. "Great—both of them."

Ten minutes later John parked his ancient green Mustang next to a shiny black RX-7 behind the theater. He wondered if it could be Kate's. It looked like something she'd drive. The old station wagon probably belonged to the janitor—he couldn't picture Kate or Venice in it.

He should check Kate out more thoroughly, considering the accuracy of what she had said. Somehow, she knew something. He saw no sign of another car, but as he stepped from the Mustang, Venice swept out of the theater door to meet him.

"She has a client, but we can wait in her sitting area until she finishes." Venice led him through the door to the rickety elevator in the back of the building.

John looked skeptically up the shaft. "We have to ride on this? Maybe I'll just take the stairs."

"If you prefer. Kate's studio is on the fourth floor." Venice pushed a button and the wooden gate opened.

"The fourth floor?" He shrugged and followed Venice inside, stepping onto the dusty plank floor. "This thing looks like an accident hoping for an opportunity."

After a noisy, creaking ascent, they reached the fourth floor and crossed the hall to the studio. As they entered, John glimpsed Kate moving around behind a screen, adjusting the lights on a matronly woman in a pink dress. He walked quietly around the room, studying the portraits on the wall.

In one of the photographs, Venice, shadowed and mysterious, gazed directly into the lens of the camera over a candle flame. Next to her hung a slim, brooding man in Edwardian evening clothes, who stared at a painting of an early Manhattan skyline. Interesting effects.

A cool blonde straight out of the twenties dominated the opposite wall. Speakeasies and the word *gams* came to mind at her pose—one knee up and one long leg stretched out to show the edge of a black garter beneath a short, fringed skirt. A curl of smoke wafted across the dark background, adding to the illusion.

John wondered how Kate would photograph him. Somehow, a computer terminal and tape recorder didn't have the same appeal as an old Underwood and a battered notepad. He turned back to Kate and her client.

From his vantage point in the shadows, John was able to study her. Today she wore a dark blue dress with her hair slicked into a tight knot above her colorless face. She was nothing like the competent woman in the gray suit he had seen at last night's meeting. Nor was she anything like the angry, tousled woman he had met at the Black Forest. She looked downright mousy. What a fraud! She ought to be wearing tiger stripes.

He couldn't figure out how she had known about the body in the lake, but she obviously had a lot of imagination. It had to be more than a lucky guess, but he couldn't picture her being involved in a murder.

Kate moved around her client, tugging the pink skirt into graceful folds, tilting the woman's face to hide a slight double chin. She stepped back to the camera and looked down into the lens, then made a slight adjustment to the tripod. "Just lift your chin a little more. That's good. Close your eyes and rest them. Keep them closed until I tell you. Now, think about your new granddaughter. Open your eyes."

The woman immediately smiled, and Kate snapped a shot. She moved a light and adjusted the camera as they chatted. "Good. Just a couple more and we're finished." She took her final shots and turned off the spotlights. "Okay, that's it."

The woman rose and walked to the desk with Kate. "Can you have the proofs ready in two weeks? Is that too soon?"

"No. They should be back by then." Kate filled out a receipt and handed it to her.

"Thanks for squeezing me into your schedule. It's kind of a last-minute anniversary present. My husband's been wanting me to do this for years, and when he told me you were doing the portraits at the bank, I decided to call you." She placed the paper in her purse and, with a nod to Venice and John, stepped through the door.

Kate turned to Venice and John. "Well, you two look as though you've been up to no good. What's new?"

"There's a new development on our case," Venice said. "I thought it best that John tell both of us face to face."

Shaking his head at Venice's words, he dropped into a chair. "The police found Kelly Landrum's body this morning. She was in Lake Jocassee, standing just the way you said."

"Oh, no!" Kate paled and sat quickly on the edge of the desk. "I kept hoping it wasn't true."

"The poor child. After we saw her in the water, I knew it was only a matter of time till she was found." Venice patted the younger woman on the shoulder. "You must learn to accept your visions, Kate. While we are truly gifted, the price we pay can be terrible, especially if you fight it."

He shifted uncomfortably. "I know you didn't want to be involved in this, but the police know it's murder now. She was weighted with concrete blocks and thrown into that lake."

Kate sucked in her breath.

John leaned forward and looked at her. "Is there anything else? Anything at all you remember that could tie in to the killer?"

Venice shook her head. "Our visions cannot be willed or controlled. They are a gift and, sometimes, a curse. We saw only that poor child's body and the water." Stopping to unhook the catch on her bracelet from the weave of her long scarf, she continued. "Did you say Jocassee? That's a long way from here."

"Yes, it complicates the police investigation. Whose jurisdiction," he said. "Kate, are you sure there wasn't anything else?"

"No . . . no. Just the dark water and her—Kelly—standing there.

It was cold in the water." She stood and crossed to the window, closed her eyes, and leaned her forehead against the cool glass. "Whoever killed her is still out there."

"You poor dear." A hennaed curl drooped over Venice's left eye. She tucked it back into place and studied Kate critically. "Your aura has turned dark red. It's the stress from all this. You aren't used to it. I am going home to meditate, and I suggest you do the same."

"In a little while, Venice. I need to finish up some work here." Kate looked over her shoulder and smiled, then crossed the room to press a quick kiss to Venice's cheek.

"Very well. See that she goes home soon, John."

John sat on the desk and turned to Kate as Venice left. "Do you really have to finish now? I'd like to talk about this some more."

"Yes, I really have to finish. This is what I do for a living, remember? And I don't want to talk about visions or Kelly Landrum anymore today."

"How about tonight, then? I could take you to dinner."

"No, I have several appointments this afternoon, and I've got a lot of work to catch up on. Look, if you really want to talk, I guess I could meet you at the Black Forest after dinner, long enough for coffee."

"Right, a meeting." He wasn't sure whether to be disappointed or relieved. "This time, though, don't bring Venice. Is seven too early?"

"That's fine. I'll see you there." She leaned over to write the time on her desk calendar. "But first we have to set some ground rules for what does and doesn't go into the newspaper. You'll have to tell me when you're being a reporter. I don't want to worry that every word I say will be plastered all over tomorrow's front page."

"Okay, we'll talk about ground rules."

"Now, if you'll excuse me, I have work to do." She began making notes in her appointment book to demonstrate. "Wait—one question. Who is the prophet from the mountains?"

"He's some hermit type who shows up about once a year, comes to save the sinners and warn us about the end of the world. And while he's at it, he accepts contributions. He calls himself Ezekiel, after the prophet. Why?"

"I saw him earlier this morning. He looked straight at me and said something about being a dreamer of dreams. It was a little disconcerting."

"I don't know much about him, but I can find out. I think he's more of a nuisance than anything. Where was he?"

"Oh, just out on the street." She shuffled some papers. "Thanks for the information. I have to get back to work now."

"Now I have a question, and then I'll go."

Kate raised an eyebrow.

"How does Venice get here? I know she lives over on Abingdon, but she got here before I did." He had a sudden urge to see Kate smile. "And her broom wasn't in the parking lot."

She rolled her eyes, but she did smile. "I'll never tell."

After he left, she crossed to the big window that faced the street and lowered the blinds, blocking the sun. The shade was halfway down when she noticed a rusty gray Buick parked under a tree on the other side of the street. She couldn't see the figure slumped in the driver's seat very well, but she was sure the car was the same one she had seen this morning near her house. At least it wasn't a truck, and no one was waving a staff in her face. She turned back to her work and forgot the car and the prophet.

Venice called just as Kate closed the darkroom door, ready for lunch. "Hello, my dear. Martin and I are going to dinner tonight and thought you might join us."

"I can't. I'm meeting John at the Black Forest at seven."

"Meeting him? He isn't picking you up?"

"It's not a date, Venice. He wants to talk about Kelly Landrum again."

"Hmmpf. It's high time you started going out and having fun. I will come by and help you get ready. Martin can pick us up at six, and we'll eat at the Black Forest before your meeting."

Venice rarely used her no-nonsense tone. Kate touched her fingertips to her forehead, knowing she was wasting her time by arguing. "No. I am not dressing up, and I want to take my car so I can leave when I want to. You and Martin may not want to stay and talk to John." That was a joke—Venice not wanting to talk to the reporter?

"Of course I will. And so will Martin. We'll take you home afterwards. I'll see you at your house at five." She hung up before Kate could say anything else.

So much for John's request to leave Venice behind. There was no point in calling Venice back. Kate knew she wouldn't answer. She slung her leather bag over her shoulder and left, looking forward to soup and corn bread, today's special at Gene's Restaurant. She wondered what else could happen.

He heard it on the radio on the way home. They had found her! How? How could that be? That lake was so deep, and he'd been so careful to put her in the deepest part. Even if he had missed the exact spot on that rainy, moonless night, he knew the water was too deep in that section for her to be found. It hadn't been mentioned in this morning's edition of the paper.

He roared into the driveway and stopped the car, leaning out the door to snatch the afternoon newspaper. The garage door had barely lifted when he shot under it and turned off the engine. He ran into the house, unfolding the paper as he went. The first thing he saw was the banner: COED'S BODY FOUND IN JOCASSEE.

Frantically, he scanned the story. How had they discovered her? A fisherman, it said. A fisherman! No one fished on the bottom of the lake in that part. He didn't believe it. Rubbing his worry stone, he thought back to that night. He had been so careful this time. It wasn't right that she had been found.

He forced himself to sit down and read carefully so he wouldn't miss anything. It must have been Kate and Venice again. They must have seen the body and told the police where to find her. The police had said it was a fisherman only to protect the women. He wondered if Kate could have picked up something, some insight, when he saw her. Seeing her was risky, but he couldn't help it.

He had to stop them. If they hadn't identified him yet, they would. He had to get rid of them. He couldn't take any more chances on their knowing he was the one.

Keep calm, he told himself. *Can't let anyone see me. Have to plan this time, no impulsive actions like the other night on the mountain. Even then, if Kate hadn't been driving that damned Mazda, she would have gone over the edge and straight down to hell, but that little road hugger had held, and Carson's truck couldn't keep up on those curves.*

His car was too easily recognized. And even though it had been dark on the mountain, Kate might recognize Carson's truck. He would have to borrow his bookkeeper's old Buick again. But not yet, he thought. Even though he always returned it with a full tank of gas, Polly had made several pointed comments about the number of times he had borrowed it recently—and how much he had been out of the office. Nosy bitch.

At least he had figured out Kate's routine, knew where she went, what she did. Venice didn't seem to have one, but she did live alone in that big, secluded house. She would be easy.

Kate had made it very convenient, living in that rough area. No one would think twice about anything that happened there. He thought about her, pounding down the pavement the other morning. She was the type who would fight back if she was mugged. Maybe it would be better if she had an accident. With the cops tracing hairs and fibers and doing DNA tests, it was better to keep his hands off her, not take chances.

— 43 —

The warehouse where she had her studio was another good place. He had checked that out, too. Yes, that was it. The idiots kept the big front doors locked, but the maintenance man unlocked the back door about seven every morning.

He started the computer and began arranging his information into a timetable. He typed in *7:30*, the time Kate usually showed up. Then he added *8:00* to the maintenance man's column. After Kate and before anyone else arrived, the man left for forty-five minutes and went across the street to the restaurant. He did the same thing every morning. The Players never showed up before lunch.

If he parked a block or two away, he could use his own car, not have to call on Polly again. Because he would be long gone when it happened, and it would look like an accident.

Descending into his basement, he thought about the situation and selected the tools he would need. Just one or two more things, and he could pick those up anywhere. He carefully replaced the tools.

Planning, that was the key. He returned to his computer and detailed his plan. He thought better when he could see the neat lines of crisp letters, marching with military precision across the screen. When he had worked it all out, he closed the hidden file in the computer and turned on his security system.

He drove to a Home Depot several miles away. It was a busy place, open late. They'd never remember him. He bought a large pair of bolt cutters and a heavy leather tool belt, rather like an apron. He was grateful for the activity. Waiting gave him indigestion.

Back at his house, he packed the tools in the belt and experimented with the bulky leather under a worn denim jacket he had taken from a Goodwill donation box—let the police try to trace that! The bottom of the belt hung out, but he found that by rolling the apron tightly around the tools, he could tie it around his waist so it couldn't be seen. That way, the tools didn't clink against each other, either. He was ready. All he had to do was pick the time. Soon.

Venice, in a blur of paisley, was waiting on the porch when Kate got home. "I knew you were on your way, so I took a chance and got out of the car."

"I'm impressed. You should get a Purple Heart for bravery." Kate unlocked the door and led the way in. "Come in."

Venice adjusted her shawl and followed Kate inside. "I think you mean a Bronze Star for bravery. You have to be wounded to get a Purple Heart." The shoulder strap of her tiny purse caught on the doorknob, and she stopped to free herself.

"Bronze, then," Kate said, kissing the old woman's cheek. "You can read photography magazines while I dress."

"What are you wearing?" Venice, suspicious, angled toward the stairway.

"I thought I'd wear the jeans without holes since Martin is going. I don't want to embarrass him." Kate didn't know whether to laugh or cry. She knew she was in for a fight.

"You're impossible. John has never seen you dressed attractively. And," Venice added in a knowing tone, "I found out a little about him today. He's divorced, but that can't be helped."

"So am I."

"Yes, but you were married to a pompous. . . ." She hesitated, then found her word. "A vampire. That's what J. B. is. He would take your life's blood if he could. You were shriveling into nothing— a nonperson—when I found you."

"I was not, and he's not that bad. But that's beside the point. I am having a *meeting* with John, not a date." She started up the stairs but could see that Venice had more to say. Still hoping to discourage her, Kate stopped with one foot on the step. "Okay. Let's hear it."

"He cooks."

"What? Who?"

"He cooks. John Gerrard is a very good cook. You should give this man serious consideration." Venice cast a significant look toward Kate's kitchen. "Wear something nice."

"I don't care if he does windows. I'm not dressing up. He won't even be there till after we've eaten. I told him I was too busy to come earlier."

"Oh, Kate. I despair of your future," she huffed, following Kate up the stairs.

It's not a date, Kate reminded herself as she stripped off her clothes for a quick shower, but she took out a bar of soap scented with orrisroot that a friend had given her. She was drying her hair when Venice's voice floated in through the steam:

"I've found something for you to wear. Hurry up."

She sounded excited, a bad sign in Kate's book. While belting her robe, she peeped out through the bathroom door. A slither of green silk lay across the bed. "Venice! For heaven's sake, we're going to the Black Forest, not the governor's ball!"

"I knew it was too dressy, but it's such a beautiful thing, and this color will turn your eyes green. I just wanted John to see you in it."

"Oh, Venice. I do love you," Kate said, hugging her. "But I'm wearing jeans." She turned back to the closet to retrieve her jeans and noticed that her shoes had been rearranged. "What have you been doing in here?"

"I just put your white shoes in the back, dear. It's after Labor Day, you know."

"Saving me from a fashion faux pas? Or is that a social blunder?" Kate pulled out her oldest jeans, grinning wickedly. "How about these?"

"Both," Venice said, taking the faded pants out of Kate's hand. She reached past Kate and pulled out a cinnamon-colored dress. "Here. This is not too dressy."

In the end, they compromised on black slacks and a black sweater. Kate put on makeup and, tired of arguing with Venice, agreed to wear her hair down, scrunched into soft curls. Standing in front of the mirror, she tugged at the hem of the sweater. It was a little stark. She reached for her jewelry box, lifted a heavy, gold chain linked to a cabochon of red agate. With a sidelong glance at Venice, she dropped it over her head, appalled to discover she had wanted an excuse to look good.

"And now you can blame it on me," Venice said, laughing at Kate's startled face in the mirror. "You hardly look cheerful, but it's better than those disgusting clothes you wear at the studio."

Chapter 6

JOHN TOOK A CORNER TABLE at the Black Forest and was studying the menu board when headlights flashed through the front window. A tan Volvo stopped at the curb, and Martin Carver got out. John watched him circle the car and open both doors on the passenger side.

The professor took a woman's hand and helped her from the front seat. Ah, damn. Venice. Then Kate got out of the backseat, laughing. Too busy for dinner, was she?

From the dimly lit corner, John watched silently as Helmut greeted Kate. The big baker seemed stiff tonight. He was reasonably polite to the professor, but to Venice he merely nodded. Strange fellow.

As the trio moved toward a table, John spoke. "Hello, Kate."

She turned quickly in his direction. "John!"

"I thought I'd have dinner here before our meeting."

"We had the same thought. I finished earlier than I expected." She blushed slightly.

"So I see." His wide smile took the bite out of his words.

Kate stood awkwardly for a moment, but Venice swept by her and greeted John, suggesting they sit together. She introduced him to the professor.

Martin said, "I think I saw you at the para group meeting last night. I didn't realize you were the reporter who called me."

"Yes, I was at the meeting. I'm sorry I didn't introduce myself, but I wanted to talk with Wolynski."

"Did he say anything? Do you think he believed Kate and Venice?" Martin raised his eyes briefly to John, then focused again on steering Venice and her long skirt between the tables.

"I don't think he did at the time, but the way the body was found may change his mind," John answered, moving a chair out of Venice's path. "I expect all three of you will be hearing from Lynne Waite."

"Wonderful. Just what I always wanted." Kate studied the menu board. "I'm hungry, and Helmut will get upset if we don't order soon."

As they returned to the table, John held a chair for Kate. She smelled good, some light floral scent, not too sweet. "I like your hair like that."

Venice's pleased smile made him wonder if she had thought he was talking to her. Kate looked pained and said nothing.

"Doesn't she—" Venice started, but Kate cut in.

"No, Venice, she doesn't." Kate's threatening tone belied the saccharine smile she directed at Venice.

John, watching, thought they were both a little strange. He must have missed something.

Martin, who had apparently noticed the exchange, started a discussion on the merits of German food, which kept the conversation neutral until Helmut returned from the kitchen to take their orders. They ordered schnitzel with potato dumplings and red cabbage. John asked, "Do you have German beer or wine?"

"This is a decent place, where young people away from home can come for good food. I serve only coffee and tea and milk. No spirits or pop." Helmut's blond hair appeared to bristle as his face reddened. "When the weather is warm I serve iced tea and lemon. That is all."

"Please, Helmut. A pitcher of tea will be fine." Kate smiled and changed the subject. "John, did you know Helmut is a skilled mountain climber? He sometimes works with the rescue teams looking for lost hikers." She turned to Helmut. "Maybe one day you could tell John about your experiences."

"Yes," Venice put in, "Helmut loves the mountains."

Helmut glared at Venice but said nothing.

"Interesting. Where do you go?" John asked, puzzled by Helmut's hostility toward Venice. Tonight he was only marginally better with Kate.

"Some of the times I climb Caesar's Head or Table Rock. I go nearby because I have only Sundays." Helmut calmed and returned to the kitchen.

"He's getting worse," Martin said, watching the kitchen door. "After his wife left, he became surly and withdrawn."

"It's too bad," Kate said. "He's really a nice fellow, but he's very bitter." She looked around the tiny restaurant at the empty tables. "This place used to be packed when Gisela, his wife, was here."

"What happened to Gisela?" John asked.

"She just walked out one day," Venice answered. "He said she went back to Germany, that she missed her family. I expect she's better off there. Helmut's a fine cook, but being married to such a man would be a nightmare."

"That's a terrible thing to say," Kate said. "He has developed this Puritan streak, but—"

"Developed?" Martin said. "He's always had it. I think Gisela got smart and left him for someone else."

They were interrupted by Helmut's bringing their food. His sleeves were rolled back over forearms that looked like small hams, and a towel hung over his shoulder. "I still must serve the food. Tomorrow I think I must have another waitress to come." When they commented on the mouthwatering aroma, he managed a brief smile, then left them.

John joined in the conversation and soon realized he was enjoying himself without thinking of his next story, but he noticed no one brought up anything connected with Kelly Landrum. He and Martin were considering the Atlanta Falcons' chances this year, when Venice, returning from the rest room, brushed Kate's shoulder. Kate jumped, sending her fork clattering to the floor.

"Oh, my dear, I didn't mean to frighten you."

"It's okay. I'm just jumpy." Kate turned to John, reminding him of their purpose. "It's this wretched business with Kelly Landrum."

John hoped to avoid discussing it in front of Venice and Martin, since he knew they would be pumping him for information. He had one or two questions of his own, based on the research he had done that afternoon. "How long have you been coming to the Black Forest? Were any of you here much last fall?"

"I came frequently before Gisela left," Venice said. "But that was over a year ago. I don't come as often now."

"I haven't come much recently." Martin frowned. "And now I remember why. The man's downright rude."

"I come with Venice sometimes since I started taking the classes at the college. Why?" Kate asked.

"Just wondered. Anyone for dessert?" John asked.

No one wanted any, and Venice stood and looked at Martin, saying, "I have to leave now. I can't stay with you, Kate. John will drive you home after you've had a chance to talk."

She kissed Kate's cheek, and she and Martin were out the door before Kate could protest.

"That was a smooth exit." John smiled, well aware of Venice's matchmaking efforts. He could see that Kate was embarrassed. "I'd be glad to take you home."

"Thank you," she said without raising her head, her attention directed at the remains of her dinner. "I'm sorry about that. I'm sure her intentions are good."

"Yes. The road to hell and all that. Don't worry about it." Checking his watch, he added, "It's still early. I was hoping you would ride over to Jocassee with me." He saw her body tense, her face tighten.

"Isn't it a long way?"

"About forty-five miles. Are you up to it?"

She drained the last of her tea and stood. "Let's go."

John, watching Kate open her wallet, knew better than to pay for her meal. He waited quietly while she paid, and then handed Helmut the money for his. They said a quick good-bye to the surly man and stepped out into the evening.

John opened the car door and scooped up a handful of papers and an empty fried chicken box, talking as he dumped them over the seat and brushed it off for her. "I'd like to know more about your visions, or whatever they are. I'm not big on this stuff, but you described exactly what they found in that lake."

"I understand. I'm not that big on it myself." She kicked aside a plastic cup and a newspaper to make room for her feet.

The Mustang coughed, then struggled to life. He turned the car toward the highway. "Have you seen anything else?"

His emphasis on the word *seen* made her wince. "Let's establish the ground rules before we talk about Kelly Landrum. I'm not used to picking and choosing my words that carefully."

"I won't use anything that isn't relevant. But I have to tell you that if something you tell me becomes relevant at a later time, I might have to use it." He refused to mislead her—after all, it was his job to tell the story.

"In other words, anything I say is fair game."

"You can't expect me to leave out something that has a bearing on the story. I can't just write around personal feelings. I either write the whole story or I don't write at all."

"What about me? Don't I have a right to privacy? Like my name—I didn't want it used. I certainly don't want any more publicity. This wacky image you're giving me can hurt my business, and believe me, I can't afford it. People, especially older people, are very suspicious of anyone who's different. And those are the ones who can afford portraits, in case you didn't know."

"I'm not giving you any image at all. I kept the part about you and Venice to a minimum."

"All right," she conceded. "It wasn't too bad, but no more."

"I might have to mention you again. If you turn out to be right about any more of this Landrum business, I would have to. I don't want to, but I don't have a choice."

"Of course you have a choice. Just don't do it." She folded her arms across her chest and turned pointedly to look out the side window.

"If nothing else turns up, I won't." He concentrated on the road, thinking the autopsy could prove her wrong and he would never have to use her name again. But he had to be honest with her. "I can't make any promises."

John drove carefully through the little town of Traveler's Rest, watching his speed. Then, as they turned onto Highway 288 in Marietta, he sped up a little. The two-lane road was open in the gently rolling hills, and in the moonlight, he could see a long way. John asked her about Helmut. "I thought you were friends. Tonight he was barely civil."

"I noticed," she said, still looking out the window. "He probably read your article and decided I was as bad as Venice. He really doesn't approve of Venice's psychic bent. Now I guess I'm tarred with the same brush, so to speak."

"I'm sorry if it caused you a problem, but I don't think the guy's stable." As they slowed to a stop in Pumpkintown, he made a mental note to find out more about Helmut. Changing the subject to Kelly Landrum, he told Kate what he knew and how few leads there had been. "So you could be providing a new lead. If what you say, or see, is right about the jealousy or anger, it has to be someone who knew her. But not a regular boyfriend or anyone her friends were aware of. What does that suggest to you?"

"I don't know. Maybe a married man. Someone who needed to keep it secret. Maybe a professor."

They crested a hill, and John said, "That's the Keowee River down there. We'll cross into Oconee County, and then it's just a few miles to Devils Fork."

Even in the fading light in the car, he could see Kate's hands clench as they crossed the river. For a second, he was sorry he had brought her, but then he considered the story and squelched the thought.

"A professor—that's good," he continued. "I thought of a married man, but not a professor. What other kind of person would want to hide a relationship with a college student?"

"What about a politician?" she offered. "They're always worried about appearances."

"Yes. She was awfully young for the average bureaucrat. Besides, most of them are married."

"Not all of them. J. B.—"

"J. B. McGuire, the state representative?" He made the connection immediately, vaguely remembering photographs with a mousy little wife hovering in the background. No wonder he hadn't recognized her. And then the divorce. The press had had a field day with the handsome politician and his quiet, self-effacing wife, but there had been hardly any photos of her, just rampant speculation. That's why he hadn't connected McGuire's wife to Kate. Ouch. No wonder she was suspicious of the press. Turning off toward the boat landing, he said, "He's your ex."

"That's him."

"Weren't you a little young for him? Does he like young girls?" His mind slipped into high gear, wondering if there could be a connection. Maybe that's how Kate knew so much—maybe she had seen J. B. with the Landrum woman and was afraid to admit it.

"Of course not! There's nothing wrong with J. B."

"What did he think about your psychic abilities? Did it bother him?"

"Wait a minute. He has absolutely nothing to do with this. We've been divorced for over a year, and I hardly ever see him. You cannot connect him with this."

"He does a lot of fund-raisers on the campus, uses student volunteers." He downshifted to second and let the engine slow them as he followed the twisting, descending road toward the water.

"That's ridiculous." She turned in her seat, glaring at him.

"You're awfully protective for an ex-wife." He stopped the car and faced her, one eyebrow raised.

"It's just that he's a nice guy and doesn't deserve to be tangled up in anything that could affect his political career. The divorce was bad enough."

"Then why did he do it?"

"What makes you think he did it?" She turned away and fumbled for the door latch. "Let's get on with this."

"Whatever you say." Remembering her flash of temper the first time they met, he backed off. He couldn't afford to alienate her just now—she was the only item of interest in what looked like a dead-end case. He told himself that was his only interest in her. Liar. He got out and walked around the car to Kate's side. Dark had fallen. "The moon is almost full, and it's clear tonight, so maybe we won't break our necks. Are you sure about this? You don't have to, you know."

"I know. I'm fine." She got out, staring over the moonlit water. "I doubt if I'll see anything. So far, things have come only through touch."

John took her arm and led her down the boat ramp to the water. "This is where they brought her out. She was about half a mile from the shore—he was probably aiming for the three rivers. Good thing he missed. It's about 800 feet deep there."

They stood in silence at the water's edge. Deep shadows disguised the outline of the rough bank; a soft night-wind ruffled the surface of the lake. Although it wasn't cold, Kate wrapped her arms around herself.

The water lapped gently against the base of a large rock near the edge of the concrete. She sat down on it, her expression blank. John pictured Kelly as Kate had described her, floating, her arms outstretched toward the dark sky.

Kate's head snapped up. "Boats! Where do they keep the boats?" She jumped up, turning as she tried to see the shoreline, and would have tumbled into the water if John hadn't caught her arm.

"What boats? What did you see?"

"I'm not sure." She exhaled, deflated. "Probably nothing. Water slapping against something. I don't know if I imagined it or saw it."

"Well, what was it?"

"I think she was being carried through the woods. She was already dead." She tilted her head back, looking at the skewed trees, and lost her balance again.

"What the hell are you doing, Kate?" John caught her again. He didn't know whether she was crazy or possessed, but she certainly needed a keeper.

"Let go!" She shook herself free, shaking her head at the same time, trying to clear it. "I'm sorry. I'm glad you're here. I couldn't tell what's real for a minute."

"Could you just tell me what's going on?"

"I was trying to concentrate on Kelly, picturing her in the lake, but then I saw the trees, sort of upside down." She described what she had seen, adding, "But I don't know if it really happened. The only times I've ever seen anything before are when I've touched something."

"Maybe you did touch something. That's where the diver who first saw her was sitting. They brought her out about there, too. Would that be enough?" He didn't tell her what the diver saw, or how sick the guy had been.

"I don't know. I'm not sure of anything anymore."

"Let's back up. You said you heard water slapping against something. And you asked where the boats are. Did you see the boat?" John peered into the darkness, blocking out the moon with his left hand. "There are no rental boats here. It had to have been a private one."

"This isn't helping. I couldn't see the boat. I don't really know if I saw anything," she muttered in disgust. "Maybe I'm losing my mind. I don't know what's going on."

"I sure as hell don't," he said. "The body had to have been in a boat to get that far out into the lake, but anyone could have put in at the Jocassee landing and gone out toward the middle. We could find out if there are any private landings with access to this lake, and who owns them. See if any familiar names turn up."

"Why would someone come all this way to dispose of her?"

"Because this lake is over a thousand feet deep in places. If he had hit the right area, she would probably never have been found. I think she must have been killed and brought directly here on that Friday night she disappeared. It was dark and rainy and—"

"Rain! Yes, I saw rain when she was being carried."

He didn't get the significance, but she seemed excited by it. Maybe it helped her confidence. They walked slowly back toward the car, with Kate twisting, walking backwards, looking up all the way.

John kept his hand out, ready to grab her if she fell or stumbled. He hoped she wasn't going into a trance or whatever these people did. She was shivering. He wished he had a jacket or a sweater to give her. "Look, why don't we come back tomorrow when it's daylight? We could try the other landing, and then maybe we'd find something."

"I have to check my appointment book. I can't think right now, and I need to talk to Venice."

"Venice? Why?"

"Because she's the real psychic. She may be a little heavy-handed sometimes, but she understands this stuff. Maybe she can explain what happened tonight." Kate climbed into the cozy litter of John's car and rested her head on the seat back. They drove in silence, passing a few lighted houses and fewer cars. It was a lonely road. Kate drifted off.

When they reached Greenville, she roused herself and told him where she lived. She was almost asleep again when he turned onto her street.

"We're here. Which house?"

"There," she pointed. "Whoops. My mother did teach me not to point." She yawned, covering her mouth with her hand.

John coasted to a stop in front of her house and turned off the engine. Looking up and down the street, he said, "I'll walk you to the door."

"Thanks, but I'm used to this neighborhood. I'll be all right."

He got out with her anyway. "By the way, I think you should know that I had some calls today asking about the psychics. Some of the callers were pretty hostile."

"I'll bet." She yawned again.

"One of them was the prophet. He's crazy. I hope you don't run into him again."

"I won't. I have appointments most of the day tomorrow."

Annoyed, he shook the water off the plastic bag holding the morning newspaper and glanced at the leaden sky. It promised rain all day. He dropped the wet wrapper in the trash can and stepped out of his shoes at the door, entering the kitchen barefoot.

Hurriedly, he downed the last of his tomato juice and cleared his cereal bowl off the table. The damp pages of the paper stuck together. He carefully pulled them apart, spread the open pages on the table, and began reading.

First the body—he still couldn't believe it had been found—and now the preliminary autopsy said she had been strangled. A prickle of fear inched across his scalp. He thought she had been in the water too long for them to figure that out. Still, they couldn't tie it to him.

Nothing was going right. Like last night—he had waited for Venice and then she had shown up with that damned professor, who had gone into the house with her.

He continued to read. Suddenly his heart lurched. The name struck him like an angry copperhead—Charlene Nelson! They had forgotten her, dropped the case, he raged, smacking the paper down on the glass table. It had been almost a year, and they had given up finding her killer. He had buried her in the woods, thinking she wouldn't be found, but that had been a mistake. Some kid and his dog had uncovered her right away. Now this Gerrard fellow was suggesting a connection between her and Kelly. There was no way he could know that. Charlene hadn't been at all like Kelly. Charlene had been a mistake from the beginning. But never mind about that; she was history. The question was, how did Gerrard know about her? Speculation? Or the women?

Carefully, he restored the newspaper to order and finished reading. Good. It didn't mention Kate and Venice at all, and no one else could possibly connect him to Charlene.

He had begun to relax when he saw it—another, smaller article on the third page, where the main story carried over. That damned Gerrard again. He described the "uncanny accuracy" of the psychics' visions of the body and how Landrum had been found, even to the dark clothing she had been wearing. The concrete blocks eliminated accidental death, lending credence to their visions. It was the women! They told the police where to find her. He knew all along it was them.

Fear gripped him. He couldn't wait any longer. They were probably spying on him right now. He should have taken care of them right away. Well, he would now, before they led the police to him.

Chapter 7

ON THURSDAY EVENING a steady, drizzling rain reminded Kate that fall was on its way. The raw air suited her mood and made her long for something hot and comforting, maybe soup. On the way home, she stopped briefly at the grocery and then, digging out two quarters from the bottom of her purse, bought a paper from the vending box.

Lately she seemed to have developed an avid interest in the news and stopped almost daily at the Quick Shop for a copy. Sundays were no longer enough. She ought to have at least the afternoon paper delivered. During the week, she didn't have time to read two a day, and mornings were too rushed.

The boarding house lot held only the usual vehicles, she noted as she turned onto her street. She saw neither dark trucks nor the mysterious gray Buick that had appeared with alarming frequency. Small comfort, she thought. *Goodness, I'm getting paranoid!*

Looking ahead, she saw several people standing on the sidewalk in front of her house. What now? Her pulse jumped a notch. She slowed almost to a stop, craning to see what had attracted them. Whatever it was, it was at her house. She parked on the street and opened her door. The voice carried over the crowd:

"Bring up a host against them, and make them an object of terror. . . ."

The damned prophet! What was he doing here? She tried to merge into the little cluster of onlookers to see. He was on her bottom step, beard, hair, and robe flying in the wind. The sudden exposure of his black Keds made him even more sinister. Should she leave? She hated to give up her own house. Before she could move, the crowd parted, and he stood before her.

"And the host shall stone them and dispatch them with their swords. He shall slay their sons and their daughters, and burn up their houses." His staff jabbed at the sky like a lightning rod. *"Thus will I put an end to lewdness in the land, that all women may take warning—"*

"What are you doing here?" Kate broke in, trying to sound strong. The wind blew harder and the rain fell faster. The man, not as old as she had first thought, looked skyward triumphantly.

His deep voice boomed out. *"Therefore thus saith the Lord God; I will even rend it with a stormy wind in my fury; and there shall be an overflowing shower in mine anger, and great hailstones in my fury to consume it."*

With his raised staff and wild eyes, he indeed looked like a prophet of old. Her heart pounded. The wind whipped his robe back. Only then did she see a spray can in his left hand. What—

A siren wailed, drawing his attention toward the street. He looked back at her, fierce with hatred. *"Yea, I will gather you, and blow upon you in the fire of my wrath, and ye shall be melted in the midst thereof."*

The prophet greeted the officer with silence. The burly policeman put the man in the backseat and told Kate's neighbors to go home, then turned to Kate.

When she gave him her name, he sighed. She was sure he knew who she was. He probably thought she and the prophet were two of a kind.

"What brought you here?" she asked the officer, ignoring the steady stream of invectives now coming from the backseat.

He leaned down and spoke sharply to the venom-spewing preacher before answering. "One of the neighbors reported a disturbance," he said, sliding into the car with the furious man. "Call if he bothers you again."

Thank goodness for the neighbors! After the policeman left, she moved the car to the rickety garage and made sure the lock on the doors behind the car was secure before she went inside.

In the kitchen, she shook the rain out of her hair, laid the paper and groceries aside, and put a pot of water on the stove. What had happened to her quiet life? What on earth had possessed her to wish for a little fun? And how had that man found her? She felt sure he'd come because of Kelly Landrum and the visions.

While she waited for the water to boil, she stowed away the few items she had bought and read the directions on a box of lentil soup mix—lentils, rice, and a small pouch of spices—to the accompaniment of her rumbling stomach. As soon as the lentils started cooking, she grabbed the paper to look for anything new on Kelly Landrum. She wondered what had drawn the prophet's attention. She didn't have to look far. The article led page three. With her attention focused on the story bearing John's byline, she absently took a slice of corn bread saved from the restaurant and popped it into the microwave.

"Oh, no!" The black words swam in front of her eyes. The prophet slipped from her mind. Quickly, she dialed Venice's number.

Venice answered before the end of the first ring. "Kate? Is that you? I've been trying to call. My paper didn't come, but I know there must be news on our case."

"Right. John has another story. Venice, listen to this! He mentions an unsolved murder from last summer." Kate, with the phone caught between her shoulder and ear, paced the length of the kitchen as she read to Venice, occasionally stopping to sniff and stir the lentil mixture bubbling away on the stove. "There's a picture of the girl. It looks like a high school yearbook photo. He says that Charlene Nelson was strangled and left under a pile of leaves and brush in a wooded area. The police have never found the killer. Oh, Venice, it couldn't be the same person."

She leaned over to turn the page and spread the paper on the countertop. Feeling a cold hand brush against her neck, she leapt back, gasping, and dropped the phone.

Venice's voice came faintly from the floor. "Kate? Are you all right?"

"I just dropped the phone." Kate, embarrassed, realized it had been her wet ponytail falling across her neck. "He says the psychics envisioned exactly what the police found at Lake Jocassee."

"I'm worried about you. I think I had better talk to Ramses again."

"I haven't finished reading." Kate paused, scanning the rest of the article. "Damn him! All kinds of crazy people are going to be looking for us. That wretched prophet from the mountain was on my doorstep tonight."

"Kate. Be careful. I have a feeling of danger. Last night when Martin brought me home, it was so strong I asked him to come in and check the house for me. Now I think it's directed at you. I don't like this."

"I'm okay. Everything's locked. But what about Charlene Nelson? Do you remember anything about her?"

"No. Just that a girl's body was found."

Venice's flat statement scared Kate. The woman must be truly frightened. The daffy old witch never, ever admitted to not remembering anything. If she didn't know, she made it up and swore the other person had the faulty memory. "Venice, I could come over if you want. Maybe it would be better if I spent the night with you."

"No, but thank you for offering, Kate. I'm fine now. It's you I'm worried about. Have you seen John again? I'd feel better if he were with you."

"I hardly know the man! I may never see him again."

"Ramses says there's a strong connection between you two. Just let it happen."

Ignore her, Kate told herself. It was absolutely pointless to argue with Venice on something like this. "Be careful, Venice. I'll call you tomorrow from the studio." Thoughtfully, she dished the lentils into a bowl and sat down to eat.

6:10 a.m.

Still dark. Time to move.

At least he had another car now, and they hadn't found the old man, so no one knew it was missing. When they discovered the body, he would get another one. No sense using his own anymore. And replacing it had been so easy. One clip with the pipe, and the guy had dropped like a lead weight. Probably did him a favor—he must have been a hundred and looked sick besides, wheezing his way to the kitchen, all white hair and liver spots. Professor Plum, he thought, in the kitchen with a lead pipe—and Miss Scarlet was next. They hadn't a clue.

Inside his garage, he lifted the hood of his new car and, using a rag wrapped around his finger, carefully wiped a smear of grime off the engine block. He rolled it in the rag and tucked it into the tool belt. On television, the cops always recognized a fresh cut because it was clean. He was smarter than that.

He drove into town, parked the car, and walked to a vacant lot behind the warehouse. It was ideal, higher than the gravel parking area at the back door and overgrown with small trees and weeds. He wanted to be in place early and make sure there were no surprises. He popped a couple of Tums into his mouth and settled down to wait, rubbing his thumb over the concave surface of the agate stone in his pocket.

Kate pulled up behind the building at 7:30 as he'd expected. A few minutes later he saw the lights come on in her studio. Occasionally she came close enough to the window that he could see her. His stomach tightened. He wished it didn't have to look like an accident.

At 8:00 the back door opened, and the maintenance man appeared. Right on schedule. He patted the tool belt and surveyed the area. Kate was out of sight of the windows, and no one else was around. He slipped out of the undergrowth, ran quickly along the perimeter of the parking lot and into the building.

He took the stairs to the fourth floor, panting. He couldn't risk calling the elevator to the first floor because of the noise. He listened at the studio door but heard nothing. She was probably in the darkroom. Turning to the elevator, he examined the door.

Although opening the door was relatively quiet—nothing like the creaks and groans of the cage in motion—this was the risky part. If she heard it, she could come out to investigate. He felt for the pry bar in his tool belt, watching the studio. If she came out and saw him, he'd pretend he'd come to see her about a picture, or he could finish her right there if he had to.

No, no. It had to be an accident.

He let go of the bar. He could keep the tool belt hidden. Fortunately, it was cool enough this morning that the denim jacket was justified. He pressed the button, and the door opened, revealing the crude wooden cage, just as he had hoped: The elevator stayed in its last position until it was called to another floor.

He waited a minute longer to be sure Kate didn't come out. He listened. Still nothing from the studio.

Entering the elevator, he pressed the "Close Door" button and climbed to the top of the open cage, pulled himself up onto the ladderlike rungs embedded in the shaft wall, from which he could reach the cables. Removing a rasp from his tool belt, he began sawing through the wire cable. It was much tougher than he had expected. He had hoped to make it look frayed and avoid a clean cut, but he would have to use the bolt cutters after all. Maybe he could rough up the cut with the rasp afterwards.

This was taking longer than he thought. He flashed the penlight on his watch: 8:27. The maintenance man would be back in eighteen minutes. Trying to judge how far to cut into the cable, he began to sweat. He cut further. The cable held. He snipped a few more strands and waited, shifting his weight on the rung ladder. Nothing. 8:31. He was well into the cable by now. What if he cut too far and it fell before he could get out? He made another tiny cut. One of the remaining strands snapped. The cut widened slightly, stretching the strands.

This was it! Quickly he slid the cutters back into his belt and took out the greasy rag. He rubbed it over the cut, wishing for more time to rough the cut with the rasp. It would look more like wear, he thought. But it was 8:34 now, too late. As he turned to leave the shaft, he glanced at the light bulb wired to the top of the cage and smiled. A quick twist and it was out. It would be worse for her in the dark. He climbed down the rungs, squeezing past the cage, careful to avoid putting any weight on it, until he reached the opening. He listened but heard nothing from the studio across the hallway. He dropped to the floor and darted across to the stairwell.

Outside, he sprinted to the safety of the bushes and crouched there as the maintenance man rounded the corner of the building. He knew he should leave, get away from the area. It would be dangerous to stay, and he had really neglected his business lately. Then Kate passed in front of the window again, and he found himself unable to move. Maybe he'd watch, just for a little while. He wondered if he'd be able to hear it crash from outside.

All morning Kate had been restless, edgy; and more than once she thought she had seen someone lurking in the bushes behind the parking lot. The phone seemed to ring every time she went into the darkroom, but it always stopped before she could get to it, adding to her frustration.

Glaring at the now-silent phone, she snapped a 400-millimeter lens onto her Nikon, edged to the studio window, and checked the bushes again, careful to keep out of sight. Raising the camera, she adjusted the focus and snapped off three quick shots. *This is insane,* she thought. *It's probably kids playing hooky from school. If so, it might make a nice shot. And if not, maybe I'll get lucky and see a face.*

But whose face?

She returned the camera to the drawer and went back to the darkroom. The publicity shots for one of the character actors with the Principal Players were due. She had promised to leave them downstairs at the theater for him to pick up this evening.

Working in the dim red glow of the darkroom, Kate fed the strip of negatives into the enlarger and adjusted it until an image filled the eight-by-ten block framed beneath it. She rolled the 35-millimeter film forward to the first of the shots she had selected. Since the players only wanted eight by tens, she used her lighter weight Nikon N70 with fine-grained Fuji film for their portraits. The Mamiya she kept in the studio for the larger portraits. Even used, she could have lived for a few months on what she had paid for the medium-format camera. But it was worth it, she reminded herself, making a mental note to pick up Mrs. Armstrong's proofs from the lab. She found the frame, made a few quick adjustments, and placed the ghostly face slightly off-center. As she slipped a sheet of photo paper into the frame, the phone rang in the other room, but she couldn't stop now. Surely the caller would leave a message this time. She started the timer and grabbed a quick sip of lukewarm coffee as the bright light burned the image into the paper.

The timer sounded and the enlarger light went out, returning the room to the red glow of the safety lamp.

She lifted the paper from the frame and slid it into a tray of developer, watching intently as the first faint shadows slowly evolved into the actor's lined face. Although it was a traditional publicity shot, she was pleased with it. This was what drew her to photography—seeing her work come to life on the blank white paper.

The phone rang again in the other room. Each time she had left the darkroom and checked, there had been no message. Probably Venice. She never left messages. *I'll call her as soon as I'm finished.*

When she was satisfied with the picture, she transferred it to a tray of fixer. She made several prints, swirling them gently in the chemical baths, until the last one reached the final stage, the stop bath. She flicked the overhead light switch and turned off the safety light before rinsing the prints in the water-filled sink. Then each print had to be squeegeed dry on a pane of glass. After plastering the dryer with the prints, she started cleaning up. The ancient dryer roared in her ears. Soon, maybe after she finished the bank portraits, she would replace it. She dried her hands and closed the darkroom door behind her. Her stomach reminded her of the time.

Back in the studio she examined the peanut butter sandwich she had brought. It looked decidedly unappetizing. Briefly she considered calling James Earl, the maintenance man, to see if he would pick up a vegetable plate for her when he went out at noon, but she was too hungry to wait. Before she could get out the door, the phone rang again. This time she answered. "Period Portraits, Kate McGuire speaking."

"Hi, Kate. It's John. Have you had lunch?"

It must be fate, she thought, glancing at the sandwich in the trash. She checked the worn khakis she was wearing. No stains. "No, I haven't."

"Good. I'll come get you and we can grab a sandwich at the Sunshine Cafe, if that suits you."

"I was just about to leave. Why don't I meet you there?" The Sunshine Cafe? Her mouth watered. She dreamed about their chicken-salad sandwiches. The sandwich shop, once tucked into the corner of a pharmacy, had gradually taken over until the whole place had become the Sunshine Cafe, but the same family still owned it. It would be a good candidate for the book on Greenville she wanted to do one day. Looking through some old photos her father had taken had given her the idea. A bit of then and now.

"I'm already in your parking lot," he said, interrupting her daydreams. "Come on down."

She hung up and ran to look out the window. Sure enough, the Mustang was down there, and John was leaning on the open door, looking up. As she waved, she remembered the figure in the bushes, but no one was visible now.

The phone rang again as she locked the studio door and turned toward the elevator. It continued to ring. She hesitated, then went on. For an instant, she thought she could hear Venice's voice, calling to her to stop. Shaking her head, she stepped into the elevator and pressed the button marked *B*. As the outer door closed, all light disappeared. *What happened to the light?* It would only take a minute or so to get down and then she would tell James Earl, she reassured herself, staring blindly into the darkness.

A slight pinging, like wire snapping above her head, sounded overloud in the descending cage. She looked up, but the blackout in the shaft prevented her from seeing. More pings. Without warning, the cage lurched and dropped a few inches. Kate grabbed the wooden gate that formed the inner door, terrified. There was another snap, louder, and Kate screamed as the elevator dropped another foot, hesitated, and then plummeted.

It plunged endlessly downward. Kate, petrified, clung to the rail. Abruptly, the cage clattered to a jarring halt, slamming her to the floor. A cloud of dust erupted around her. Stunned, she lay there for a second, trying to catch her breath and determine if she was dead or hurt.

Aachoo! She couldn't stifle the sneeze that erupted into the dust.

The elevator box creaked. Cold sweat broke out on her forehead. *Don't panic!*

Trying to think, she looked around and saw the faint outline of a wide door. The top of it was only a few feet above the floor of the cage. In the narrow gap between the ill-fitting upper and lower sections of the freight door, she thought she could see a strip of green, the color of the Principal Players' carpet on the second floor.

Two more floors to the basement—it could fall again! Fighting panic, she inched her way across the dirty floor toward the remains of the wooden gate. The top bar was on the floor with her, and one end of the lower bar rested on top of it. The cage creaked again and she froze. *Would it hold?*

From below, she heard the door open, and James Earl's voice echoed up the shaft. "What happened? Is anyone up there?"

Another voice sounded in the background. She heard James Earl say he thought the elevator had fallen, and then John was there, shouting, "Kate? Are you all right?"

"I'm here," she called, barely above a whisper. She was afraid to answer for fear the noise alone would disturb the elevator's tenuous position. "I think I'm okay."

"Don't move. We'll get you. Just stay perfectly still." She could hear John telling James Earl to call the fire department as his voice faded out of range.

Hours seemed to pass before she heard John say, "We're here, Kate. James Earl is opening the door now. He has to override the safety lock. We'll have you out in a minute."

His calm voice continued. "The fire department's on the way. Just stay still. Okay, he's opening the door now."

Light poured in as the gap between the horizontal freight doors slowly lengthened. Kate, still on her hands and knees, held her breath, her heart pounding. The elevator creaked but didn't move.

As soon as the door rose above the floor of the suspended cage, she saw John. Only about three feet separated her from the opening, but she had to get under the cage's broken door. She guessed it to be about eighteen inches off the floor at the highest point. Slowly she shifted her weight from knee to knee until she crossed the space. She reached for his outstretched hand, her lifeline. "John, pull me out."

"No, Kate," James Earl said. "The fire department said not to touch anything. They'll be right here. Your friend here made me open the door. I'm going to wedge this board against the wall of the shaft under the elevator. It will hold until the firemen get here."

Kate barely heard him. She could think again, and she wasn't staying here a single second longer than she had to. "You pull me out or I'll jump." Drawing up her right leg, she carefully shifted onto her foot.

"Hold on," John said. "Just a few more minutes. I won't let go. I can hear the siren now."

"No. Help me, John." Beneath her whispered words, the terror she felt was clear.

"Give me your other hand." John held her left hand steady, supporting her as much as he could while she eased all her weight onto her right foot and got her left foot under her.

Although ice water ran through her veins, she could see beads of sweat on his face.

"Are you sure you want to do this, Kate?"

She nodded. She launched herself forward in a flat racing dive. John jerked back and pulled at the same time. Kate flew through the opening, scraping her back on the bars of the door, and crashed into him. He staggered but managed to stay upright, catching her in his arms. The elevator creaked but stayed in place.

When the firemen arrived on the second floor, John was sitting against the wall in a metal folding chair, holding Kate, who was still shaking. She sat on his lap with her face pressed against his neck. He rubbed her back while James Earl hovered nearby, stepping back and forth over the length of two-by-four he hadn't used.

After the initial jumble of explanations, she forced herself to let go of John and face the firemen. John stood and eased her into the chair.

One of the firemen gently checked her for injuries, especially her legs and ankles, while another questioned her. The medic lifted her shirt and examined the scrape on her back. "You may be a little tender, but I think it's okay."

With the firemen's calm concern, she gradually pulled herself together, assuring them that she was all right, and described what had happened.

James Earl and the others were peering into the shaft, now illuminated by several flashlights. One of them snagged Kate's shoulder bag from the floor of the cage and handed it to John.

"Can you tell what happened?" John asked an older fireman who seemed to be in charge.

"Only what stopped it. There are safety devices built into it that kick in when the elevator exceeds a certain speed. From what little I can see, it looks to have been pretty well maintained. We'll have to get somebody from the elevator company over here to examine it with our inspector and figure out why it fell. It's really unusual."

John looked up the shaft but couldn't see anything. He didn't want to think it was anything other than an accident, but he had a bad feeling. "As soon as you know what caused it, give me a call, will you? It might be important." He scribbled his home number on the back of a business card and gave it to the fireman. "Home or work, anytime."

"Sure thing." The man read the card and stuffed it into his pocket. "I've seen your name in the paper. Why does something like this interest you? Nobody got hurt."

Checking to be sure the emergency team had Kate's attention, John answered, keeping his voice low. "It's possible there's a connection to a story I'm working on. Check it carefully, will you?" He didn't want to get into any lengthy explanations, and he didn't want to scare Kate unnecessarily.

The fireman frowned, squinting into the darkness above the cage, then looked over at Kate, who was still in the chair where John had left her. He leaned closer to John and lowered his voice. "Does that mean you think this might not have been an accident?"

"Maybe. It was only a thought." He too looked at Kate. Her eyes looked like burnt holes in a sheet. He ought to get her out of here. "But I wouldn't want to take any chances, just in case."

"I'll be sure they check," the fireman promised.

The paramedics wanted to take Kate to the hospital to check her out and to X-ray her ankles, but she flatly refused, insisting she was fine. Shrugging, they advised her to stay off her feet, watch her ankles. As they picked up their gear, the younger one turned to John. "Keep an eye on her. She's a little shocky."

"Let's get out of here." He scooped Kate up in his arms and carried her down the hall to the front elevator, the one the Principal Players used. He could feel her tensing up as she realized where they were going.

"Wait! I can walk. Let's use the steps." She tried to wriggle out of his arms.

He tightened his hold and said, "Dammit, Kate, you ought to go on a diet."

"A diet?" She stilled, and her voice rose over the two words.

"Right. You weigh a ton!" He huffed as he punched the elevator button with his elbow, turning Kate away from the door. He squeezed her slightly. "A little pudgy, aren't you?"

"I am not pudgy! Put me down, you pig."

To the women of his acquaintance, an extra ounce was anathema, and the word *pudgy* had the power to start a fistfight. As he had hoped, his remarks distracted her long enough to overcome her immediate trepidation. The smooth hydraulic lift arrived quietly behind her.

He stepped into the elevator with her.

When she realized where they were, she tightened her arms around his neck and buried her face against his collar. "John," she whispered. "I don't want to do this."

"Hang on, honey. This one's perfectly all right, I promise you." He pressed his cheek to the top of her head, then grinned and shook his head slightly. She smelled like chemicals again.

Before the elevator stopped they could hear Venice. "What do you mean, the elevator fell? Where's Kate? Is she hurt?"

Two of the firemen, trying to get past her, were pointing to the elevator when the doors opened.

Kate sighed gratefully when John stepped out onto the solid floor. "Here I am, Venice. I'm fine."

"Oh, Kate! I was so afraid!" The old woman, tears running down her cheeks, threw her arms around both of them. "I knew something was wrong. I've been trying to call you for hours."

John managed to get Kate, with Venice clinging to them, to the nearest bench. "If we don't sit down, I'm going to drop you. The two of you are a bit much."

Despite his good-natured grumbling, he neatly sidestepped Venice and placed Kate gently on the seat in the lobby. "Are you sure you don't want to go to the emergency room and let them check you?"

"She doesn't have insurance, and she can't afford it," Venice told him.

"Venice!" Kate admonished, embarrassed. "If I thought I needed to, I'd go. What I need is to get out of here."

"How about some Kentucky Fried Chicken?" John asked Kate. "I'll take you home, and we can pick it up on the way. Venice, why don't you come, too. Maybe you could stay with Kate this afternoon. She's not supposed to be on her feet. Later, I'll get someone to take her car back to her house."

"Fine," Kate said. "Thank you."

Venice nodded, taking Kate's bag.

"Okay, here we go again." He picked her up once more and took the stairs to the basement, while Venice followed.

"Kate, didn't you hear your phone ringing? I have felt all morning that you were in danger, and I called several times. You *said* you would call me."

"I heard it, but I was in the darkroom. A message would have been nice. What, exactly, did you see?"

"Malice. A threat. I woke up to a feeling of danger. Tell me what happened. Whatever it was, it wasn't an accident."

When they reached Kate's house, John carried her to the front door. "What the hell is this?"

They all stared at the scarlet letters sprayed across her door: HARLOT.

"That must be what the prophet was doing here. He had a spray can with him. I didn't notice the door then, but you'd think someone would have seen it. I wonder if he's been back here." Kate glanced around, as if expecting him to leap out of the bushes.

"What prophet? That crazy preacher?" John asked. He remembered the man's telephone call after Kate's name appeared in his article. Had mentioning her name really caused all this?

"He was here when I got home yesterday, but I went in the back. This is the first time I've seen the front door." Tears rolled down her cheeks.

Venice glared at John. "You did this, young man. I hope you realize what danger you've put her in."

"It's no one's fault. It would probably have come out one way or another," Kate said, wiping her tears away. "Sorry, it just overwhelmed me for a minute."

"You may be right, Venice. I'll find out more about the prophet." John quietly accepted blame and didn't remind Venice of her role as catalyst. He was much more concerned about the danger to Kate.

Chapter 8

"HELLO?" Kate mumbled into the phone, not opening her eyes.

"What the hell are you up to now?"

The voice in her ear registered immediately, jerking her fully awake. She sat up. "J. B.? Is that you?"

"Of course it's me! And how did you get involved in a murder? You're no damned psychic."

"I'm not involved. And how did you know?" she asked, shoving her hair out of her face as she kicked off the covers.

"The Sunday *Times Herald*, Kate. The front page. John Gerrard, that's how. He called yesterday to ask some stupid questions, like did I have anything to say about your involvement in that coed's murder. He even asked if I had ever met her! Now I'm involved, just because I was married to you."

"Oh, no! J. B., I'm really sorry." Kate reached for the clothes she had dropped on the floor last night, pulling them on as she talked. "I didn't know he'd use your name. I hoped he wouldn't use mine again."

"I tried to get you last night, but you didn't answer." His rhythmic footsteps echoed through the line as he paced the length of the phone cord. "Why the hell did you tell him about me? I've warned you about the press before. Is this some sort of revenge?"

"Of course not! And I didn't tell him about you. Well, not exactly. We were just talking. He wasn't supposed to use it." Temper shot through her like an electrical spike. *You're dead, Gerrard.*

"Kate, why are you even talking to him? Do you know who he is?"

"What do you mean, who he is?"

"Gerrard's the reporter who broke the statehouse scandal last year. And before that, the padded contracts for county roads. He wins prizes. He's a crusader." J. B. was livid now; she knew that crisp, controlled tone.

He continued, "Once he gets his teeth in something, he never lets go. You stay away from him, and keep my name out of whatever it is you're doing. You're going to ruin me yet."

"I'm sorry, J. B. Things have just . . . just gotten out of control."

"*You're* out of control, Kate. You have been for the last year." He hung up.

She fell back on the bed, thoroughly dejected. Nothing she did with J. B. was ever right. Her mother would probably call next, all because she had mentioned J. B.'s name in a private conversation. Damn reporters! She'd spent eight years under their watchful eye, and she didn't deserve their attention now. Her anger surged again. She snapped upright on the bed and snatched the telephone directory out from under a stack of books, knocking them over. Fanning the pages to *G*, she found John's number and punched it into the phone.

On the third ring, the mechanical sound of his answering machine kicked in. She could hardly hold back her words through his brief message. Her temperature reached flashpoint. The tone was still sounding when she started. "You bastard! What are you trying to do to me? Don't you ever use my name again, and don't come near me."

She slammed the receiver down, hoping that somehow the sound would be recorded and hurt his ears when he got the message.

The throbbing in her temples increased as she told herself John hadn't done anything special Friday, didn't deserve her gratitude. After spending most of yesterday propped up on a pile of pillows on her friend Gwen Gordon's couch, she had come in late last night. Gwen had wanted her to spend the night, but Kate wanted to be in her own bed. Aspirin had eased the ache in her ankles and sent her into a deep sleep. At least until the phone rang. She hadn't lost her temper like this in years—probably not since she had met J. B. He had a way of squelching her "tantrums," leaving her feeling embarrassed and immature.

She hobbled down the stairs. Perhaps after coffee she would go get a paper. Maybe that would clear her head. She stopped at the answering machine in the kitchen and, smiling nastily, turned it on. She would disappear for the day. Then she wouldn't have to deal with John or her mother, whom J. B. would surely call.

Her mother, Dorothy, had long ago formed a conspiracy with J. B. to keep Kate in line. Dorothy saw him as an ideal partner for her difficult daughter. Kate had met her future husband at a political debate when she was in college, the year after her father died. J. B. was twelve years older than she, a handsome attorney with political ambitions. Dorothy thought his conservative outlook and traditional lifestyle would curb Kate's "Bohemian" impulses, his calm and reasonable manner would overcome her quick temper.

Kate had spent eight years trying to please the pair of them. She had juggled the demands of a job she hated in J. B.'s family business with his heavy social schedule. She must always be at his side, supportive, loving, and above all, inoffensive—and let's not forget ready to entertain at the drop of a vote. *Naughty, naughty, Kate. Sarcasm is such a petty weapon.*

At a dinner party one night, Venice, recently returned from Europe, had waltzed in. She had known Kate's father and, years before, had met Kate, whom she described as an undisciplined teenager with a camera hanging around her neck. "You've let your mother and that prancing goat you call a husband leach all the life out of you," Venice told her after they had run into each other a few times.

Kate didn't know what to say. She vaguely remembered Venice and knew her father had liked the woman, but she couldn't imagine why. She ended up mumbling something unintelligible and tried to get away. "Good-bye, Mrs. Ashburton."

"You're an adult now. You may call me Venice. Your father was a fine man. I never liked your mother." Venice could be blunt when it suited her.

Somehow, the two women kept bumping into each other. Venice asked about Kate's photography, and Kate told her that J. B. had gotten rid of her old Nikon and replaced it with a little instant camera because the manual F-2 took too much of her attention. Inwardly, she cringed. She could still hear herself whining to Venice, "He was right. In the back of my mind, I still had this stupid idea of being a photographer. I could never have done it. I just don't have a head for business."

Months later, when Kate told her she had moved out of J. B.'s house, Venice had confessed her part in what she considered Kate's resurrection. "After hearing about the camera, Ramses and I fumed over it," she had said, "searching for some spark of life, appalled at your apathy."

Kate popped a piece of hard bread into the toaster and poured another cup of coffee, smiling. Dear Venice.

She had never admitted to apathy, but looking back from where she was now, she thought maybe Venice hadn't been far off. If a hint of her temper surfaced, J. B. had twisted her words until he convinced her she was being childish and unreasonable.

"Now, Kate," he would say. "You might want to do a little more reading on the subject before you sound off. You wouldn't want to look foolish in the papers." She could feel his hand on her hair now.

Her mother's voice chimed in like an echo. "Kate, you're overreacting as usual."

The phone rang. When the answering machine picked up, Kate heard her mother's voice again, and she groaned. It was still the same tone. "Kate! What have you gotten yourself into now? Call me the minute you get home."

Exactly what she had expected. Dorothy had adored—still did, for that matter—J. B. and continually reminded Kate of how lucky she was to have him.

Venice thought Kate had been patted quietly into oblivion. But not quite. She had surprised both herself and Venice one night at a political get-together. J. B. had been speechless—for a short time.

Was I really that much of a wimp? Kate wondered as she retrieved the toast. She tapped it on the counter. It cracked in two. Shrugging, she spread it with jam. She was out of butter.

Kate knew Venice would gladly have turned J. B. and his mother-in-law into toads if she'd been able, but they both knew that any real change would have to be effected through Kate. Venice had taken every opportunity to waken Kate's benumbed mind. The scene played in Kate's mind like the rerun of a soap opera.

The Awakening, as Venice called it, had taken place one night when Kate and J. B. were at a big fund-raiser. J. B. was running for reelection to the state legislature, and Kate stood dutifully beside him as he chatted with an old, powerful state senator. The senator, well beyond his alcoholic limit, reached for another cocktail, staggered slightly, and knocked a tray of drinks from the hands of an elderly waiter.

The drinks, complete with maraschino cherries, spilled over the senator's tuxedo. "You clumsy fool!" he roared, calling the man names and cursing.

"I'm sorry, Senator." The embarrassed waiter tried to apologize.

"Get out. You're fired, you—"

"It wasn't his fault, Senator," Kate interrupted. "You bumped into him." She plucked the drink from his hand and gave it to the waiter with a smile. "Here. You'd better get another round. Maybe ginger ale."

Then she turned to the senator. "Sir, I think you should calm down. Why don't you—"

He cut her off. "J. B., keep your wife out of this. And I want you to personally take care of that waiter. See that he's fired."

"Yes, sir," J. B. said. He turned and said softly to Kate, "Don't worry. I'll find him another job."

"J. B., you can't have that old man fired. He's worked here forever. Besides, he didn't do anything. Your drunken friend of a senator did it."

J. B. hauled Kate outside and turned on her. "What's the matter with you? This isn't one of your little tea parties. You have no idea what's at stake here."

"My little tea parties? *My* little tea parties?" She had exploded. "Those are *your* damned tea parties. I'm just the resident plastic wife. And I do know what's at stake. The man's life—"

"Be quiet! And don't be so dramatic. It's not his life but my career we're talking about." J. B. had been so angry and trying so hard not to attract attention that he hissed.

Kate snapped back, "You know damn well what I mean. That old man takes pride in his work. He's been here as long as I can remember. You can't allow this to happen, J. B."

"I said I'll get the man another job. You're being unreasonable, Kate." His voice took on the paternal tone Venice had commented on so often, the father patiently explaining to the child.

"No, J. B. Use your almighty reasoning on the senator. Make him see reason."

"Welcome back, Kate," Venice had murmured.

Until then, Kate hadn't been aware that Venice had followed them outside, blatantly eavesdropping.

In the end, J. B. had persuaded the senator to change his mind, but that small battle in the country club parking lot was the turning point of the war, and Venice was quick to take advantage.

Choking down the hard toast, Kate smiled. Venice should have been a general. With all the subtlety of Wellington at Waterloo, she had begun her campaign to restore Kate's confidence. Six months later, J. B. withdrew in defeat and Kate moved out.

J. B. and Dorothy had let her know how much she had hurt them with her selfish decision to leave him just as his career was taking off. J. B. wanted to keep it quiet, sure that she would come back as soon as she found out how difficult life would be on her own. But as soon as the press got wind of it, he had intimated her infidelity, never saying anything outright, of course. The press had driven her into hiding for a time, but J. B. wasn't important enough to sustain their interest for long.

Outside the window, a blue jay flapped excitedly around the bird feeder, sending the smaller birds into alarmed flight. The jays reminded her of rowdy teenagers. A yellow figure slunk into view. Tom, the neighbors' cat. He was too old and stiff, had too many war wounds to hunt, but he kept trying.

Like that old waiter. If he had only known what he started with that one drink. She should have written him a thank-you note. Shaking her head, she flexed her sore ankles, sympathizing with both the cat and the waiter.

She hadn't wanted to hurt J. B., had asked for nothing. She

had a savings account in her name and a small inheritance from her grandmother that, if she was careful, would see her through the first year while she was getting started as a photographer.

And the first year was difficult; clients were few and far between, especially paying clients. Buying the RX-7 was her only real indulgence. Venice was probably right in saying it was a symbol of freedom—the last car J. B. would have chosen for her.

After the divorce, when her mother had moved to Atlanta to be near her people, Kate had suffered all the guilt her mother had wished. But she had to admit, especially today, that it took some of the pressure off to have her a hundred and thirty miles away.

And now, Kate thought, now that she had finally gotten things together and her photography was getting some attention, she wasn't going to be manipulated for anyone's benefit. Certainly not John Gerrard's.

While she soaked in a hot bath, the phone rang. It rang as she wound Ace bandages around her ankles and again as she started downstairs toward the kitchen. She continued to ignore it and fixed the inevitable peanut butter sandwich to take to the studio, examining the bread carefully for nascent penicillin. The Principal Players needed some more prints, and she wanted to have a few more of her own photographs ready for an upcoming exhibit at Caesar's Head, the state park in the mountains.

The warehouse was deserted when Kate got there. She unlocked the door, let herself in, then walked carefully up the steps to the main floor and, taking a deep breath, made herself step into the paneled passenger elevator the Players used. This was bad enough. She would never go near the freight elevator again.

If John hadn't made her get on this one Friday. . . . Crushing the kindly thought, she focused instead on his betrayal. She got off on the third floor where the Players stored props and scenery. Taking the last flight of stairs slowly on her tender ankles, she was truly grateful when she reached the fourth floor.

Knowing the Players would show up for a rehearsal later, she left her studio door unlocked. Sometimes Gwen and a few of her fellow actors wandered up to say hello. More importantly, they shared food if anyone brought something special.

After resting a few minutes on the sofa with her feet propped up, Kate pushed herself up and limped across the floor to her desk, tossing the leather purse to one end. She admired the glittering dust particles that rose through the morning light. A little housekeeping wouldn't hurt, she thought, surveying the large room. It looked more like a home than a business—not surprising, since she had used the den furniture J. B. had given her when she moved out. That bit of generosity wasn't surprising either—she had picked it out herself, and his first step toward bachelorhood had been to have a decorator eradicate any trace of her.

She spent ten dutiful minutes with a dust rag before she allowed herself to go into the darkroom. Once there, she forgot everything as she developed a roll of pictures she had taken of Gwen, who was starring in the next play, and printed a couple of contact sheets. The camera adored the gorgeous blonde. If Gwen came by today, she could choose the shots she liked, and Kate could make the prints. After hanging the contact sheets up to dry, she left the darkroom to mark her calendar and put on a pot of coffee.

"Hi. Mm-mm. Smells good." Gwen stuck her head around the corner of the studio door. She had an unfailing sense of timing, even when they were children. "Did you make enough for three? Venice is on her way up." Not quite touching her lips to Kate's cheek, she asked, "How are you feeling today?"

"Much better. Thanks for all the pampering yesterday."

"Anytime. You've had a bad run lately." Gwen glanced downward.

Kate, catching the look, pulled up the leg of her jeans and waggled a bandaged ankle at her. "Cute, huh? But much better."

"See you got your name in the paper. Again." Gwen poured a cup of coffee and handed it to Kate before fixing her own and arranging herself gracefully on the couch.

"And J. B.'s.," Kate said. "He called during an apoplectic fit this morning."

"Do I detect a sour note? What did he do?" Gwen asked. "Wake you up?"

Venice popped in and sat down beside Gwen, puffing from the flight of stairs.

"Yes, but he was justified. I should never have mentioned his name," Kate said, rising from her chair.

"I'll heat some water for tea, Venice. Kate, you stay in that chair," Gwen said, gently shoving her back down. "Forget J. B. As soon as he gets over his initial panic, he'll be delighted with the publicity. After all, he wasn't accused of anything. Now he'll have a chance to say something pompous for the press."

Gwen dismissed J. B. with a flick of her wrist. "Oh, Kate? A little something you didn't mention yesterday—the reporter Venice told me about. I find it very interesting that you didn't tell me about the other evening with him. I told you about Thomas."

Yes, she had, and Kate had only said she had met him, hadn't mentioned his asking her out or told her friend that he reminded her of J. B.

Gwen plugged in the electric kettle for Venice's tea and leaned against the desk, intrigued. "Did he take you to look at his etchings—maybe galley proofs in his case—before he took you home?"

"No, he didn't. He took me to Lake Jocassee to pick my brains for his next article."

"Is he the one who wrote this morning's article?"

"Yes, the snake," Kate answered.

"Who's Thomas?" Venice asked, heading off a tirade.

"Thomas Andrews, a marvelously handsome fellow I met recently. He seems to be very comfortable financially. Dresses well, drives a swanky little Jaguar." Gwen straightened and moved a neat stack of magazines to the other side of the coffee table to make room for her cup.

Venice and Kate both knew that after a brief, ugly marriage, Gwen was deeply suspicious of men, fearing that they were only interested in her money. She wanted someone with money of his own so he wouldn't care about hers.

"You may know him, Venice," Kate said, glad to forget John, even though she couldn't work up much enthusiasm for Thomas. "He takes classes at Poinsett. I met him in marketing."

"Oh, yes, I know him. I've met him several times. Actually, it's his mother I know. His father died when Thomas was about eight or nine. She and Thomas were very close. She always talked about her 'devoted son.' And a year or two ago, after all those years with just Thomas, she up and married Lyle Border, a charming fellow. She always seemed rather weak and clinging, to me. I suppose that appeals to some men." Venice smiled at Gwen. "But I do think the first husband left them in good shape financially."

Relief flitted across Gwen's face, but she said nothing more about his fiscal status. "Are you sure about his mother? I had the impression she had died."

Venice straightened and raised an eyebrow.

"Right, right. I'm sure you're right. I guess I misunderstood." Gwen looked like a cat with a whole salmon, practically purring, and added, "He asked me to go to Atlanta with him for a big dinner his company is giving in a couple of weeks. He called this morning. It's on a Wednesday, so it won't interfere with the play. We're leaving as soon as he finishes work the Tuesday before the dinner."

"Wow! That was fast. You only met him a week ago," Kate said.

"True, but we really hit it off. He talked me into breaking a date this weekend." With a coy smile, she batted her eyelashes at them. "He doesn't want to share me."

Kate couldn't think of a smart comeback. She found Thomas a bit stiff, conceited. She wished someone else would show up for

Gwen. Changing the subject instead, she said, "I just finished your pictures, Gwen. The contact sheets should be dry. I'll bring them out, and you can see if you like any."

Venice and Gwen were whispering when she returned with the pictures, limping slightly. "No plots, you two. I'm fine."

"Here, see what you think of these." She spread the sheets on the desk and pointed to one. "This is my choice. I like the expression in your eyes." She handed Gwen her loupe.

The three women huddled over the film-sized frames, passing the small magnifying lens back and forth for several minutes while they dissected the shots.

Finally Gwen settled on two, and Kate circled them with a red grease pen. "I'll have them ready before the play opens."

"Fine."

"I have to go now," Venice said. "I just stopped in to see how you are. Read the article, Kate. I'll talk to you about it another time, when you're calmer. Ramses told me that you were having a bad morning."

"He probably guessed when he read the paper." References to the thousand-year-old inhabitant of Venice's crystal ball always set Kate off.

"Don't be sarcastic, Kate. It doesn't become you." Venice gave her a quick kiss on the cheek and turned to the door. Frowning, she turned back as the door closed. "Gwen, don't rush into anything with Thomas Andrews."

"Don't worry, darling. He's a real gentleman." Gwen moved to the mirror and twisted a mauve lipstick out of the tube. Making a moue, she touched the color to her lips.

As soon as the door closed behind Venice, Gwen turned to Kate with a knowing smile. "She told me all about your reporter. Are you seeing him again?"

"Never, the bastard."

"Well, well, well! He must have really hit a nerve."

"You can't trust him!" Kate snatched the contact sheets from the desk and stuffed them into a manila folder marked *Carter*. "I called him this morning and told him what I thought. Only, I got his answering machine, so I couldn't say it all. Did you read his article today?"

"Yes. Did you?" Gwen kept her eye on the folder Kate was mangling. "The autopsy showed just what you said—Kelly Landrum was strangled."

"I was so mad after J. B. called that I didn't read it." Kate sat heavily on the desk and massaged her temples. She whispered, "Everything I saw was real. Why is this happening? I'm afraid to go to sleep at night for fear of what I'll see."

"Why don't you come stay with me for a few days? Maybe you could get some rest." She put an arm around Kate's shoulders.

"No, I'm all right. I would rather be at home."

"At least J. B. wouldn't find you at my place. You're still letting him manipulate you." Gwen assumed a stern look and took the folder from Kate's hand. She withdrew her photographs and put them in the correct folder. Placing it carefully back on the desk, she said, "Stop worrying about him. I was serious about the publicity—he's going to eat it up. And meanwhile, you're eating up the guilt. Has your mother called yet?"

"Yes, but I let the answering machine take it." Kate grinned. "I'm not answering the phone today."

"Good," she said. "Are the nightmares the same as the visions? Have you seen anything new?"

"No, they're all the same. I don't think they'll stop until the murderer is found. I'd like to find out more about Charlene Nelson, but I have no idea where to start."

"John Gerrard could help you. Why beat your head against the wall when he probably has all you want at the newspaper?"

"There has to be another way. I'll never see him again." She frowned, surprised at the feeling of depression that washed over her.

"So phone him. It wouldn't have to be social. If you want the information, you know where to get it. You think he used you. Use him." Gwen pressed her cheek against Kate's. Smoothing her gray silk shirt, she said, "Well, my fans are waiting. I must fly."

Kate closed the door behind her and took a stack of prints from a bulging folder on the desk. Flopping down on the sofa, she flipped idly through the outdoor shots she was considering for the exhibit at Caesar's Head, but her concentration was gone. The aluminum wrap on her peanut butter sandwich caught her eye; she doubted if it would make her feel better.

Kate was drinking coffee when John walked in. She spluttered something unintelligible before he got the first words out. He could see her surprise and anger.

"I got your message," he said, before she could recover. "If you had been home or had your answering machine on, you could have read the article last night. After the autopsy proved you right, I had to use your name. I tried to reach you—"

"It wasn't only my name, but J. B.'s." Kate jumped up, slamming her chair into the wall behind the desk. "I told you not to use his name! How could you do that?"

"Now wait a minute. I never said I wouldn't use what you told me. It's my job to print the facts, and the public has a right to know *all* those facts." He slung his jacket on the sofa as he crossed the room to the desk. "As a journalist—"

"Don't give me that right-to-know crap. I thought we were having a private conversation when I was stupid enough to mention J. B. You're one of those sick people who focus on a mother crying for a dead child. It's *not* the people's right to know. It's none of anyone's business."

"If you don't want to know, don't read. But if I pick and choose which facts to tell, it becomes an editorial, expressing my personal views. It's no longer an objective report." He was preaching now and he knew it, but he wanted to make her understand. "My responsibility is to tell the whole truth, not a whitewashed, selective version. And whether you like it or not, you described a murder that no one else saw." With his hands spread on the desk, his face was only inches from hers. He could see the fire in her eyes; even her hair seemed to spark. He tapped her hand with his forefinger. "You—"

"Ouch!" Kate jumped as the static electricity arced between them. "Don't touch me."

He straightened and looked down at her. She was glaring across the desk at him, her fiery hair crackling around her—a witch if he ever saw one. "Could we talk calmly about this?"

"How can I if you're going to print everything I say?"

"That's not what I meant. I was talking about—"

"People get hurt when you print private things, but you don't care about that, do you?" She leaned farther over the desk, challenging him.

"Silence is what hurts. Covering up the truth can be as bad as lying. If it weren't for the press, this country would be in a hell of a lot worse shape. That's why—"

"What do you know about it? You could destroy an innocent person with your ruthless disregard for privacy."

Making an effort to keep his voice low, he snarled at her. "Don't interrupt me again." He leaned down so that they were almost nose to nose, letting her feel the heat of his anger. "And where do you get 'ruthless disregard'? What about the 'ruthless disregard' of the politicians and power brokers? What about the innocent people crushed by their machinations?"

"You're the one who's unreasonable—you'll print anything that might sell another copy, no matter who gets hurt." She glanced around her desktop.

Probably looking for something to throw, the unreasonable witch. "I print the truth, and I intend to keep on doing it. When I stop, I won't be a journalist anymore."

He wanted to shake her. Instead he turned and snatched his jacket. "This is stupid. You're too stubborn to listen, and I'm too mad to talk."

He left, slamming the door behind him.

Chapter 9

STARING AT THE DOOR, Kate sank to the sofa, drained by her outburst. Her chest heaved. She held her hands in front of her, watched them tremble. She didn't know which surprised her most, the biting anger she had given way to or John's equally angry response. As the scene replayed itself in her mind, she considered the brief exchange, satisfied she had held her own.

Perhaps their disagreement had been a little heated, but he hadn't treated her like a child. He hadn't condescended to her. It had felt good to blow off like that for a change. All the tension of the past weeks had built to a monstrous weight, constantly pressing down on her. Unexpectedly light and free, she laughed aloud.

The studio door opened silently, and a woman stepped in, catching Kate in mid laugh.

Flipping open a wallet to display her identification, the woman smiled and introduced herself. "Ms. McGuire? I'm Detective Lynne Waite from the Greenville Police Department. May I come in?"

"Of course," Kate choked out. She smoothed the faded jeans over her hips, wishing she had dressed better. Waite, an attractive woman with short, honey-colored hair, looked entirely professional in a dark blue suit. Kate stood aside and gestured toward the sofa and chairs. "Please sit down."

"As I'm sure you know, I'm here about Kelly Landrum." Waite sat, looking perfectly composed, and asked, "Have you had good news? That was a happy laugh I heard as I came in."

"Oh, that." Kate inwardly cursed the blush that warmed her cheeks. "I just figured something out."

"Don't be embarrassed. In my business, that kind of joy is rare."

She seemed sincere, and Kate liked the way her eyes crinkled at the corners. Maybe this woman would take her seriously.

The detective continued. "I read John Gerrard's piece this morning, and then I talked with Officer Wolynski about the parapsychology meeting he attended last week. I'd like to ask you a few questions. Is that all right with you?"

Kate nodded.

"First, I want to understand about these visions and how they come to you. Can you tell me about it?"

Kate, after a few confused starts, gathered her thoughts and did her best to give a coherent explanation, ending with the last time she had touched something of Kelly's. "Until this business, the experiments were sort of fun, nothing serious. Then, when I picked up the sweatband, I felt like I was the one being strangled."

"Had you ever met Kelly Landrum? Maybe taken a class with her?"

"No. I've only taken two, so I would remember."

"What were these classes?"

"Business law and marketing."

"Kelly Landrum was a business major. Do you know anyone who knew her?"

"Not that I know of."

"Let's talk about the lake. Have you ever been to Jocassee?"

Kate hesitated, wondering if she and John should have gone there. "Not before they—before she was found there."

"Have you been since?"

The question made her feel vaguely guilty. Maybe it was closed to the public or something. "Yes, I have."

"Why?"

"I . . . I just wanted to see it. See if I could learn anything there."

"Did you?"

Kate described what she had seen, leaving John out of it, and then added, "But it wasn't quite the same as the other times. I don't know whether I imagined it or it was real."

"How about Charlene Nelson? Did you know her?"

"I don't think so. The picture in the paper looked old, but I would have recognized her." A coldness settled over her. The implications of the question were all too clear. "Is there a connection?"

"It's possible," the detective said, her expression grim. Then she stood and held out her hand. "Kate, I have to tell you I don't put much stock in these visions. Besides, they aren't specific enough to tell me anything. But that doesn't mean everyone thinks the same way. The person who did this is probably unstable and may see you as a threat. Be sure to keep your doors locked and take a little extra care for a while."

Waite took a step toward the door, then stopped, looking back at Kate. "Did you know Kelly Landrum rented the house you live in when she first came to Poinsett? She was only there for a few weeks before she moved on campus."

"In my house?" Kate was stunned. "Maybe that's why I keep

getting these visions. I must be constantly touching things she handled."

"It was almost three years ago. I just thought you'd like to know." Waite closed the door gently behind herself.

Kate flung herself down on the sofa, rubbing her forehead. How had she ever gotten into this mess? If John hadn't put her name—and Venice's—in the paper, would that have changed things? No, because it wouldn't have changed the visions.

Waite's warning ran through her head. Would Kelly's murderer see her as a threat? The falling elevator—was that an accident? And what about Venice? *Venice!* She ran back to the phone and punched in the number.

It rang several times before Venice answered with a question in her voice. "Kate?"

"How did you know it was me?"

"I just got home," she said. "What's wrong, my dear?"

"Nothing. Detective Waite was just here. She warned me to be careful about security. I guess all the publicity brings out the crazies. Venice, the murderer may see us as a serious problem." She hated to frighten her but felt she had little choice. If something happened to Venice because she hadn't passed on Waite's cautious advice, she would never forgive herself.

"Oh, well. It's to be expected," Venice said, apparently unconcerned. "But don't blame John. After the autopsy proved us right, he really had no choice. Are you calm enough to talk about it yet?"

Kate sighed, defeated. So much for scaring her. Venice's only concern seemed to be for John. It was clear that she thought Kate completely unreasonable. "Go ahead, Venice. I'll listen. I'm sorry I was so rude earlier."

"He called me to explain before the article appeared. He wanted to warn me. He also asked if I knew where you were. He'd been trying to reach you."

"I forgot to turn on the answering machine," she mumbled. But she wouldn't give up so easily. "Was warning us supposed to make it all right?"

"It's more than most reporters would have done. You can't blame him for doing his job," she said. "I have to go now, Kate. Mrs. Batson is coming for a reading, and I have to prepare."

"Okay. Just be careful, Venice," she said. "I'm going home now."

By eight, the answering machine had recorded two hang ups and two messages, one from a woman who wanted Kate to find "something precious" for her and another from a man who thought he had a ghost in his house. He wondered if Kate could tell him why the spirit couldn't rest. Nuisance calls, but not frightening.

She double-checked the locks on her windows and carefully shoved home the simple brass bolts on her doors. She stacked her glass bottles at several strategic places around the house and, for good measure, carefully balanced a kitchen utensil on top of her precarious homemade alarms before she got into bed. At least she'd have warning if someone entered her house.

Another restless, dream-haunted night caused Kate to oversleep. Fortunately—or maybe not, considering her bank balance—she had no appointments today.

She chose to indulge herself with a leisurely morning. Too bad she didn't have any donuts. Idly sipping her coffee, she stared out at a beautiful day and thought about Charlene Nelson. What would happen, she wondered, if she touched something of hers? Would there be any trace of her left? The woman had been dead for more than a year. Kate decided to go by the newspaper office and look up the stories on Charlene Nelson. That way she wouldn't have to ask John for help.

She dressed quickly in a bright madras skirt and blouse, but she took time with her makeup, carefully hiding the shadows under her eyes. She planned to get to the *Times Herald* building around lunchtime, so John should be out. Nevertheless, she found herself checking the mirror when it was time to go.

At the paper, she was directed to a large room called the morgue, the repository for past articles. She asked a young woman at a desk for help in locating stories related to Charlene Nelson.

"Right over there," the woman told her. "See that man with dark hair? Right where he is."

Kate turned just as the man looked up. He stood quietly, watching her. She couldn't leave, would have to face him. "Hello, John."

"Kate," he said.

He wasn't going to make this easy. She swallowed. "I came to look for the articles on Charlene Nelson."

Holding up the file in his hand, he said, "This is most of it."

"May I see it? I wanted to. . . . Is her family here in Greenville? I'd like to talk to them." She looked at the file, then raised her eyes to meet his. "I'm sorry about yesterday, John. I don't agree with what you did, but I shouldn't have lost my temper. I guess I got a little carried away."

"I may be a little touchy on the subject myself—I don't usually slam doors on my sources." A slow smile started across his face. "How about some lunch? We can discuss the terms for a truce."

The sudden lift in her spirits was out of proportion to the casual invitation. "Okay." *Watch it, McGuire, and for heaven's sake, keep your mouth shut.*

He returned the file to its place and picked up a notebook. "I have the Nelsons' address. I'm planning to see them this afternoon. Want to come? We could go after we eat."

She gave him a long, assessing look. After all, she told herself, he *had* tried to call before he published that miserable article. "Sure. We can take my car. It's right out front, and the meter will run out soon."

A meter maid was approaching the shiny RX-7 when they reached it. "This can't be yours, Gerrard," the woman said. "It's too clean. And besides, there's money in the meter." She moved on to the next car.

"You're all heart, Joyce," he said, sliding into the car. Fastening his seat belt, he turned to Kate. "How about the Main Street Grill? It's close."

"Sure," she said over her shoulder. Taking advantage of an opening in the traffic, she backed into the street.

He looked around the clean interior and whistled. "Look, I'm sorry about that scene in your studio. I know I sounded like a pompous ass," he said. "I meant what I said, but I guess I didn't say it very well."

"I didn't handle it well myself. Let's forget it." She smiled at him, a little sheepishly. She didn't want to spoil the day. "Have you—"

"Is there anything—" he asked at the same time.

They laughed, and John said, "You go first."

"Okay. I was going to ask if you've found anything new about Kelly or Charlene." Kate whipped into a parking space close to the little restaurant.

"Nothing."

They left the car and walked over to the wide plate-glass windows, checking the crowd. "They're pretty busy," he said, holding the tall glass door for her. "How about conjuring up an empty table?"

"You can be assured that I'm no witch," she said, winding through to a small table in the back.

"How so?"

"Because you don't have any warts on your nose."

"What luck," he said, rubbing his nose. "But I do want to know if you've had any more . . . visions? Insights?"

"I don't know what to call them either. Venice says visions. But whatever, it's just been more of the same." She picked up the menu, practically drooling, and wondered how much money she had with her. She hoped they took charge cards.

A waiter who looked as if he should still be in high school brought an iced cranberry tea for Kate and an Amstel for John, then flipped open a pad and took their order. When John ordered a chicken burrito with green chili sauce, the boy asked, "Extra sour cream, Mr. Gerrard?"

"Yes. Thanks, Scott."

After Scott left, Kate gave John an amused smile and raised an eyebrow. "Mr. Gerrard?"

"Shows respect."

"Or age."

"I considered the possibility, but opted for respect." He took a long drink of the cold beer. "Better for my ego."

"Ah." She smiled, then looked down, using her forefinger to trace a swirl in the condensation on her glass. "Tell me about the Nelsons."

"Last summer there were three of them. Mom, Pop, and Charlene's sister, Rita. He was a foreman at a textile mill, Mom stayed home and baked cookies, and Rita was just out of high school, summer job at McDonald's. Nice, ordinary family."

His face had a somber, reflective look that puzzled Kate, but from his flat, expressionless tone, he could have been reading the phone book.

Then he added, "Completely unprepared for what happened."

Kate saw the flicker of pain in his eyes. Behind the emotionless voice, he cared.

"I gather you met them," she said. "Did you cover the story?"

"Yes. It's not my usual beat—I seldom cover overt local crime. Someone was on vacation, I was handy. Same thing this time. Jan's on vacation, and Dave has a broken leg."

Scott returned with their food.

The sight of the black-bean tostada and the faint aroma that wafted under her nose caused Kate's stomach to rumble. She hadn't realized how hungry she was. She took a bite and sighed. "This is wonderful."

Kate ate steadily, but John managed an occasional comment. When she finished, he said, "I like the way you eat—with enthusiasm."

Her plate was clean. A satisfied smile lit her face. "I was planning on peanut butter."

"Then I've done my good deed for the day." He picked up the check and took a worn leather wallet from the pocket of his jeans. "Are you ready?"

"Yes, thanks." Since she couldn't pay for either of their lunches, it seemed wise not to argue.

At John's direction, Kate turned off Main Street and followed Augusta to Mills Avenue. She made several turns into a mill village, where paint and landscaping gave the houses character. Most were neat and well kept, but at the end of a small street, one stood out like a bag lady at the mall.

"Is that it?" she asked.

He nodded, and she stopped at the curb. They got out and stood for a minute, looking at the place. On one side of the frame bungalow, an aluminum canopy shaded a dusty green van. Weed-choked shrubs marked the path to the front door. The blinds were drawn, the curtains closed, giving the house a secretive air.

"It didn't look like this a year ago." He looked down at Kate. She looked thinner. Murder had taken its toll on all of them. The shadowed look she'd had that night at the para group meeting had returned. She moved closer to him, but he knew she wasn't aware of it. He shortened his stride to match hers and took her arm. "I'm not going to mention any of your psychic stuff, but if you have any questions that won't scare them, ask."

Rita Nelson opened the door for them. "Come in. I told them you were coming." She gestured toward the darkened room behind her. An older woman with short gray hair pointed a remote control at a softly murmuring television set, and the orange-skinned characters faded away.

The man, slumped in a worn brown recliner, continued to stare at the screen. His hands were folded across his stomach; light from an overhead fixture glinted off his scalp through thin strands of hair.

"This is Kate McGuire," John said as he stepped into the room. He bent down in front of the woman, taking her hands in his. "Hello, Mrs. Nelson. May I ask you a few questions? I don't want to open old wounds, but something has happened, and I need your help."

Kate followed him in and, at Rita's nod, slipped into a stuffed chair on the other side of the silent man.

The woman held tightly to John's hands. "I know you don't mean no harm, son," she said, "but there's not no more we can tell. Harlan here don't talk to nobody nowadays, and Rita don't know nothing."

"I'd like to try again, though," he said, sitting on the sofa beside her without letting go of her hands. "Do you know about the girl who was just found in Lake Jocassee?"

"Heard it on the TV," Harlan said, still staring at the screen.

"It's possible that the same person who . . . took Charlene from you . . . is responsible for her." He tried to avoid using the words they hated, words that pierced the heart. He caught Kate's eye and saw that she understood.

"Is this one rich? Maybe the police'll try a little harder this time," Harlan answered, turning to John. "They didn't find nothing, just quit, when we lost our girl."

"Mr. Nelson, the police checked out everyone they could connect to Charlene. So did I. There was never anything to go on. That's why I want to try once more. Maybe we can find a link between Charlene and Kelly Landrum, someone who knew them both." He placed Mrs. Nelson's hands gently on her lap and sat back. "Rita, can you think of any connection Charlene might have had with Kelly Landrum? She was a business major at Poinsett and worked at the library there."

"I never heard of her before this."

"Can you think of anyone whom Charlene wouldn't go out with, someone who was very interested in her?" John asked.

"No. She went out with lots of boys." Softly she added, "She was real popular."

He had noticed Rita checking out Kate's bright clothes. The poor kid had a drab gray look. Everything about her seemed dull. "What are you doing now, Rita? Are you in secretarial school?" On a hunch, he asked, "Are you dating anyone?"

"No," she said quickly, darting a glance at her father. "I'm working at the mill."

"What the girl's saying is, I ain't worked regular in the last year. She's helping to take care of her mother and me." Harlan, without taking his eyes from the blank television screen, slumped further into the chair. His voice had a rusty, lifeless tone. "Rita's all we got now. She don't go out much."

Kate looked from one to the other and listened, saying nothing.

"Rita, you ought to go on to school like you planned," John said. "You're what? Nineteen? Twenty? You should be getting out, enjoying life." He directed his words to Rita, but the message was for her parents. "I learned a lot about Charlene last year. She wouldn't have wanted you to sit here and do nothing. She would have told you to get on with your life."

Harlan snapped out of his trance. "You stay out of this. Whoever took my first daughter is still out there, and he ain't getting the other one. She stays right here, or I know where she is every minute." His voice rising, he sat upright in his chair and glared. "If we was rich, they'd have done caught the son of a bitch."

"Harlan!"

"It's all right, Mrs. Nelson. But maybe one of you knows something that can help catch him. You might save the next woman." John leaned forward. "Do you have any personal items, maybe a gift from a boyfriend, that we could see?" He nodded toward Kate. "Maybe Kate would have some ideas."

"Or perhaps some letters or papers." Kate spoke for the first time.

"There's—" Rita began.

"There's nothing of Charlene's we're giving out. Nothing we got left that can help." Harlan stood. "Now you upset my wife and my baby girl. You'd best be leaving."

"I apologize if I've upset anyone, Mr. Nelson." John held out his hand. "We'll go now."

The older man hesitated, then shook John's hand briefly. "Don't mean to be hard on you, son. But there ain't no one going to catch that. . . ." He looked at his wife and let the sentence trail off.

"I understand, but if you should think of anything, will you give me a call?" John handed his card to Mrs. Nelson.

"Good-bye," Kate said. She quickly scribbled her home number on the back of one of her cards and slipped it to Rita, whispering, "Please call if you think of anything."

The girl took the card and looked back at her father. She bit her lip but didn't say anything.

Chapter 10

"YOU DRIVE." Kate handed John the keys and got in the passenger side. She wanted to think about the Nelsons, and she figured John wouldn't strip the gears or wreck the car on the way back to the newspaper office. She wondered if he had known those people before. He didn't sound as if he had grown up here, but there seemed to be a connection. His sympathy and caring were genuine, more than she would have expected from meeting them for a couple of interviews.

"You look tired," John said. "Let's go for a ride, clear out the cobwebs. I know a nice place to sit and think."

"Okay," Kate agreed and turned her face toward the window to catch the warm rays of the afternoon sun, content to be a passenger. Her eyes closed, and within seconds, she had drifted into a dreamless sleep.

When the engine stopped she looked around, surprised. "How did we get here? Is this Paris Mountain?"

"Yes, we're at one of the remote picnic areas. You missed the ride." He handed her the keys but made no move to get out of the car. "But as it only took twenty minutes, you might want another nap."

"I'm sorry. I keep going to sleep when I'm with you. I don't know why." But she did know—she felt safe with him, able to relax. *As long as you're careful what you say.*

"I don't want this to sound wrong," he said, "because, in an unusual way, you're beautiful. But you have a tense, edgy look. Maybe *haunted* is a better word."

She didn't know how to answer a left-handed compliment like that. "Let's go for a walk."

They left the car, and John took her hand to help her down the short, steep bank where the path left the road. She didn't need the help, but she needed his touch. When the path leveled off, he kept her hand. As the trail wound through woods and over rocks, sometimes narrowing so that they had to walk single file, he occasionally changed hands or held his hand on her back. But always, he kept a reassuring hand on her.

Turning off the main path, they followed a trail beneath a canopy of oaks and stopped to watch three mallards glide down to the water. Kate began humming softly, slightly off-key.

After a minute, John asked, "'Smoke Gets in Your Eyes'? I'd have figured something more current for you."

"That, too, but I love the old tunes—Porter, Gershwin, Rodgers and Hammerstein. My dad played them endlessly." She smiled. "I'm surprised you recognized it, the way I sing."

"I'm no Pavarotti, although I sometimes forget that in the shower."

"Opera? That's a surprise."

"I'm half Italian." John stopped in a patch of sunlight beside the lake. He spotted a fallen log at the edge of the clearing and kicked it several times.

"What are you doing?"

"Scaring away the snakes." He gave her a funny little half-smile. "I'm a city boy. You know, the concrete jungle. I hate snakes. I'll take the homeboys anytime." He brushed off the surface and said, "Let's sit down."

"Okay, now that I know it's safe." She sat down on the log beside him. "Where did you come from?"

"Philadelphia, the city of brotherly love." He couldn't keep the hint of bitterness from his voice. Abruptly changing the subject, he asked, "What do you know about hockey? Beyond Wayne Gretzky."

She filed away the Philadelphia reference for later. "I know who he is—the Canadian hunk who sold out to sunny California."

"Hunk?" he snorted. "He's retired, but his is still the only name anyone down here knows. What do you know about *hockey*, the game?"

"It's a game where frustrated roughnecks chase a tiny little ball around, looking for excuses to club each other with those mis-shapen golf clubs they carry." She pursed her lips, trying to look prim. Wild red hair did not add to the picture.

He just laughed at her. "Never been to a game, huh? I love it. My brother-in-law plays for the Philadelphia Flyers. What about college football, the old Southern standby?"

"Converse. No football." *Converse*, she thought, *the lovely college in Spartanburg where I met J. B.* She didn't want to think about that, not today. "Ever swim in a lake?"

"No, not much. There aren't many where I came from. Mostly a lot of crowded city pools." He tossed a rock into the water, watched the ripples spread. "Been sailing a few times since I moved here, had one or two unplanned swims in Lake Hartwell."

"Pools are nothing like a lake. It's wonderful, especially in the early morning, when the mist is still on the water," she said, looking over the small lake. Selecting a flatish stone, she skipped it a couple of times across the top of the water. "You don't have to worry about the snakes—they won't come anywhere near you. They don't like you, either."

"They swim?" He sounded horrified.

"Well, of course," she said, checking to see if he was serious. She thought maybe he was. She skipped another stone. This one hit several times before it disappeared into the green water.

He watched closely, then selected a similar stone and threw it. It sank immediately.

"You have to put a spin on it, City Boy." She showed him how she held it, how she threw it off her forefinger to keep it horizontal and give it a spin.

He threw another. It skipped once. Kate cheered. After he had made a couple of mildly successful tries, she found a perfectly shaped stone and handed it to him. "Here's one. You can do it," she said, carefully arranging his fingers around it. Her face was animated, all the shadows gone.

"Right, Coach." He drew back and let it fly, just as she had instructed. The rock bounced across the surface of the water. He held up his hand. She slapped it, palm to palm, laughing.

The sun was low in the sky when they started back. Watching her, he said, "You look more relaxed than I've ever seen you. I'm glad we came."

"Me, too."

They stopped in comfortable silence at a picnic table and watched the tangerine glow of clouds caught in the sunset.

Kate looked down at the big warm hands holding hers. They were square and practical, a little rough, a few calluses, but gentle. With a sigh, she withdrew. "It's getting late. We should go."

He slid off the table and stepped back to look at her. "I know a place where you can get great Italian food. How about it?"

"Great. I'm starving." She smiled and jumped off the table. "I feel wonderful. Thank you for bringing me."

"I needed some time to relax, too," he said, ruffling her hair.

She whirled out of reach, laughing, and took off, calling confidently over her shoulder, "Race you to the car. Last one there buys dinner!"

He had longer legs, was stronger, but she bet the only time he ran was to get the phone. She flew across the park. He almost caught her at the bank by the car park when she lost one of her shoes. She slowed, but then kept on going, and he stopped to pick it up.

"That's going to cost you, McGuire," he said, panting, when he reached the car. She was sitting on the hood, swinging her bare foot. "Looks like your ankles have recovered."

She threw her head back and laughed. "You're just a sore loser. And yes, I'm fine."

"Here's your slipper, Cinderella." He caught her ankle with one hand and brushed the dirt off her foot before sliding the dusty blue flat over it.

"Thanks." She liked him. Liked the clean smell of him, the warmth of his brown eyes, his gentle humor. A nice, caring guy who would sell his sister for a good headline. What was he?

Abruptly, she slid off the hood and, turning to unlock the car, said, "We had better forget dinner. I need to work tonight."

"Oh, no you don't. You can't weasel out on me now." He opened the passenger door and got in. "You owe me for that shoe trick."

Kate started the engine before she answered. "All right, but you still have to buy dinner." She cruised slowly through the park, telling herself she could handle one dinner with him.

John directed her to a small street in the downtown area where older homes of all sizes and styles sat comfortably side by side.

The tree-lined street looked decidedly residential, Kate thought. So where was the Italian restaurant? She felt her stomach tighten; she hadn't been in a situation like this since she had met J. B., and that had been more than ten years ago.

"That's it," he said with obvious pride, pointing to a house almost hidden behind a row of cedars.

"You think somebody stole their sign?"

"Sign? What sign?"

"The one that says 'Italian Restaurant—Great food.'" She looked out the car window toward the house, a narrow brick with a steeply pitched roof. Exposed beams crossed the stuccoed gables, giving it a Tudor look.

"Who said restaurant? It's my house. But it does have some of the best Italian food in town," he said. "Come on in. I'm still working on it—will be for the rest of my life, I think."

Kate hesitated.

He smiled. "Should I be flattered or offended? Come on, I'm harmless."

She locked her car and followed John.

The soft twilight disguised any signs of disrepair, and the sharp angles of the roof gave the house an interesting look. More interesting than galley proofs, she thought, recalling Gwen's comment. It was strange, going into a man's home like this, a man she hardly knew. She had been in a couple of apartments when she was in college, but then J. B. had come along, and there had been no one in her life since. At least she had her car, could leave when she wanted. Feeling a bit like Little Red Riding Hood being lured by the Wolf, she watched John as he sorted through his keys.

He looked innocent enough. Actually, he looked very good. Watching him, she began to feel more like the Wolf. She turned away and reached over to shake the railing. "Hmm, pretty solid. I'm impressed."

"You may not be when we get inside." He unlocked the door and flipped a light switch. "Watch out for the paint trays."

"How long have you been working on it?" she asked.

"About a year, off and on."

The house smelled faintly of fresh paint. The entrance hall, a surprising deep salmon, was accented by snowy white woodwork. The dark wood floor was partly covered by the edge of a paint-spattered drop cloth that extended into the next room. Skirting a ladder, she walked across the cloth into the living room. Two walls were a dingy white, but one was a softer, paler version of the entrance-hall salmon. The wall surrounding a large diamond-paned window was half finished.

"The colors are beautiful. Not what I expected."

He laughed at her awkward compliment. "The colors make a nice background for your hair."

Was he serious? She put a hand up and felt her hair, wild now from the wind and the run. Too bad. She wasn't going to a mirror to fix it.

He turned on the next light. "I haven't decided about the dining room yet."

"What other colors are you using in the living room?" she asked.

"The sofa's upstairs for safekeeping. It's dark green with some of these colors in the pattern," he said, indicating the salmon walls. "You'll see—it's on the tour."

She shrugged uneasily and suggested, "Maybe, uh, dark green in the dining room?" She made a little coughing sound. "To lead from one room to the next, sort of."

"Kate, you're doing everything but drawing circles on the floor with your toe. Uncertain? You?" It clearly surprised him.

"I don't know much about decorating." She hated herself when she mumbled.

"Is this the same woman who scorched my eyebrows when she found out I was a reporter? Who blasted me over privacy rights?

Who taunted me and raced through the woods today?" He spoke to the air, waving his hand.

"Come on, I'm not that bad." But she wished she'd never mentioned his colors. Scenes with J. B. flashed through her mind. She really was a wimp.

He laughed and gave her a skeptical look, opened a swinging door for her. "The kitchen was my first project, for obvious reasons." He patted his stomach. "Let's eat before we finish the tour."

"Yes, let's." She looked around the big kitchen. A stained-glass lamp hung over a scarred pine table, giving a warm, comfortable glow to the peach walls.

"Here, have a glass of tea while I cook." He took a pitcher from the refrigerator, filled a glass with ice, and poured cold tea over it. "Sugar and sweetener are on the table. Help yourself."

She sniffed at the glass. "Mint. I love it." She added sweetener, stirred the tea, and held the glass to her forehead for a moment, enjoying its cold touch, watching while he pulled things from the cabinets and the refrigerator. He seemed at ease, as if he knew what he was doing and was comfortable with it.

"Are we having bacon and eggs?" she asked, checking the ingredients. "I didn't know that was Italian."

"Something like that." He added a spoonful of olive oil to the pasta water. "What I'm doing doesn't take long."

In a surprisingly short time, he had two bowls of salad on the table. She left the chair and moved over beside him to see better when he started frying the bacon in small pieces. "What are you making?"

"Fettucine alla carbonara. My mother usually made this or a frittata on Sunday evenings. No one worried about cholesterol back then."

They made small talk while he cooked, and the time passed quickly. "Why don't you put some music on," he said. "Dinner's almost ready."

"Okay." She had seen the equipment in a corner of the dining room. His system looked manageable, so she knelt to select a CD. Although he leaned toward opera and classical, he had a broad selection. She finally chose an old Lena Horne recording and slid the disc in as the mixed aroma of bacon and Parmesan cheese reached her.

She returned to the kitchen to see him deftly cracking eggs by popping them on the counter with a flick of his wrist. He dropped the egg into his other hand, letting the white slide through his fingers into a cup, then dropped the yolks into the pasta mixture. An empty cream carton sat on the counter next to a butter wrapper.

She could almost see the calories simmering in the skillet. She inhaled deeply. "Mm-mm. That smells wonderful."

He washed his hands and returned to the stove, quickly stirring in the yolks. After a minute, he turned off the burner and brought the creamy pasta dish to the table. "Let's eat." He took a bottle from the refrigerator. "Wine?"

She nodded and he poured her a glass of chilled Frascati. They ate slowly, exchanging occasional comments. By the time Lena got to "Stormy Weather," Kate was swaying to the music, a blissful look on her face. She finished the last bite and closed her eyes, savoring the rich taste. "You may be my new best friend. Do you cook often?"

"Occasionally. What's your contribution going to be?"

"I'll take your picture." She cocked her head and studied him. "Let's see. Not in a chef's hat. Maybe gloating over a table covered with cholesterol—cream, butter, eggs, you know. And something red—tomatoes, apples. And long, spiky pasta." Warming to her theme, she continued, "Of course, there would have to be a worm in one of the apples."

"That's low, McGuire. And for that, plus the shoe trick, you get to do the dishes."

"Sore loser." Laughing, she started clearing the table. "I'm doing this only because you cooked. It has nothing to do with my fleetness of foot or your lack thereof."

He waited until she had filled both hands with dishes. "My revenge," he said, stepping in front of her. Catching her around the waist with both hands, he dropped a light kiss on her lips.

"The dishes!" she gasped.

He saved the teetering crockery by placing his hands underneath hers to help hold the two stacks upright, keeping her hands pinned. This time, his kiss was longer.

When she caught her breath, she said, "Could we at least put the dishes down?"

Warily and without taking his eyes off her, he put the dishes on the counter. "I don't trust you, McGuire."

"Then we're even." She smiled and wrapped her arms around him, pulling his head down to hers. As the kiss deepened, all thoughts of mischief disappeared.

Kate slowly withdrew and turned to the sink. She watched it fill with warm, soapy water while she struggled with her equilibrium. Then she started on the dishes. John stayed behind her, close enough that she could feel the heat from his body. She wanted to feel his arms around her again, to be pressed against his chest. Was it only yesterday she wanted to kill him?

She said, "Why don't you sit down? This will only take a minute, and then we can talk about the case."

He didn't answer, didn't move. What was he waiting for? She could think of nothing to say. How could she have gone from a shrieking shrew to a lusty wench in such a short time? After another minute of silence, she raised her head and looked warily over her shoulder.

John stood right behind her, waiting for her to turn around. He brushed her lips lightly with his and grinned. "You're right, I can't be trusted. Want some coffee?"

"I'll remember that. And yes, I'd love some coffee." She concentrated on finishing the washing up while he measured out the coffee.

They worked in silence for a few minutes, careful not to touch each other, and then sat back at the table with their coffee.

A faint breeze wafted through the window, and Kate lifted her hair off her neck, letting the night air cool her hot skin. For two weeks she had been trying to get her mind off Kelly Landrum. Now she couldn't seem to keep her mind on the woman. "The Nelsons didn't have much information."

"No. I didn't think they would, but it was worth a try."

"Did you meet them when you did the story on Charlene?"

"Yes. Why?"

"It seemed like you had sort of a special feeling for them. You were very sensitive to them."

"They had been through a bad time, that's all." He shifted on the chair. "What do you know about Helmut Kusch?"

Kate couldn't decide whether he was uncomfortable or uneasy, but something caused the abrupt change of subject. Now it was her turn to be uncomfortable. She didn't want to talk about Helmut. "I know he's a nice guy who's had a hard time."

"Charlene Nelson worked for him before she got the job at Business Express." He watched her closely.

"Oh, no." *Surely not Helmut.* He couldn't be involved in something so heinous. "Gisela must have been there then. She left last fall. That's about the time I started going there with Venice. I know he's a little peculiar, but he couldn't be a murderer."

"Why not? He knew Charlene, almost certainly disapproved of her. And he may have known Kelly—a lot of the Poinsett students go to the Black Forest to eat." He sipped thoughtfully, staring at his coffee, then cut his eyes to Kate. "Maybe he and the mysterious Gisela were having trouble. How do you know she went back to Germany?"

"Because he told me. And he was devastated by it. John, I know him. He's a genuinely nice person, just different."

"Is J. B. a genuinely nice person, too?"

Kate blinked. "J. B.? Why, yes, of course. He's—"

"According to the people I know, he's a slick, manipulative jerk."

Her expression caused John to throw up his hands in mock surrender. "Okay, okay," he said. "We won't talk about him." He added "for now" under his breath as he left the room to put on some more music.

"I heard that. Not now, not later, not ever." She hated to spoil their easy mood, but she had no intention of discussing J. B. with John.

Billie Holiday's wistful voice floated out on the breeze. Dimming the light, John pulled Kate into the empty dining room. "Dance with me."

"No, I—" she began, melting into his arms, unable to resist. Shaking her head ruefully, she smiled and let herself drift to the slow, bluesy notes.

Finally she said, "John, this has been a lovely day, the best I've had in quite a while, but I really need to get home now."

He let her swing away from him. "Okay. If you'll drop me at the paper—my car, remember? I'll follow you home."

"Of course I'll take you to your car, but I can get home all right." She picked up her purse and fished out her keys.

He locked the front door and followed her to her car and got in. "With everything that's been going on lately, I'd feel better if I saw you safely in."

She knew he had something on his mind, but what? "What are you thinking? It's okay. Even the prophet has been quiet since the police took him away."

"The prophet? Have you seen him again?"

"No, not a glimpse. He's probably gone back to his cave by now."

"He's more than a crazy fanatic. He comes down from the hills about once a year to raise money for his 'mission.' Calls himself Ezekiel, but the police know him as Aaron Youngblood. He has a record. Minor disturbances, mostly, but he's been in some nasty bar fights."

"I'm being very careful. After that lunatic the other night, I even stick to the main roads."

"What lunatic?" He turned to face her, switched off the car's radio. "Tell me."

"Nothing really happened," she said, alarmed at his reaction. "It was after the para group meeting when Wolynski came. Some fool in a pickup truck tried to run me off Paris Mountain. Fortunately, my car was made for roads like that, so I scooted by on the shoulder and left the SOB in the dust."

"Why didn't you tell me? Did you report it?"

"Why would I tell you? It was hardly a news event. And no, I didn't report it. I had no proof, no information. And they already think I'm nuts. The guy would have been long gone. He probably lived up there and was already in bed sleeping it off by the time I got home."

"Oh, Kate." That was all he said, but his tone reminded her of her father when she had done something really stupid.

"What's wrong? What did I do?"

"It's not you," he said, reaching over to gently massage the back of her neck. "I have a very bad feeling about this."

What could she say? She, too, had bad feelings about it. She turned into the *Times Herald* parking lot and stopped beside his Mustang, unsure again. "Good night, John."

"I'm following you home, and I'm coming in with you to check your house. Accept it." He left her and quickly got into his car.

Chapter 11

IF SHE HAD WANTED TO, Kate might have lost him on the back streets, but since he knew where she lived, it would have been pointless.

John left his car parked on the street and glanced quickly around as she pulled into the ramshackle garage. He edged past the car and carefully locked the door behind the Mazda. The garage touched the house at the corner, forming an offset extension. A wooden door almost beside the car door led to the narrow backyard and, a short distance away, the back door of the house. White roses vied with rampant honeysuckle in an effort to strangle an overgrown hedge of privet; together, they created an impenetrable barrier around the perimeter of the yard. That and two large oaks, plus a number of scrubby volunteers struggling upward through the hedge, separated Kate from the neighboring houses. The thorny barricade could keep out marauding lions. It would be nearly impossible to get into—or out of, he mused.

Under the light of a bare bulb in a porcelain socket, he checked the lock on her back door. "It would be a lot easier to get through your door than your hedge." He frowned at the simple skeleton-key lock. A thin curtain barely obscured a view of the kitchen through the tall glass panes in the upper half of the door. *But, hey! Why bother with the door?* A set of triple windows stretched invitingly across the back of the house. Feeling the need to make some comment on her deplorable lack of security, he said, "You at least need a good dead bolt that opens with a key. Anyone could break the glass and open this slide bolt. Is the rest of the house like this?"

She shrugged. "See for yourself." It did look a little flimsy. "I have a very effective early warning system."

"What, a goldfish?"

"No snide remarks, Gerrard. And no, no pets." She turned on the kitchen light.

The first thing he noticed was the number of doors. The kitchen, not all that big, had four. And where there wasn't a door, there was a window. The windows all seemed to have large panes, the kind one could easily break and enter through. The only thing lacking was solid walls. He looked further. Aside from a large worktable in the center, the dining room had a triple window, two doors, and a wide opening to the living room. A few easy steps put him in front of a green love seat angled across a corner between two windows. A quick inventory around the room showed him another triple window, a single window, fireplace, stairs, an open hall, and the front door. "Kate, why don't you just leave the front door open? This whole place is a clear invitation to a burglar. The dining room windows, conveniently hidden from the rest of the world by the jungle around your yard, would be my choice. The backyard is the most secure place in it. My suggestion is to move or camp out back."

"Well, that's reassuring. However, I will, in the future, include the dining room in my early warning system."

"Which is?"

"Bottles stacked mouth to mouth at critical points, such as a few inches in front of a door. When touched, however gently, they crash with a suitably loud noise." Taking him into the kitchen, she placed a glass soft-drink bottle upright on the floor a few inches in front of the door. The second bottle she carefully balanced upside down on top of the first. Then she opened the door, very slowly, barely touching the bottles. They toppled immediately, sounding like breaking glass. "If you're really worried, I could add a tin can or two. That should increase the volume."

"Okay, McGuire. It works. But if someone seriously wants in here, that won't stop him. You must sleep upstairs. Can you get down the steps and out before someone reaches you?" Without thinking, John brushed a strand of hair from her face and tucked it behind her ear.

After hearing about the truck on Paris Mountain, and with what he suspected about the elevator, he believed someone meant her harm, probably wanted her dead. He knew he had contributed to the danger she was in by publishing her name in his articles, but at the time, he hadn't felt that he had a choice. If he had it to do over. . . . But, of course, he didn't.

He watched her fiddle around the kitchen, wiping away imaginary crumbs. She was clearly unused to having a man in her house. He had thought she must have gotten a bundle out of J. B., but why would she live where she did? She couldn't be the promiscuous adulteress the press had made her out to be. And what was it Venice had said about not having insurance? He would figure it out.

Wasn't that what he did best? Invade people's privacy? He'd

never had any qualms about printing a story before. Now he found himself reexamining his standards. Maybe there *were* gray areas, times when printing the whole story did more harm than good. He shouldn't let what happened to his father color everything, every decision he made.

She stood by a cabinet, a sponge in one hand, watching him. "If I thought someone was in this house, I'd go out my bedroom window. It's over the back porch, and I could get down from the roof. But thank you for worrying." A small smile touched her lips, reflecting in her gray eyes.

Sliding his hand around the back of her neck, he pulled her toward him and lightly kissed her forehead. "Be careful, McGuire."

Kate thought she could spare a couple of hours away from the studio this morning. Business was hardly booming right now. Although she didn't believe Helmut Kusch could be involved in the murders, in fairness, she thought she should check out John's theory about Gisela. She supposed she would have to start by questioning his neighbors, but it seemed dishonest to sneak around behind Helmut's back. Unfortunately, she couldn't think of any other way. Maybe she would hit the neighborhood gossip on the first try. Venice, who knew everything, would know where he lived and what kind of area it was.

Venice didn't answer the phone. She could be in the bath or outside, Kate thought, as she continued getting dressed. She called again, but there was still no answer. Maybe she was talking to Ramses. The third time, she let the phone ring a dozen times before hanging up. She checked the clock on the microwave. 7:50.

Wondering what could have dragged Venice out before eight, Kate turned to the phone book and looked up Helmut's address, resigned to going in blind. She would spend a couple of hours at the studio and then go. If she could wait until eleven, Helmut was sure to be at the restaurant, and then she would see what his neighbors had to say—if any were home on a weekday morning. Maybe Venice would turn up by then.

Promptly at eleven, with the help of a map—still no response from Venice—she found the subdivision and, finally, the street and Helmut's house. The neat, boxy brick appeared to be one of the smaller designs. Precisely laid out flower beds and trees lined the outer edges of the front yard. A green lawn, its smooth perfection unmarred by leaf or twig, spread across the center. Kate bet the lace curtains visible in the windows were leftovers from Gisela.

Only one neighbor's house looked promising. A tricycle, a

wagon, and various toys blocked the sidewalk leading to the front door. Kate rang the bell.

A plump brunette in a denim jumper and sandals warily opened the front door but left the storm door closed. Small hands clung to her knees, and a curly-haired toddler peeked out from behind her skirt.

Kate introduced herself as an old friend of Gisela's and, explaining that asking Helmut was a bit awkward, asked if the woman knew where she was living now.

"No, I don't know anything about them." With disapproval written all over her, she quickly closed the door.

Feeling twice as guilty as before, Kate turned to the house on the other side of Helmut's. She'd been wrong about the house with the toys. Maybe this one would be more productive. She might as well try.

Plywood covered the steps to the porch, creating a ramp. Pots of scarlet geraniums flanked a neatly painted green door. A cheerful place, it had a well-loved air. The handicap ramp made her think someone might be home. She rang the bell and stepped back, hoping this person was less suspicious than the young mother.

A tall, white-haired man came to the door. "Yes?"

Again, Kate gave her story about being an old friend of Gisela's who didn't want to ask Helmut about her.

"Oh, yes, I understand. Mr. Kusch can be a bit intimidating, can't he? My wife knew Mrs. Kusch better than I did. You should talk to her. Come in. I'm Herschel Stern." He held the door for Kate and gestured toward a wide archway off the small entrance hall.

"Oh, I don't want to intrude." She hesitated at the door.

"No, no. Lila would love to see you. She doesn't get out much these days, and she enjoys company." He led Kate to the living room and stopped before a frail woman in a wheelchair. "Lila, this is Kate McGuire. This is my wife, Lila."

The pride and love in his face as he introduced the still-lovely woman touched Kate. Lila Stern sat in a soft halo of light, framed by a picture window filled with blooming plants. A bag of potting soil and a watering can sat on a small table by her right side. She placed a small trowel under the fingers of her left hand, which rested in her lap, and, brushing her right hand against her skirt, held it out to Kate. The gentle smile that illuminated her face completed an irresistible picture. Kate forgot Gisela.

After taking her hand and exchanging brief greetings, Kate took a business card from her purse and handed it to Mr. Stern. "Your wife is beautiful." Turning back to Mrs. Stern, she said, "I'm a portrait photographer. Would you let me get my camera from my car and take your picture? It would be my pleasure—certainly no charge."

He responded with an enthusiastic "yes" at the same time his wife said "no."

"Come, Lila. It would mean a lot to me to have a picture of you as you are now. You grow more lovely every year." He bent and, taking her right hand in his left, lifted her other useless one to his cheek. She turned luminous eyes to him. They seemed to have forgotten Kate's presence.

"If it pleases you, my dear," she whispered.

Kate slipped out, feeling like a voyeur. Quickly gathering her camera bag from the floor of the car, she ran back to the house, knocking before she entered. If she could capture that inner radiance. . . .

For the next hour, Kate talked with the couple while moving around to different angles, changing exposures, and switching between the Nikon with color film and her father's ancient Leica, which was loaded with black and white.

Finally Herschel remembered Gisela Kusch. "Didn't you want to know how to reach Mrs. Kusch?"

"Mrs. Kusch?" Lifting her head from the tripod she had just lowered, Kate looked up with a blank expression. "Oh! Yes. Gisela. I'm sorry, I had completely forgotten."

"Are you a friend of hers?" Lila asked, frowning slightly.

Kate found herself unable to lie. "Not really. I'm just looking for her. I need to know where she is," she added lamely, not wanting to explain John's theory or mention the murders to these gentle people.

Lila looked at her for a minute. "I trust that you have a good reason for asking, Kate, so I'll answer your question. I've received two postcards from her since she left. She and her husband live in Charleston. Of course, she would prefer that Mr. Kusch not know where she is."

"Husband? Charleston? I thought she went back to Germany."

"That's what Mr. Kusch wanted people to think. Although theirs was not a match made in heaven, he was shocked when she left him. Had it not been for the embarrassment of her involvement with the meat salesman, I believe he would have accepted it much better."

At least Helmut hadn't murdered his wife, Kate thought.

A short time later she left the Sterns, promising to return with the photographs next week. She envied their relationship, the closeness developed and nurtured over many loving years. Her parents would never have been like that, no matter how long they lived. She wondered how Venice and her husband had been. She knew Venice had loved him.

Thinking of Venice reminded her. Where would she have gone so early? Kate stopped at the first phone booth she came to. She let Venice's phone ring for a long time.

She returned to her car, worried. "Where are you, Venice?" Maybe John had heard from her. She could also tell him to cross Helmut off his list. She got out and returned to the pay phone. The newspaper switchboard put her through to John. He hadn't heard from Venice. She told him briefly about the Sterns.

"You were crazy to go there, Kate. What if Helmut is the killer and he finds out you're checking on him? Just because his wife is alive and ran off with another guy doesn't clear him. If anything, it gives him a better reason to go off the deep end.

"Look," he added, "I know you're worried about Venice. Why don't I meet you at her house, and maybe we can all get some lunch?"

Kate thought John must be worried, too, if he wanted to meet her at Venice's. Most of the time, he tried to avoid her.

Abingdon was a quiet street, overhung with the branches of ancient trees. Large old houses in a variety of styles sat on acres of lawn, discreetly hidden by hedges, fences, and graceful evergreens. Kate hadn't realized how isolated each house was from its neighbor. She turned in at Venice's wrought-iron gates, increasingly alarmed.

Alarm turned to panic when she saw the rear end of Venice's Cadillac in the open garage behind the house. Kate slid to a halt in the gravel drive and, leaping from her car, ran to the front door, calling to Venice. At Kate's touch, the door swung open. For an instant, fear took her breath away. Then, with her heart thumping madly, she plunged into the dim interior of the house, calling, "Venice! Venice!"

She found her in the study Venice used for readings, sprawled on the floor in a pool of blood. Unable to utter a sound, Kate fell to her knees beside the prone woman. Gingerly, she touched the still form, seeking some sign of life.

"My God!" John's shocked voice sounded over her shoulder. Kneeling beside Kate, he took Venice's hand and placed two fingers over the inside of her wrist. "Kate, she's alive. Call 911!"

Still on her knees, Kate grabbed the phone from the desk. Between her shaking hands and the tears blurring her sight, she could hardly punch in the numbers, but she managed to tell the dispatcher what had happened. Turning back to Venice, she saw

John carefully cover her with an afghan he'd pulled off a chair.

"I know I can't move her," he said, "but she feels so cold. Shock and loss of blood, I guess. Whoever did this is long gone. I would guess it happened last night. Stay here. I'll go watch for the ambulance."

The police and the paramedics arrived within seconds of each other. While the paramedics dealt with Venice, and one of the officers checked the house, Kate and John went into the living room with the second officer. Kate couldn't concentrate on the questions directed to her for watching over her shoulder for Venice. A short time later, one of the medics stuck his head in the door and told them which hospital they were going to, adding, "She was wearing a wig. It probably saved her life."

The first officer came back to say the back door had been jimmied. "Definitely not a pro. The lock is old and would have been easy to open."

Kate and John looked around the house with the police but couldn't tell if anything was missing. Obvious targets such as a television set and several pieces of silver had not been disturbed. Kate hardly listened. John did most of the talking and suggested the police notify Detective Waite, in case there was a connection to the Landrum murder.

"Oh, she's that psychic!" the first officer said. "Yeah, someone might think she knows something, whether she does or not. The guy was probably waiting for her when she came home. That purse on the floor indicates she'd just walked in."

Although Kelly Landrum's killer had been in the back of her mind, Kate hadn't fully faced the possibility of their being in danger. She clutched John's arm for support as a wave of nausea rose to her throat and cold sweat broke out over her forehead. He quickly sat her in a chair and shoved her head between her knees, brushing her hair out of her face. The policeman brought her a glass of water from the kitchen.

After the police finished, Kate picked up Venice's purse and keys. Stopping at the desk, she saw the crystal ball that Venice insisted housed Ramses's spirit. On impulse, she lifted it, cradling it in her arms, christening it with her tears. "What happened here, Ramses?"

"Why don't you take it to her at the hospital?" John suggested. "She might find it comforting. Come on. I'll drive and we can get your car later." He locked the house and, taking Kate's keys, locked her car.

In the hospital, on the way to the elevators, Kate suddenly swerved, almost tripping John. "Wait, I have to get something," she said, darting into the gift shop.

He expected her to come out with flowers. Instead, she held a helium-filled balloon—a large purple heart.

John stayed in the hospital waiting room with Kate, holding her hand and bringing her drinks. He asked if there was anyone who should be notified. Kate thought of Martin Carver, but she knew of no one else. John called the college and, telling the switchboard it was urgent, had a message delivered to the professor in class.

As they waited for news, Kate alternately paced the floor and huddled next to John.

Martin, breathless, ran in just as the doctors came out to explain Venice's injury and talk with them.

"She's resting comfortably. She has a concussion, and she's lost a lot of blood, but the injury is not as bad as we first thought. She had her hair pinned up under the wig, and that, with the wig, protected her skull somewhat, cushioning the blow. It didn't do nearly as much damage as it might have.

"Now, if we can keep her from getting pneumonia," he continued, "I think she'll be all right. She's conscious, but groggy. She doesn't remember what happened, and I don't want her upset. You can see her, one at a time, for a few minutes—but no questions."

"This is hers," Kate said, holding up the crystal ball. "I think it would comfort her to have it. Is it all right?"

The doctor looked blankly at the ball but agreed.

Kate slipped in and put Ramses on the table beside Venice, then tied the purple heart to the foot of the bed. "Venice?"

Venice opened her eyes and greeted Kate with a weak smile on her colorless face. She seemed almost transparent. Her gray hair with the shaved patch and bandage added to the fragile picture. She saw the purple heart floating above her and smiled. "You remembered."

"For being wounded in action. Yes. And I brought Ramses to stay with you." Venice brightened when Kate showed her the ball. Kate gave her a quick kiss and left the room, letting Martin go in.

A few minutes later, Martin, looking only marginally better than Venice, came out, shaking his head. "A bad business. Someone needs to stay with her. What if he tries again?"

No one had to ask who *he* was.

"I'm going to talk to Detective Waite," Martin said. "She might be able to assign someone to stay here. At least she can make an official request for the hospital to keep an eye on her. If not, I could get one of the nursing students from Poinsett. The doctor would let one of them stay." Martin left them to go to the nurse's station.

Before they left the hospital, Kate left a message on Gwen's answering machine.

Martin arranged for a male nursing student to spend the night with Venice. "In case her attacker returns," he explained, "I feel having a man in attendance would be more discouraging than if a woman was with her." He also had a notice posted at Poinsett, canceling tonight's para group meeting, and talked with Detective Waite, extracting a promise from her to stop by later in the evening when Venice would feel more like talking.

John drove Kate back to get her car. "I'll be back in time for dinner. Be careful, Kate. You won't be as easy a target as Venice, but that won't stop a murderer."

"Believe me, I'll be careful. I have to go by the studio and run a few errands. Then I'm going home and barricading the doors until you come." She was amazed at how easily she had accepted his presence in her life.

"You shouldn't stay by yourself. I have a spare bedroom. Why don't you stay at my house?"

"I'll try to get Gwen, but if I can't, I'll take you up on your offer," she said. Did she just want to be with John, or was she really scared to stay in her house alone? Where was her vaunted independence? What was happening to her?

"Tonight," he said, dropping a quick kiss on her forehead.

Kate, having no appointments, locked herself in at the studio and checked the answering machine for messages. There was only one. The timid voice belonged to Rita Nelson, but the girl asked that Kate not call her house. She said she would call back. Maybe Rita had something for her. Anything!

Looking at her hands, Kate's pulse quickened. Touching something of Charlene's was a long shot, but what else did she have to go on?

Working in the quiet theater building held little appeal, and after unloading her film and trying Gwen's number once more, Kate left the studio. She hoped Rita would try her at home.

Still feeling guilty about checking on Gisela with Helmut's neighbors, she rejected the idea of picking up something for dinner at the Black Forest. Maybe she could cook something simple. Or better yet, she thought hopefully, if she had a few things in the house, maybe John would cook.

Vegetables. She needed vegetables. Her diet was lousy, she knew. Maybe if she put a little more effort into it, she would feel better, be more clearheaded. Heaven knows she hadn't been thinking clearly lately.

The parking lot at the Farmer's Market was full, so Kate pulled into the adjacent parking lot at Maitland Pharmaceuticals. At this hour, people were beginning to leave for the day, and she would only be a few minutes. She slipped her wallet into her pocket, leaving her purse on the floor of the car, and started toward the market, when a battered gray Buick caught her eye. It looked like the one she had seen so much of recently, right down to a place on the driver's door where the paint had worn off, exposing the rust-stained metal. It had to be the same car, she thought, wondering to whom it belonged.

Intent on the car, Kate almost missed the man unlocking the green Jaguar a few spaces down. She turned to ask him about the Buick.

Chapter 12

DAMN! It was Thomas Andrews, Gwen's new friend. At least he could give her the information she wanted. "Thomas. Hello," she called, signaling for his attention as she walked over.

"Kate." He nodded, a rather stiff smile on his face. Standing motionless beside his car, he waited as she approached him.

Maybe he was embarrassed or put out about asking her out, especially if he knew she and Gwen were friends. He certainly seemed uncomfortable. She felt a little awkward about it herself. Well, she couldn't do anything about it now. She just wanted information. "Do you know who that gray Buick belongs to?"

"Yes. Polly Sherwood, one of the bookkeepers here."

A woman? She hadn't considered that. She studied the car. It must be the same one. "Do you know where she lives?"

"I have no idea. Why do you ask?"

"I just wondered. I thought she might live near me," she answered. She couldn't think of a plausible excuse, but continued her questions anyway. "What does she look like? How old is she?"

"I guess she's in her forties. Short, with grayish hair." He paused and then, with a puzzled look on his face, added, "She's a nice person."

"Is she married?" She was sure a man had been driving the car.

"I believe she's divorced. Are you thinking of asking her out?"

Startled, Kate turned from studying the gray car and saw that he had been joking. She forced a small laugh. "I know this sounds strange. I thought I'd seen this car lately, and I wondered who owned it."

"Polly." He shrugged. "How was your appointment the other day, Kate? I'm sorry you had to rush off."

"Oh. It was a portrait—went well." She wished her friend would find someone else, but if Gwen were to continue seeing him, they'd have to get past this. Thomas was extremely handsome, in a neat, almost fastidious way. Here he stood, in his three-piece suit, leather briefcase in hand, beside his very expensive car. There was nothing wrong—most women would jump at a chance for a date with him. Maybe she would have if it weren't that he reminded her of J. B.

Awkwardly she turned back toward her car, the vegetables forgotten. "I have to be going, but thanks for asking."

Empty-handed, she returned home.

John was sitting on the top step of her porch. "Your railing's about to self-destruct. You'd better get your landlord to fix it before someone falls through it."

"I've been meaning to call, but I forget when I'm at work during the day." She unlocked the door and let him in. "I meant to pick up something to eat, but I forgot that, too."

"No matter," he said, following Kate to the kitchen. "The police haven't learned anything about the attack on Venice. I checked before I left the office. Tell me what those people said about Helmut."

"There is absolutely no way Helmut would hurt Venice. I don't care what Gisela did, or how upset he was. It's not Helmut."

"Okay, I'll accept that for now. You know him, I don't. But tell me about this morning anyway." He watched Kate open a cabinet and peer in for a minute, then close it and move to another.

"There's nothing here to eat." Too distracted by her stomach to respond, she abandoned the cabinets and moved to the refrigerator. "I don't cook much."

"Let me look. We can come up with something." John, with confidence born of ignorance, gently shoved her aside and looked in at the bare shelves. Half a loaf of whole-wheat bread, a couple of cartons of yogurt, a jar of mayonnaise, and one lonely plastic container. "Geez! You really don't cook." He opened the container. "Yuck! What's this?" he asked, staring at the round brownish lumps.

"Eye of newt," she said solemnly.

Bravely, he touched the congealed mass with a finger and stuck it in his mouth. "Lentils," he said, smiling.

"Really?" She peered into the dish, widening her eyes. "Maybe that's why you're not sitting on a lily pad, belching 'ribbit.'"

"Pack your stuff, Witch." He ruffled her hair with his knuckles. "We can pick up some fried chicken on the way to my house."

Kate followed John in her car, idling in the parking lot while he ran into a country-style restaurant for the chicken.

At his house, she trailed after him into the kitchen and dropped her small gym bag in the corner.

He handed her a bunch of grapes. "Wash these while I heat some leftovers to go with the chicken."

She turned from the sink, the grapes dripping in her hands, and was surprised to find he had already filled the plates on the table. Was he that fast, or was she that slow?

Kate selected a leg from the bowl of chicken. John rolled his sleeves to his elbows and took three pieces. "In the morning I want to go to the Oconee County Courthouse and make a list of property owners around Lake Jocassee. Duke Power Company still owns most of the land, so there shouldn't be too many."

He took a long drink of tea and polished off a thick thigh. "It's likely to have been someone with access to a boat already docked there. I can't imagine pulling a boat all the way out there on a rainy night—it would attract too much attention."

"And wouldn't hauling a boat imply planning?" Kate pushed her plate back and toyed with the grapes. "I think he did it in anger, just got carried away."

"Yeah, you're right," he said, popping a grape into his mouth. "So now that you've been fed, tell me about your morning."

She told him about the Sterns and then, with a dreamy expression, said, "He kissed the back of her neck when he turned her back to her window garden."

They carried the dishes to the sink, and John plunged his hands into the hot soapy water, passing the cleaned dishes to Kate. She rinsed and dried in silence, still thinking of the Sterns and how she would display the photographs of Lila.

"Hey, come back," John said, waving his hand in front of her face. "How are your ankles?"

She blinked and turned to him. "I'm not ready for any serious running—unless it's in a good cause—" She rubbed her stomach. "But they're okay. That little distance at the park didn't hurt."

Holding her hand, he led her into the dining room and flicked the switch on the CD player. "Let's dance."

Kate stepped into his arms as Louis Armstrong's rich voice crooned the first mellow notes of "What a Wonderful World." By the time they reached the last song, Kate could hardly keep her eyes open.

"Let's go up," John said.

The solid wooden stairs gave no sound. There would be no telltale creak if an intruder crept up in the night, as there would have been in Kate's house. She wondered if Venice, who still couldn't remember what happened, had had any warning.

When they reached the top of the stairs, John took his hand from hers. The sudden withdrawal of warmth left her a surprising sense of loneliness. He opened a door that led to one of the front bedrooms, then flipped the light switch. "I haven't done much upstairs. Just shoved some stuff in here and closed the door. I can make up the bed and put a lamp in here for you."

Under the harsh glare of the single overhead bulb, he glanced into the bare room. "I didn't realize how inhospitable the room might seem to a woman. Until now, my brother-in-law, who didn't even care if the bed had sheets, has been the only one to use it."

"It's fine," she said without thinking. She looked around at the empty walls lined with packing boxes, the dusty hardwood floor. The narrow bed, its bare mattress covered in striped ticking, had a forlorn look. Safe, but lonely. She didn't want to be lonely. She could feel the heat of John's warm, solid body behind her. She glanced over her shoulder at the squarish hand resting on the light switch, remembering the feel of it at her waist.

"Actually," she said, clearing her throat, turning to face him, "I don't want to sleep here." She didn't want to sleep alone—she wanted to stay with him, wanted him.

"You shouldn't go home, Kate. Why don't you take my bed. It's a little better, and I'll sleep here."

"I think your bed sounds good," she said, turning off the light. Aware of her heart pounding in her chest, she took his hand in hers and pressed it against her cheek. "But don't bother with this one."

"What did you have in mind for me?" he asked cautiously.

Why did he have to be such a gentleman? Couldn't he help her out here? "Hmm," she said, closing her eyes and holding her wrist limply against her forehead. "It's coming to me now. I see two people. They're in a large bed. . . ."

Laughing, he slid his arms around her. "I like your vision, Witch," he said and leaned slowly down to her, watching, giving her a last chance to withdraw.

She smelled the pleasant scent of him, could see the shadow that marked his beard at the end of a long day. Her eyes closed as he came too near for focus. His warm lips touched hers, gently, and then harder as his arms tightened, enclosing her. Sliding her hands over his shoulders and around his neck, she pressed her body to his.

He stepped back and took her hand as he led her across the landing into his room. Leaning down, he pulled a shirt off the back of a chair and draped it over the small bedside lamp, dimming the light, bathing the tired walls in a mellow glow. Silently, he faced her again. His eyes never left hers as he reached for the front of her blouse. Kate's breath caught in her throat as she felt his fingers move down the buttons, felt the soft breath of cool air against her skin. Heat rushed through her blood like fire through a tunnel. She leaned into him.

The seductive aroma of coffee drew Kate from sleep. Awareness dawned and she remembered where she was. Behind her hand, she yawned widely, opening her eyes to sunlight and a steaming cup on the nightstand. Tucking the sheet under her arms and her hair behind her ears, she pushed herself up against the pillows.

Waking up in someone else's bed was a new experience, or if not new, long forgotten. John was not in sight, for which she was grateful. She ought to be up and dressed before he returned, but the lure of fresh coffee was too strong, and she flopped back against the pillows with a sigh. She savored the coffee—having it served to her in bed seemed downright decadent.

John called up the stairs, "Breakfast in ten minutes." The soaring notes of a soprano followed his voice. The aria, whatever it was, was beautiful.

Mmm, I think I'm in love. Kate sighed and stretched, reluctantly setting aside the coffee cup. *Joke! That was a joke,* she reminded herself. Her gym bag sat on the floor beside her. *Is this man for real?* she wondered, dressing quickly in her darkroom clothes.

"Good morning," she said from the kitchen door, holding her empty cup. "Am I in time?"

"Barely." Holding the coffeepot in one hand, he snaked his arm around her waist and kissed her. Then he filled her cup. "I let you sleep as long as I could. I have to leave soon, and I didn't know if you had any appointments this morning."

He made everything seem so natural, her morning-after awkwardness completely disappeared. She wanted to tell him how much his easy kindness meant but couldn't find the words.

"Thank you." Sliding into the chair he held, she added, "For everything. It's the first time I've really slept since this all started." She reached for the milk and sniffed, peering into the glass pitcher. "It's fresh. You're an amazing man, John Gerrard," she said as she poured it over a bowl of Special K. *All those vitamins! How like him.*

He smiled, then sobered. "Be careful today, Kate. I called Venice's room—"

"Venice! Oh my goodness, I forgot about her," Kate whispered, appalled.

"You're hardly awake. It all would have come back soon enough. Anyway, Martin Carver answered. He said she had a good night, but she's still having a lot of pain and is groggy. She told Lynne Waite she doesn't remember anything."

"Detective Waite?"

John nodded, grinning. "Last night. Apparently Martin was able to make his point with Waite. She's very concerned and said for you to be careful. Venice told her not to worry, you were with me."

"How did Venice—" She broke off, shaking her head. "The same way she always does, I guess."

"Well, maybe not. I told Martin yesterday that I was keeping you with me. I doubt if he'll let Venice out of his sight again. This really scared him."

"They've been friends for years. I guess neither of them has anyone else to worry about."

"Kate, they're a lot more than friends."

"They are?" she asked, surprised. "How do you know?"

"Watching them together. You're probably too close to see it," he said, finishing the last of his coffee as he stood. He took a steel ring from his pocket and worked a brass key off. "I've got to go. Here's a key to the front door. I'm going to Oconee this morning, but I should be back by lunch. Promise me you'll be careful."

She took the key, a little dazed. *Martin and Venice. My goodness.* "I will. Call if you find something. I'll be at the studio after I see Venice."

Martin rose from the bedside chair to greet her. When Kate saw Venice lying there, so pallid and frail, tears filled her eyes. "Oh, Venice," she whispered, leaning over to kiss her.

Venice raised her hand to Kate's cheek. "I'm going to be fine, Kate. Don't worry. Just take care of yourself."

Aware now, Kate noticed how tenderly Martin dealt with Venice, holding the straw so she could sip water, smoothing her hair, adjusting the pillow. *John's right, he loves her.* Just before slipping into sleep, Venice gave him a smile so full of love that Kate felt like an intruder.

After a few minutes with Martin, she left. Seeing them and the Sterns had given her a new perspective on love and marriage. Maybe happily-ever-afters were possible with the right person and a lot of effort. She knew it took effort, no matter how right the people were. Still dreaming, Kate wound through the hospital corridors and left.

When she reached the parking lot, a big red-faced man in sharp creases and starch stood beside the fender of a BMW which was nose to nose with her Mazda. Ignoring him, Kate approached the driver's door of her car. He attacked like an outraged mother. "Is this your car? If you've damaged my car, I'll sue! It's brand new!"

"I didn't hit—"

He cut her off. "Do you know what this car cost? These bumpers alone are worth a fortune. I'm calling the police."

"Sir, if you'll just—"

Looking her up and down, taking in her worn jeans and stained shirt, he ranted, looming over her. "You're probably on drugs or something. Don't think you can get out of it!"

"Quit yelling!" Temper replaced shock. Hands on her hips, she faced him. "Your car isn't hurt. I barely touched the damn thing."

"You'll pay for this! You give me your name and address right now." He reached for her, and Kate sidestepped away from him.

As he got in her face, Kate could smell the liquor. "Sober up and look around you, mister. There's nothing wrong with your car, and I'm not giving you anything!"

He grabbed at her again, then stopped, raising his eyes. "Ahem. Well, you should be more careful." He turned quickly and walked to the other side of his car and got in.

Kate, surprised at his sudden withdrawal but pleased with herself, turned back to her car, almost bumping into a T-shirt-covered bosom. Startled, she looked up.

Kelly Landrum's roommate towered over her, grinning. "You're pretty tough for a little thing. I guess it's that red hair."

"Josephine Wardlaw! Well." Kate felt her ego deflate like an old balloon. "I guess I know what changed his mind."

"You were doing all right till he decided to get physical. It was probably his wife's car." The big woman laughed.

"Listen," Kate said, "I know we didn't hit it off too well before, but I really need to talk to you about Kelly."

"Tell me what your interest is in all this, and I might." She folded her arms across her chest and leaned against the car, crossing one ankle over the other.

"Okay, fair enough." Kate took a deep breath. "Have you been reading John Gerrard's articles?"

"Yeah. So?"

"I'm Kate McGuire." She waited to see if the name would register.

"Ah, the psychic. Well, this ought to be interesting."

Kate explained briefly what she had seen. "I know it sounds crazy. It does to me, too. But I'm sure the murderer knew Kelly and was jealous, or angry. Do you know if she was seeing someone in secret? Did you ever see her with anyone when she didn't want you to?"

"I never saw him, but I'm sure she was dating someone. She was practically engaged to Bill Norris, the basketball player, but he went back home to Georgia for the summer. That's why she didn't want anyone to know about the other guy."

"Of course!" Kate smacked herself in the forehead. "I never

thought about Kelly being the one who wanted to keep it secret."

"Yeah, and Bill was due back the week after she disappeared."

"That's it! She was trying to break it off, and he didn't want to let go."

"Makes sense, if he's nuts. That's a little extreme for most people, don't you think?"

"Yes, but most people don't kill. I think he *is* nuts." Kate smiled at the other woman, fished a card out of her bag, and handed it to Josephine. "Thanks. If you think of anything else, would you let me know?"

"Why? You playing girl detective?"

"Not exactly. It haunts me. I have to find out what happened to her. And he just attacked my friend Venice. That's why I'm here."

"Yeah, I read about that in this morning's paper."

"You did? It was in the paper?" Kate frowned. "Damn him. Now he knows Venice is alive!"

"Damn who? I can guess who knows the woman's alive."

"John Gerrard, that's who!"

Kate fumed all the way up the steps to the studio. How could he put Venice in danger, just for a story? Unlocking the door, she tossed her bag and the newspaper she had just bought onto the desk and snatched up the phone. John had gone to the courthouse in Oconee County. She was forced to settle for leaving another nasty electronic message.

Just as she hung up, the phone rang. Knowing it couldn't be John, she willed herself to sound pleasant. "Good morning, Period Portraits. May I help you?"

A soft voice whispered, "Is this Kate McGuire?"

Rita! "Yes. Rita?"

"Yes. I can't talk now, but I'm going to the grocery in a few minutes. Can you meet me at the Winn-Dixie on Mills Avenue? The one by Kmart?"

Kate guessed she was at home and didn't want her parents to overhear. "I'll be right there. Ten minutes."

Rita hung up without saying any more.

Chapter 13

MIDMORNING TRAFFIC made the trip more like fifteen minutes, but Kate spotted Rita, standing by a pile of pumpkins, right away.

"I thought you'd see me here," Rita said, nodding at the pumpkins. "I brought you some of Charlene's things. It's letters and pictures and things from her desk. Do you think any of it will help?" She kept looking over her shoulder, shifting from foot to foot, as she handed Kate a shoebox tied with twine.

"I hope so." Kate hugged the box to her chest, feeling the excitement build.

"Could I have them back, you know, after you look at them?" The poor girl looked miserable.

Kate's heart ached for her. "Of course. Can I keep them for a couple of days?"

"Yes. No one will notice." The fear of exposure faded. Her eyes bright with tears, she focused on Kate. "Have you and Mr. Gerrard found anything yet?"

"Not yet." Kate wished she had something to offer, but she couldn't lie to the girl. "Rita, do you know if Charlene was dating anyone more than others, or if there was anything unusual about any of her relationships?"

Rita looked at her for a minute before answering. "I don't really know, but I think she went out a few times with someone who was different, maybe older."

"Different how? Can you think of an example?" Kate's heartbeat kicked up a notch. This was the man, she was sure of it. "Anything at all."

"A few times she got really dressed up, and then she would say she was meeting some girlfriends and go out in her car. She seemed to be kind of excited, but trying to hide it."

"Why would she hide it?"

A quick, conspiratorial smile flashed over Rita's wan face. "Dad's very strict. He wouldn't have let her go with someone he didn't approve of. She's had to sneak out before. I helped her sometimes."

"Did she ever mention going anyplace different?"

"No, that's the odd part. I asked where she was going, and she said, 'Nowhere, and I'm tired of it.' She sounded unhappy about it. I wished I hadn't asked. It spoiled her mood." Rita looked up, adding, "But she had a couple of dates with someone else right at the end. Larry Crawford. He picked her up at the house. My dad liked him. He worked with Larry's dad."

"I guess the police checked him out."

"Yes. It couldn't have been Larry." She blushed, then stared at the pumpkins, looking more miserable than ever.

In a burst of insight, Kate asked, "Rita, are you seeing Larry now?"

"I want to, but Dad won't let me date anybody. I know it's because he's afraid for me, but. . . ." Rita's voice changed into a sniffle as a tear rolled down her cheek. "Please find out who killed Charlene. He's killing the rest of us, too."

"I'll try, Rita." Kate, feeling hopelessly inadequate, handed her a Kleenex.

Rita blew her nose and straightened, wiping the back of her hand across her eyes. "I'm sorry."

"Don't be. I understand." Kate racked her brain for anything that might give them a clue to the killer. "Can you think of anything at all that would help describe the man? Like, maybe she suddenly got interested in something different or started talking about some unusual activity?" Kate knew she was clutching at straws, but she couldn't think of anything else.

"No." Rita rubbed the side of her nose and scratched an ankle with her foot, thinking. She shrugged helplessly, then brightened. "But she did say something about a car once. It was only a week or so before she— We were out and this red convertible pulled up beside us. I said that was some car, and she laughed and said I should see what she'd been riding in. That's not much, is it?"

"I don't know. Maybe there'll be something in the box."

"I have to go. Someone will see us and tell my parents. They'll guess it was you," she said, her gaze flicking to Kate's hair.

"I understand. I don't want to cause any trouble. How can I contact you to give the box back?"

"Don't. It'll just set Daddy off again," she said. "Can I call you on Monday? That's my next day off, and I usually go to the store after lunch."

"That's fine." Impulsively, Kate hugged her. "Thank you, Rita. It was good of you to do this."

The girl scurried into the store and disappeared.

* * *

Kate couldn't wait to get into the box, but aware that it held memories and fragile links that meant so much to Charlene's family, she didn't want to risk losing anything in the car. She waited until she got back in the studio.

Before she had a chance to open the box, Gwen tapped lightly on the door and waltzed in. "Kate, you ought to keep that door locked."

"I forgot," she said, putting Charlene's box aside. "Did you get my message about Venice?"

"Yes, I came here from the hospital. Martin said I just missed you. The doctor came while I was there. He's going to let Martin take her home this afternoon."

"Great! Maybe I should plan to stay with her."

"No, Martin has arranged for a couple of off-duty cops to take turns, and he'll be there." Gwen added, "Detective Waite set it up. She told Martin it was worth it if it would keep him and John Gerrard off her back."

"John? What does he have to do with it?"

"He agreed to plant that article in this morning's paper if Waite would get someone to watch Venice. I think Venice is really frightened since the attack. She and Martin were all for it." Gwen looked at Kate, puzzled. "Didn't you know?"

"No! You mean they're using Venice for bait?" She sprang from her chair. "What are they thinking?"

"I think I know why they left you out," Gwen said, arching an eyebrow. "Kate, it would have been in the paper in the Crime Beat section anyway. Martin said John bargained with Waite to get protection for Venice. He said he'd print the story any way she wanted it as long as Venice would be safe. Do you think whoever attacked her wouldn't notice that no murder was reported?"

"Ah, dammit." Kate sagged back in her chair.

"What have you done?" They had been friends since childhood. Gwen knew her too well.

Kate muttered, "Called and left a rude message. Very rude."

"I have to say, your temper's been getting the best of you lately." Gwen softened her unsympathetic words by adding, "But you've been under a lot of strain. He'll probably understand."

"I hope so. By the way, how are you and Thomas doing? I saw him yesterday."

"Oh, Thomas." Gwen turned to the window for a second. "He's turning out to be rather intense. We have a date tomorrow night. If he doesn't lighten up, it may be the last one."

"Oh, Gwen." She knew that in spite of Gwen's glamorous lifestyle and the attention she received, the gorgeous woman was lonely. "I'm sorry it didn't work out."

"Flash in the pan, that's all." She shrugged. "I have to go. I just wanted to see how you're doing." On her way out, she tapped the brass key slot with a long fingernail.

Kate got the hint. As soon as the door closed, she locked it and returned to Charlene's box. Carefully sifting through the contents, she selected a sheet of pink stationery and held it for a moment, trying to let her mind go blank. Nothing. She opened the letter and found a note in a round, childish script, thanking "Cousin Charlie" for a Michael Jackson album.

Maybe she should check first to see if there was something in the box Charlene might have handled frequently or kept close to her. She lifted out the contents carefully, placing the items on the desk. Nothing seemed intensely personal. A card from Business Express with a telephone number scrawled on the back drew her attention. Concentration brought only a faint feeling of pleasure. Envisioning some tall, dark man answering, she dialed the number.

"Maitland Pharmaceuticals," a woman's voice said.

"I'm calling from Business Express," Kate lied. "Can you tell me if our delivery truck has already been there today?"

"Not yet. He usually comes after lunch."

"Thank you," Kate said and quickly hung up. Maitland was just one of their customers. Nothing there.

After several fruitless attempts with other objects, she turned her attention to the photographs at the bottom of the box. There were several of Charlene. In spite of their poor quality, Kate could see that she had been a pretty girl, obviously full of life. In most of them, she was clowning or posing with friends. In a drugstore photo package, Kate found several taken at a party. The prints had a murky, greenish cast. *Printed with dirty chemicals*, Kate thought, disgusted. But the sheer joy expressed in one caught her eye. It should have been a really good picture.

Dancing barefoot on a tabletop, Charlene had her head thrown back, laughing. Her skirt swirled around her legs in a blur of color, and one hand arched above her head, gypsy-style. Light sparkled on her gold hair and a wide silver bracelet. An earring glinted at her ear.

Kate stared at a group of upturned faces, all watching the exuberant dancer. Even though they were difficult to see because of the dark print, their rapt expressions were apparent. Charlene drew all eyes. But as Kate handled her things, sadness for the loss of this bright girl was the only feeling that came to her.

The negatives were still in the package. Kate wondered if the Nelsons would like an enlargement of the little photo. She was sure Rita would. When she went back in the darkroom, she would see what she could do in black and white. If it looked good, she would send the negative to the color lab she used. They could do wonders if there was anything at all to work with.

Carefully replacing everything in the shoebox, she shut it in the back of a file cabinet.

Now John. She looked at the telephone. It was past time for lunch, which her stomach reminded her she had missed. He ought to be back. Wishing in vain that somehow his voice mail had lost her earlier message, she dialed his office. "You have reached—" Kate hung up. She would try again from home.

Excuses and justifications played in Kate's mind on the drive home. There were none. "No way, McGuire. Admit it. You're a bad-tempered bitch. Grovel and get it over with."

The door still smelled of paint from the fresh coat John had given it. It needed another. The mocking HARLOT still showed, if faintly. The key turned easily in her front door lock, snapping her to attention.

She froze. *Had it been unlocked?* She wasn't sure—she had been operating on automatic. If someone was there, she would hear a creak or a footstep—something—she told herself. She dropped her bag at the door, wanting her hands free just in case. Her heart thudding in her chest, she stepped cautiously into the living room. A ceramic vase lay against a corner of the sofa. Magazines littered the floor, as if someone had taken a wild swipe across the top of the low coffee table.

Shaking, she crossed into the dining room. The mutilated remains of the pictures she had been considering for the Caesar's Head show were scattered over the work table, a few on the floor. A faint stirring of the air from the open door caused tiny bits of the paper that had been her acceptance notification to drift slowly to the floor. Shards of frosted glass surrounded naked fluorescents in her light box.

She halted, surveying the wreckage, her breath coming short and hard. *Calm down.* At least she still had the negatives.

A torn and crumpled photo of fog-shrouded trees fluttered from the table to the floor at her feet, precipitated by her passing. She bent to pick it up, then stopped. She had seen enough crime flicks to know she shouldn't touch anything.

Holding her breath, she picked her way through the debris to the kitchen. Cabinet doors stood wide, and the contents of the open drawers lay on the floor. Kate's hands shook as she dialed the police. "Detective Waite, please."

"She's out right now. Can someone else help you?"

Kate explained about the intruder to another detective and asked that he pass the information to Detective Waite.

He didn't sound too impressed, but he promised to send someone to check.

Kate was afraid he would write it off as a simple burglary. "Please call Detective Waite. Tell her it's connected to Kelly Landrum, and give her my name."

"McGuire." He placed the name; Kate could hear it in his flat voice. "You the one with the visions?"

"Yes." She ground her teeth. "And the other woman involved was nearly killed yesterday," she snapped.

That got his attention. He said he would send someone out right away, and although he still sounded skeptical, he promised to notify Waite. "Don't touch anything, Ms. McGuire."

She hung up and dialed John's number, her earlier phone call completely forgotten.

"Gerrard," he answered.

"John, he's been here. He's been in my house! I called the police."

"Are you sure he's gone? Get out of the house. I'm on my way." His voice trailed off, the connection broken as his last words sounded.

She wasn't ready to go upstairs even though she was certain the killer was long gone. Holding herself tightly, she went to pace on the front walk as she waited.

Within minutes, she heard the uneven roar of John's Mustang. He braked sharply at the curb and was out of the car before the engine died. "Oh, Kate!"

She threw herself into his arms as he reached the sidewalk.

A patrol car arrived, parking behind John, and two uniformed policemen got out. Kate recognized Paul Wolynski. So did John, who held out one hand to the young officer, keeping Kate tight against his side with the other arm.

The second policeman, an older man with a long, sour face, introduced himself as Officer Dill. Kate had to bite her lip to keep from giggling. Adrenaline did not have a good effect on her.

She told them what she had seen and that she had left the house after using the telephone. "Except for tearing up some of my photographs and smashing the glass on my light table, I think he just made a mess, but I didn't go upstairs."

The officers asked her to wait outside while they checked the house. Dill added, "You, too, Gerrard." Apparently he also recognized John.

Kate felt an excessive amount of fear, considering what she had seen. Nausea clutched at her stomach. "It was him." She started to shake again.

John kept his arm around her, watching her through narrowed eyes. "I got your message. Didn't your mother teach you not to use words like that?"

Kate winced. "I'm sorry. I don't know what's wrong with me. Everything seems to set me off."

"Understandable, considering. But I hope it wears off soon." He kissed the top of her head. "You smell better today. I like it."

"You should. It's your shampoo. After you left, I took a quick shower." She smiled, realizing he had successfully distracted her. Again. "I didn't have time to come home before I went to see Venice."

Wolynski signaled to them from the doorway. "No one's here, but there's something upstairs you should see. Be careful not to touch anything."

Kate hesitated, then took a deep breath and started up the steps, John right behind her.

Dill was waiting at the door to Kate's bedroom. "It's a good thing you weren't here last night, Ms. McGuire. Somebody doesn't like you very much." Watching her, Dill abruptly moved out of the way, giving her a clear view of her bed.

Kate's eyes widened and her knees sagged. The air left her lungs in a rush, and her stomach contracted as if she had been punched. John locked his arm around her and pulled her against him.

A large kitchen knife protruded from the mattress. Multiple stab wounds pierced the sheets, and polyfoam from the pillow littered the room like wool from a shorn sheep. Shreds of lace and nylon hung from her dresser drawers. Above it all loomed the word *BITCH*, scrawled across her mirror in lipstick letters. The ruined tube lay open on the dresser.

"Waite's on her way. She'll want to talk to you. Don't touch anything," Dill said again. He took a ballpoint pen from his pocket and retrieved his clipboard from a chair. "You up to answering a few questions?"

"Outside." Glaring at Dill, John turned Kate and led her down the steps. "She doesn't need to stand here in this mess."

"Just don't touch anything," Dill said.

"I never want to touch any of it again," Kate said, her teeth chattering.

"How about the kitchen? Can I make her some coffee?" John asked over his shoulder.

"The fingerprint guy will be here soon. Better not." Wolynski stepped aside to allow them room to pass at the bottom of the steps.

"How did he get in? Do you know?" John asked Wolynski as he led Kate to the porch. The officers followed.

Dill answered. "Cut a hole in the dining room window. Very small, very neat. He reached in and unlocked it, climbed in, and closed the window." The older officer leaned against the porch railing and, frowning, quickly straightened when it wobbled beneath him. "You ought to have that fixed."

Kate nodded absently at the loose rail, intent on their information.

John said, "He's learning. He butchered Venice's door."

Wolynski took up the story. "Yeah, I saw that. We almost missed the window. He probably let himself out the front door. My guess is that he did the pictures and the coffee table stuff on the way out, just a last token of his esteem. Is that knife upstairs yours?"

"I think so. It looks like one of mine."

"We'd better let Detective Waite talk to you."

"It's easy enough to guess." John tightened his hold on Kate. "He expected to find her in bed. When he didn't, he lost it. That's why the bedroom's torn apart."

"Yeah, that's how we see it, too," Wolynski said. "He was regaining control, cooling, when he went downstairs. The destruction's less savage."

Waite and her partner, a tall dark contrast to her fair coloring, arrived, joined them on the porch. She spoke briefly to Kate and John, introduced her partner as Jamal Burnett, and turned away to speak quietly with the two officers. Gesturing for Kate and John to wait, the four of them went into the house.

Kate folded her arms tightly across her midriff and began pacing, her head down.

"Your neighbors are out," John said, indicating people across the street in clusters of two and three. One wizened little woman on the porch next door had turned her chair toward them, unabashedly staring as she rocked. He glanced at the black Timex on his wrist. "I guess a lot of them are coming home from work now. I wonder if anyone saw or heard anything."

The lab man arrived in another marked car, a Blazer with CRIME SCENE UNIT written on a gold band, and pulled up behind Wolynski's black-and-white cruiser, causing a ripple of excitement to spread through the growing group of watchers.

John slowly perused the faces. "Kate, do you know who lives around you well enough to pick out anyone who doesn't belong? These creeps often return when they can hide in a crowd, to see the results of their handiwork."

She quickly scanned the knots of people. Cold waves undulated through her stomach at the thought. "I don't think he would be here. With what Rita and Josephine have told me, I think he would stand out in this crowd."

"Rita? Nelson? When did you talk to her?" John's attention switched back to Kate. "And who's Jo— Ah!" he interrupted himself. "The roommate. What have you been doing, Kate?"

"I ran into Josephine at the hospital this morning, and Rita called as soon as I got to the studio." She started to explain, when Lynne Waite came out of the house.

"Let's go inside. We can sit in the living room now." The detective motioned them to follow her. "Kate, John, we'll need your fingerprints and those of anyone else who's been here recently. Frankly, I don't think we're going to find anything. There's nothing on the glass where he broke in, and Debis, the fingerprint guy, thinks the perp was wearing gloves. There are some indentations—and a concrete block he used as a stepping stone—in the soil under your dining room window, but nothing distinct enough for a print. This is a very careful person."

"Kate has had some other 'accidents' that you should know about," John said.

"What?" the detective asked. "When?"

"I didn't connect them with anything at the time." Weary and confused, Kate wilted like a rose out of water. "But now I don't know."

"Is that what I think it is on your front door?"

Kate nodded.

"That doesn't look like an accident to me. How did it get there?"

"That prophet from the mountains." Kate told her about running into him and then finding him in front of the house. "I guess the officer could tell you about it."

"He will, as soon as I get back to the station." Waite called to Burnett to join them.

The tall detective clattered down the wooden stairs and pulled up a chair near Waite. Kate and John sat together on the sofa. Kate sneezed.

"It's the fingerprint powder. It'll go away soon," Waite said, balancing a steno-style notebook on one knee. She turned to her partner. "There's more, Jamal." She nodded at Kate to continue. "All right. From the top. Let's hear everything this time."

Kate told them about the car on the mountain and the elevator, about the feeling that someone was outside the studio that morning. "I snapped a few shots with a long lens, but I don't know if anything will show up. I haven't developed it yet."

Waite excused herself briefly to make a call. Her voice carried from the kitchen. "I want that report from the fire department."

For her partner's benefit, Waite asked Kate to repeat what she had said at the studio Sunday about the parapsychology group and the visions.

As concisely as she could manage, Kate told them. She tried to keep any emotion out of her voice, but an underlying quaver crept through.

Skepticism written all over his handsome face, Burnett refrained from comment, asking instead, "Did you have any connection with Kelly Landrum before this? Do you know anyone who did?"

"Not directly, except that Detective Waite told me she used to live in this house." Kate started as the big detective jumped up and strode to the steps.

"Hey, Wolynski! Come down here a minute," he called. The young officer appeared immediately. "Tell us what happened that night you went to the meeting at Poinsett. The one where Ms. McGuire had her 'vision.'"

Kate shook her head at his emphasis on *vision*.

Wolynski, as carefully as if he were on the witness stand, described the meeting. It sounded like a scene from a grade D movie. Kate was just grateful that he didn't describe Venice's outfit.

Burnett watched Kate but said nothing as Wolynski's story ended. He nodded, dismissing Wolynski, and said to Waite, "I don't know about psychic powers, but she's probably convinced the killer that she knows something."

"I agree. And while it looks like this"—Waite gestured toward the upstairs—"is connected to Kelly Landrum's death, we need to rule out any personal motives. Are there any rejected lovers or upset business associates, anything like that?"

Kate's heart sank. If they questioned J. B., he would be furious, but she would have to tell them.

John sat quietly beside her, taking it all in, his surprise evident when she told them she'd had only had a few dates since her divorce.

"Did you turn down anyone who was especially persistent?" Waite asked, her blue pen poised above the small notebook.

"I don't think so. Most of them accepted it with unflattering ease." The corners of her mouth turned up in a wry smile.

John asked. "Who cuts your grass? Have you had any work or repairs done in the house? What about the studio?"

"I do it all. If it's bigger than I can handle, James Earl, the maintenance man at the warehouse, helps me. If the house needs serious work, the landlord takes care of it. A contractor remodeled the inside when I first moved in, so it hasn't needed anything much."

"A contractor?" John repeated. "Here? There's a big difference between the inside and the outside of this house. Someone's done a lot to a rental in a—" He stumbled, looked at Kate. "In a less expensive neighborhood. Who owns it, Kate?"

"I don't know. Someone bought it right after I moved in and had the inside redone. The rental agent said the new owner needed a tax write-off."

"Save it, Gerrard." Waite scribbled something on her notepad and flipped the page over. "Let's get back to this business."

"Tell me about this James Earl," Burnett said.

"James Earl Withers." Picturing the slow, kindly man, Kate smiled. "He's helpful, quiet, pleasant—"

"No, it's not him," John said, shaking his head. "I saw him when Kate was trapped in the elevator. It scared him to death."

"I'll decide that for myself." Waite frowned at him and nodded at Kate to continue.

"If he works at the Principal Players warehouse," Burnett said, "he knows you and Ashburton, and he could easily have tampered with the elevator—if that wasn't an accident."

Unconvinced, Kate told them what little she knew. "He was working there when I moved in with my studio. I think he was laid off from one of the mills. Gwen Gordon would know."

There wasn't much else to say, and they wrapped it up quickly. Waite and Burnett rose together.

"Whatever this is about," Waite said, "someone is very serious. Are you staying with Gerrard?"

"Yes, she is," John answered. As the detectives turned to go, he added, watching for their reactions, "Kate ran into Josephine Wardlaw at the hospital this morning."

"Wardlaw? The roommate?" Burnett asked. "What was she doing there?"

"I didn't ask," Kate replied. "I just saw her in the parking lot. She was very friendly." Surely they didn't think Josephine had anything to do with it.

"She's big enough," John said.

Burnett glanced at Waite. "Maybe," he said noncommittally.

They do suspect her! "No, no, it's a man. I'm sure of it," Kate protested. Over the last week, her feelings about the killer had jelled. She was certain now.

"We haven't ruled out anyone yet. Tell us about seeing Wardlaw," Burnett said.

Kate told them, including the incident with the BMW driver, but she left out the visit to the dormitory. It couldn't help their investigation, and it might make them think worse of both her and Josephine. She had a feeling Burnett didn't trust either one of them.

She started to tell them about visiting the Nelsons and meeting Rita, but John tightened his fingers on her arm in a barely perceptible signal.

"Kate, whatever you do, be careful," Waite warned. "Gerrard may be a pest, but he's not stupid. Stick with him."

"Debis will be finished in a few minutes, and you can have your house back," Burnett said. "But Lynne's right. Be careful. Whoever did this will be back—and my guess is soon."

Chapter 14

AS THE TWO DETECTIVES DROVE AWAY, John turned to Kate. "You're too tired and I'm too hungry to start cleaning up now," he said, brushing his thumb lightly over the shadows beneath her eyes.

"If they finish soon, I'd like to at least make a start." She glanced at the house. "I guess I need a new mattress."

"You won't need it until they catch the guy, for sure." He draped his arm over her shoulders and started slowly back inside, dropping a light kiss on her cheek. "While we wait, you can tell me about Rita Nelson."

Debis, a lanky stick of a man, met them at the door with Wolynski and Dill in his wake. "We've finished here, Ms. McGuire. We'll send you a list of the items we removed."

At the bottom of the porch steps, Wolynski turned back to them. "Be careful."

John closed the door and followed Kate into the living room. "Now. Tell me about Rita."

"That poor, sad girl. She had to sneak out to give me a box of Charlene's things—letters, some photographs, stuff like that." Kate rubbed her eyes, then leaned down and retrieved a copy of *Outdoor Photographer*, its bent pages fanned over another magazine. "Damn him! Look at this," she said, waving a *National Geographic* with a torn cover.

She put aside the thought of him, here, touching her things. The knife. At least the police had taken that—no one had suggested she touch it, and she was grateful. Ignoring the ugly scene upstairs, she began straightening and picking up with John. "Charlene was a pretty girl. In the pictures, she looked so full of life."

John, gathering mutilated photographs from the dining room floor, listened as she described the contents of the box. He dumped the scraps on the table and wiped a smudge of black powder off one of the pictures, frowning. "You don't get anything from this stuff?"

"I wish I could," she said, working her way toward the kitchen. "I don't usually see things. And when I do, it's usually just a quick flash. And I can never find my own things. I lose coffee cups and keys all the time. This is so different. I've never had anything like the intense visions that came with the sweatband. And I hope I never do again."

John followed her into the kitchen, dropping his collection of trash into the waste can. "Why don't you pack some things, and then we can get something to eat. We can clean up tomorrow and see about fixing that window."

"Good idea." His casual use of *we* warmed her. "Suddenly I'm ravenous. Would you like to go to the Black Forest? I'd like to see Helmut, in case his neighbors have told him I was checking on him. I want to apologize. This spy business isn't for me. I feel horribly guilty about it."

"Don't. But I'd like to see Helmut, too. See how he reacts to you. Having his wife run off with someone gives him *more* reason to dislike women, not *less*. And if he was already disturbed, that could have been the blow that sunk the soufflé, so to speak." He grinned, ruffling her hair, and pushed her out of the kitchen.

"Is this a professional hazard? Bad metaphors?"

"Okay, okay." He laughed, then sobered as they neared the stairway. "Why don't you let me get your clothes? Just tell me what you want, and you can wait down here."

"No. I can do it." She didn't want to face her ravaged room, but neither was she ready for John to be picking out her underwear. Anyway, she needed to see what was salvageable. Grabbing her gym bag, still sitting beside the door where she had left it when she came home, she gave John a parody of a smile and marched up the steps. He followed her.

Except for the bed, the actual damage wasn't as bad as she had thought. A few blouses and some slacks lay on the floor in front of the closet, as if he had grabbed at them in passing. Mostly, things were thrown around the room. Some of her underwear had been torn apart, but most of it had just been raked out of the drawers.

While John leaned against the door frame and watched, she quickly stuffed a bra and some panties into the satchel. As she picked up a scrap of peachy lace, a queasy wave hit her stomach. Her throat tightened. A clenched fist gripped the panties, while a knife, held tightly in the other hand, slashed at them. Eerily familiar hands reached for her neck as rage swept over her like a hot wind. She staggered back, clutching her throat.

"Kate!" John grabbed her, folding her in his arms, stroking her back as she pressed her face to his chest. "What did you see?"

She pushed herself away and straightened. Still a little shaky, she cleared her throat and then, husky-voiced, said, "I'm okay. It was just his hands, and the violence of his anger. He wanted to strangle me, even though he was holding the knife. I still can't see his face."

"But you could see his hands? Describe them."

"Big. He was wearing thin gloves, the kind doctors wear. The knife was in his right hand." She shivered, pressing a hand to her stomach.

"How about a ring? A watch?"

She shook her head.

"Picture the hands. Any hair showing above the gloves?"

"Dark sleeves down to the gloves. Nothing else."

"So we know for sure there won't be any prints."

"I don't think so." She realized that he accepted her vision. Amazing. Amazing how gratifying it was for him to believe her.

"Come on, Sherlock. We need to eat. Get your clothes and let's go. Don't force me to look in your refrigerator again."

"After we eat, I want to check on Venice. She must be home by now." Kate took a pair of khakis from a hanger and a blue chambray shirt from the floor. Pausing, she surveyed the closet with its drunken spill of clothes. A silky buttermilk shirt slithered to the floor. She snatched it up and slung it over her arm, nodding to John. "Let's go. I dread seeing Helmut, but it's something I have to do. This day can't get any worse."

They dropped her car and bag at John's and returned to the Mustang. He cleared a stack of papers off the front seat and then drew her into his arms. "I'm glad you were with me last night."

Damn her eyes! Did Kate think she could hide from him? He had to get her; she kept edging closer to him. He knew it, could sense it. He had to find out where she was staying.

And Venice was still alive. How? How could she possibly have survived that blow? He had hit her hard, squarely on the head. She had just crumpled and collapsed, with not so much as a whimper. At least she hadn't seen him—he was sure of that. Maybe he'd get lucky and she would lose her psychic ability. So much for Venice.

It was Kate he had to get rid of, but how? He took the Browning nine millimeter out of his drawer and carefully laid it on the table, placing the magazine beside it. Fourteen shots. He wasn't all that good with a gun, had bought it only for protection, but if he were close enough, it would do the job. He would have fourteen chances. Anyone could do it with that.

He hated having to resort to a gun. He hated Kate, and he wanted it to be more personal. It *was* personal, especially now, when she had tricked him. She should have been home. It was her fault he'd lost his temper. She should have been home.

He could feel things closing in on him. This time he had to get it right. Maybe he'd contact his new friend, create a little diversion.

Customers occupied two of the tables in the Black Forest. A woman in khakis and a plaid shirt stood beside one, holding a small pad and a pen. She looked up when John and Kate entered. "Have a seat. I'll be with you in a minute."

They took the table farthest from the other diners. "He must have found a waitress," Kate said. "Even though she doesn't look like one."

The woman, tanned and athletic looking, came to their table and gave them an easy smile. "Hi. I'm Nan. Been here before?"

Kate nodded, finding herself smiling in return.

"The menu hasn't changed." The woman nodded toward the blackboard. "What'll you have?"

After they ordered, Kate said, "Would you tell Mr. Kusch that Kate McGuire's here? I'd like to see him if he has a minute."

"Thought you might be. He's not very happy with you, but I'll see what I can do." She tucked a sun-streaked hank of hair behind her ear and crossed to the swinging doors in long, easy strides.

John watched her go. "She must know him pretty well. She seemed to know all about you."

Nan returned with tall glasses of iced tea and a small bowl of sliced lemon and mint. She winked at Kate. "I'm working on him."

By the time Nan brought their food, Kate's appetite had waned. She looked up at the woman and nodded toward the kitchen. "Is he very angry?"

"Don't worry. He'll be fine by the time he gets out here, and he's all bark anyway."

Kate cut her schnitzel into small pieces and stirred them around on her plate. "I can't eat," she announced, slapping her napkin on the table. "I'll go to the mountain."

"Sit down, Kate. You can't go back there. This man may be a murderer, and if so, you're high on his list."

"I don't believe it's Helmut. He's surly, not psychotic."

The kitchen doors swung wide and Helmut appeared, filling the space. He marched quickly across to them and stood over Kate, red-faced. Wiping his hands on his apron, he said, "So. You are not such a friend after all, eh, Kate? Why do you snoop around my house?"

"Oh, Helmut, I'm sorry. It's these awful murders—I had to find out what happened to Gisela."

"Murders? You think I had something to do with that?" He

rocked back on his heels, dropping the apron. "You think I killed Gisela?" The big man sank into a chair, stunned.

"No, she doesn't," John said, rising to his feet to deal with this mountain of a man. "I'm the one who wanted you checked out because of the connection with Charlene Nelson, and I figured you could easily have known Kelly Landrum, so many students come here."

"I cannot believe it. Charlene worked here only for two months. She was a good girl, very hardworking. I would never hurt her."

Kate laid her hand over his. "I'm sure you wouldn't. But I couldn't just depend on my feelings."

He carefully lifted her hand off his and stood. "Eat your dinner, Kate. We will not speak of this again." There was a certain finality to the way he returned to the kitchen.

"I've lost him. He'll never forgive me." Kate was miserable.

"He'll come around," John said. "Give him time."

"No, I don't think he will."

Nan came out of the kitchen, her friendly smile replaced by a disapproving glare. "Helmut said dinner's on the house, but you shouldn't come back. You really hurt him. I thought you were nosy. I didn't know you thought he was a murderer."

"I don't," Kate cried. "I just had to be sure."

"You're wrong about him. He's a nice guy who was married to a flighty bitch, that's all. He's told me all about it."

A dark-haired woman in blue jeans answered Venice's door. "Hello. I'm Officer Capello." She asked for their identification, but Martin overheard.

"It's okay," he called. "They're the good guys."

Kate and John found Venice on the divan, propped on pillows. Martin rose from a chair close beside her. The officer returned to the far corner of the room and picked up a book, leaving them to talk.

Kate kissed Venice, gently squeezing her hands. "I'm so glad you're home. How are you feeling?"

"Much better, my dear. Much better indeed." She turned to Martin, smiling. "Shall we tell them?"

"Yes," he said, lightly stroking her cheek. "Venice and I are going to be married as soon as she's able."

John shook his hand and turned to Venice, planting a big kiss on her lips. "Terrific. I'm happy for you both."

"Wow! This is a surprise," Kate said, hugging Martin. "Has this been a long time in the making, and I was just too dense to see it?"

"Too long. I've been after her for years, but it took this little incident to make her see how precious time is," Martin said. "Now we just have to keep you two safe until it's over."

"That reminds me," Venice said as she took a small velvet pouch from the coffee table. "Kate, Ramses wants you to have this. He said to keep it with you."

"He did, did he?" Loosening the string tie, Kate slid a small crystal sphere about the size of a golf ball out of the blue bag. She held it up to the light. A small formation near the center suggested an eye. "It's lovely, Venice. Thank you. And Ramses, of course."

"Just keep it with you. Ramses thinks it will be important."

They talked a few minutes more, but Kate, not wanting to spoil their happy evening, didn't mention the break-in at her house or her run-in with Helmut. After a short time, Venice's eyelids drooped and she yawned behind her hand.

She still looked pale to Kate. "I don't think you'll feel like going to Caesar's Head Sunday."

"Oh, I'd almost forgotten. Martin, I was going to the art show with Kate this weekend." At his nod she continued. "I'm sure we'll be able to go."

While Kate said good-bye to Venice, John reached into the pocket of his jacket and took out some folded papers. "I'd like to leave you some homework," he said, handing the papers to Martin. "This is a list of property owners at Jocassee. Maybe you and Venice could look it over when you have a chance, see if you recognize any names. We figure the killer had to have known the lake area well and have easy access to a boat."

"Yes, of course." Martin anchored the list to the coffee table with a cloisonne cat. "It will be more interesting than the cryptograms in the paper."

"Take care, you two," John said, shaking Martin's hand. "Call if you need us."

The policewoman followed them to the door and whispered, "Detective Waite told me what happened. I'll be here till midnight. Then Paul Wolynski is coming. Don't worry. We'll take care of her."

As Kate and John turned out of Venice's gates, she asked, "What did you give Martin?"

"The list of property owners around Lake Jocassee. None of the names rang a bell for me, but when you feel like it, you can go over them. Maybe you'll recognize something."

Although he didn't think it likely that the killer knew Kate was staying with him, John checked the house carefully when they went in.

Kate yawned at the kitchen table. "Let me see the list."

"Why don't you wait until morning? You look ready to drop," he said from the refrigerator. "Wine? Milk? Tea?"

She rubbed her eyes. "A glass of wine would be nice."

"And maybe a little something to eat?" He waved a plastic-covered bowl in front of her. "Leftover pasta."

"Mmm, wonderful." While he crushed garlic, she got two plates from the cabinet and collapsed into the chair, shoving her hair back from her face. "Dinner wasn't a success tonight, was it? We weren't exactly best friends, but I hate losing Helmut. I think I'm definitely persona non grata at the Black Forest now."

"For a while, anyway," he said over his shoulder as he dumped the congealed lump of pasta into a pan coated with olive oil. "I'll introduce you to Mama Rosa's tomorrow. I think Italian pastries have more calories. You'll love it."

She groaned as he dropped a chunk of butter in with the pasta. "I need to run in the morning. I may have to add a mile."

"Skip it. You can afford a couple of pounds."

"The other day you said I was fat."

He left the stove and leaned over her, circling her with his arms. "You know why I said that."

"It was very effective. I forgot all about the elevator. You sure know what buttons to push." She tilted her head back and kissed him, nose to chin.

"I have two sisters," he mumbled against her lips.

"Two sisters?" She turned to face him. "Where?"

"They're both married. One lives in Philadelphia—she's married to the hockey player—and one in New York City. Gina, the one in New York, has two kids."

"Where did you grow up? How about your parents?"

After a moment of silence, he said, "I lived in South Philly," as if it was significant. He did a short push-up off the back of Kate's chair and looked at the floor, thinking. "My mother's still there," he told her.

Kate remained silent, giving him time, aware that he was struggling. She put her hand over his, sensing his pain. Maybe his father had died recently. She felt the familiar pang, the one that would never entirely leave her, as she remembered her own father.

John raised his head and looked at her, seeming to come to a decision. "I grew up, all right. The summer I was sixteen, I became the head of my family, my mother and my sisters."

It may not have been wise, but she had to ask. "What happened to your father?"

"He blew his brains out. He'd been fired from his job, couldn't get another."

"Oh, John. Over a job!" It was inconceivable to her.

"Not exactly. He was an accountant. He discovered some kick-backs, payoffs, crooked deals involving the company he worked for and its backers—three local politicians who didn't take the news well." He paced the length of the kitchen, running his hand over his hair, then stopped to stir the pasta. "They accused him of embez-zling the money himself, and he couldn't get anyone to take his story seriously. They threatened to send him to prison. He went to the police and to the papers, but you know the story—you can't fight City Hall."

"They got away with it?"

"For about ten years." His grim tone held a message. "The worst part was the feeling of guilt that we all shared—my mother and sisters and I. As if, somehow, it was our fault, that we had failed him. It took us years to see that he was so caught up in his prob-lem, he didn't think of us at all. Suicide in these circumstances is a selfish act, one where your problems push out everyone and every-thing else."

There was nothing she could say to lessen his pain.

He reached out and touched her cheek, smiled a little. "It's all right now. We all got past it."

Calculating the time, she asked, "Was that your first investiga-tive report?"

"Second. I chose one to practice on before I went after them."

"What happened?"

"Two went to prison, probably out by now. The Mob took out the third. He tried to turn state's evidence, do a little trade."

"Good for you." She stood and wrapped her arms about him, hugging him fiercely, wishing she could absorb some of his pain. "That's why you always print the story."

"I at least check out what I'm told. If there's something there, yes, I print it." He let her go abruptly and turned back to the stove, added a generous spoonful of capers to the skillet. "But maybe there *are* a few gray areas, times when something would be better withheld."

For John, that was a major concession, and it went straight to her heart.

"Let's eat." He turned off the burner, tossed the pasta with fresh Parmesan cheese, and placed it in front of her.

She had no idea leftover pasta could be turned into such a good dish. After they ate, Kate stood and picked up her plate. He took it and pushed her gently back into her chair. "I'll do them tonight." He turned on the stereo system, slid in a few CDs, and programmed his favorite songs. He came back, humming, and quickly cleared the table. The man deserved a medal.

"I can last a few more minutes," she said, swaying in her chair to Susannah McCorkle's seductive voice. Kate, sleepy now, sang with her. *You go to my head.* . . . She yawned and lifted her hair off her neck. John's lips brushed her nape, sending a shiver down her spine.

Chapter 15

JOHN'S ALARM WOKE THEM BOTH. He sat up and turned on the lamp. Kate, lying on her stomach, moaned and pulled the pillow over her head.

"Talk to me for a minute," he said, pulling his jeans out from under Kate's T-shirt. "Then you can go back to sleep. I have to go to the office and get some things I'm working on, but I'll come right back and work here. I have a deadline."

Lifting the corner of the pillow, she mumbled, "Go on to work. I'm going to the studio, but I'll lock myself in."

"I don't want you by yourself." He stood, stepping into the jeans. "It's not safe. I'd take you to the office with me if I thought you would come. Can't you go to the studio this afternoon? I'll go with you after lunch."

Pushing the pillow off her head, she opened one eye and peered up at him through a tangle of hair. "No. I have deadlines, too. The Caesar's Head show is Sunday, and I have to reprint a lot of those pictures. Fortunately, most of them were still at the studio."

"Kate, this guy is serious. Just wait a while for me. Maybe I can borrow a laptop and go with you."

"Dammit, John, I'm not Venice." She turned over and pulled the sheet under her arms, giving him a baleful glare. "I can take care of myself."

"Don't kid yourself," he said. "I'm an average guy, and you couldn't even slow me down if I wanted to take you."

She snatched the pillow and swung it at him. "You couldn't catch me."

He blocked it and dived for her as she rolled to the other side of the bed. He yanked the sheet off and grabbed her. They struggled briefly as John tried to hold on to her while Kate twisted and wriggled to escape.

He pinned her with his weight, breathing harder than the fight warranted. "Now who's caught?"

"Good question, Gerrard," she said, her eyes sparkling as she pulled him down to her, reveling in the feel of his warm flesh against hers.

The second time he got up, he didn't bother with the jeans. "Okay, now you'll have to get the coffee while I shower."

"You mean you were going to make coffee? I would never have let you distract me if I had known." She threw a pillow at his retreating back and retrieved her big T-shirt from the floor. As she pulled it over her head, a solid arm snaked around her, trapping her inside the shirt with her arms over her head.

"That's twice, lady." He nuzzled her through the soft knit, his warm breath tickling her ear. "Promise me you'll stay here until I get back."

"You dog," she said, working the shirt down her arms. "You'll never get to work. Go get your shower while I get the coffee."

From the kitchen she could hear faint singing. She cocked her head and listened. Italian. He really did sing opera in the shower. She popped some bread into the toaster and moved to the hallway to listen. The words sounded like *dio mes oh dee* to her. She'd have to ask the name of the aria and listen to it.

By the time she returned to the bedroom with coffee and burned toast on a tray, John was buttoning a blue oxford-cloth shirt. He had shaved, but his hair was still wet and tousled.

He watched her pad barefoot across the room, her hair wild, the T-shirt barely grazing her thighs. He wished he could take the day off. She wasn't going to wait for him, he knew. Pushing it would only cause a fight.

He lifted a white mug, inhaling the steaming fragrance. He raised an eyebrow at the toast but didn't comment, just took a piece, leaning forward to keep the blackened crumbs from falling onto his clothes. "You're a rare woman, Kate McGuire," he said, planting a crumb-laden kiss on her cheek.

Kate smiled, munching her own toast between mouthfuls of coffee. She held up a crust. "Extra-crispy, just the way you like it."

"It's terrific, but I think I was talking about chicken," he said, taking a worn corduroy sport coat from the closet.

"What does *dio mes oh dee* mean? What were you singing in the shower?" she asked, following him down the steps to the front door, cradling her coffee.

"*God has answered my prayer.* I must have been smelling the toast. It's from Verdi's *La Traviata,* 'Di Provenza il mar.' A father reminding his son of his home by the sea—more of those good intentions gone wrong."

John opened the dead bolt and turned back to her. "Kate, at

least let me know if you go anywhere other than the studio."

"I will." She lifted her arms and wrapped them around his neck, hugging him tightly.

John, glancing in the hall mirror behind her, grinned. She was a hard woman to leave.

At eight o'clock on Sunday morning, John stood in Kate's driveway with his hands on his hips, studying the car. They were trying to pack the Mazda. It wasn't designed for haulage. "Do you have to take all this? Don't they supply anything?"

"This is my first show. I don't know," she said, looking at the card table and cooler they couldn't squeeze in.

"Look, let's just take my car, too. You take the pictures, and I'll follow you with the table and chairs and the cooler. There's no way everything's going in this, including me." He wasn't happy about going separately, but neither of their cars was adequate.

A horn drew their attention. The rear end of Venice's big Cadillac crept up the concrete tracks toward them and stopped. Martin got out and walked around to the trunk.

Venice called from the passenger side, "Hello, you all. I knew you would have a problem carrying your pictures and equipment."

"I don't know that this show is a good idea" Martin said, looking up at the blue October sky, "but if we're all together in a crowd of people, what could happen? It's a beautiful day, and I know Kate needs the exposure for her work."

"What do you have in the cooler, Kate?" Venice asked. "Peanut butter sandwiches?"

"Not exactly," she said, wishing she hadn't told John she'd bring their lunch. It had seemed like a good idea at the time, but she'd worked all day yesterday to finish remounting her photographs and hadn't had time to get anything. She'd only remembered this morning and had tossed in a loaf of bread—with only a few green spots—and a jar of Jif. She wondered if John would consider extra-crunchy peanut butter a substitute for extra-crispy chicken. Still, there was always food around these outdoor shows—she hoped.

John gave her a suspicious look and asked, "Do we need to pick up some chicken, Kate?"

"No, John," Venice said over her shoulder as she freed her skirt from the spikes of a low-growing holly. "We brought a picnic lunch for all of us. You should know better than to rely on Kate for food."

They packed the trunk, and John and Kate slid into the back with Venice's big picnic basket on the seat between them. John immediately lifted the lid and sniffed. "Venice, are you sure you want to marry Martin?"

"Yes, I am. It's a wonder Martin hasn't starved without me. He's almost as bad as Kate."

"I've had to loosen my belt a notch already," Martin said, easing out of the drive.

The car climbed slowly up the twisting road under the overhanging greenery, with Kate and Venice pointing out the trees that had already turned to brilliant autumn colors. In two or three weeks, Kate thought, she would be seduced by the display and come back for a day of shooting. Maybe John would come and carry the camera bag and tripod. She turned to look at him and chuckled silently. He had his hand in the basket.

Venice would catch him. She should have been a mother; she had eyes in the back of her head. "Close it, John," she said from the front seat, apparently still focused on the scenery. "You can have something after Kate's show is set up."

"Yes, ma'am." He closed the lid and sighed loudly.

They arrived in a crowd of vans and trucks, maneuvering among people carting boxes and fancy cases into the picnic area. Kate found her assigned space and stood looking at the rocky area. She was located at the edge of the woods near the end of the exhibitors. "I like this. It's perfect. I can prop the framed prints on the rocks in odd places. That way you can discover them, almost one at a time, instead of being hit with a whole row at once."

John brought the picnic basket and the table and then went back for the cooler and chairs. He slung the camera bag over his shoulder at the same time. "What do you keep in here? Rocks? I think I'll have to make another trip for this thing."

"It's easy to see where your priorities are, Gerrard," Kate said. She and Martin carried the boxes packed with photographs.

"Did you bring any money, Kate?" Venice asked, watching from her perch on a smooth rock.

"Money? I've got a couple of dollars," she answered, wondering why Venice needed money.

"Not for me, dear. For a practical person, you can be quite dense." She took a large envelope from her purse and held it out to Kate. "To make change. These *are* for sale, aren't they?" she asked, waving at the pictures.

"Oh. Thanks, Venice. I didn't think of that." She looked around for a place to put the money. "Do you really think anyone will buy them?"

"Yes, I do. Take the cookies out of the tin, John. She can use that for a cash box."

Kate arranged the photographs on the rocks, exchanging and moving the images, looking for the most advantageous mix. The rocks were nice, but the black-and-white prints didn't show up well. From a few feet away, the display looked dull.

"Here," Venice said, pulling the scarlet shawl off her shoulders. "And I have a scarf in here somewhere." She dug through her purse and came up with a length of gold tissue silk.

"Venice, you're wonderful," Kate said, draping the shawl over a rock. She let the scarf fall loosely across the middle and then placed several of the pictures on the scarlet backdrop. She stepped back to admire the effect, her eyes shining. "Perfect!"

"It looks great," John said. "I'd like to have a couple of those sepia prints for the living room. I've developed a sentimental attachment to the smell." He grinned over Kate's head at Venice. Munching a chocolate chip cookie, he leaned over to study a barn on the edge of collapse. It appeared to be held upright by a tangle of vines clinging to its side. A lone cow peeked out through the open door. "This reminds me of your garage, Kate."

"That's why it's secure. No one would try to break into it, for fear it would fall on them." She tweaked the shawl and moved one of the pictures an inch to the right. She tilted her head, squinting at the presentation, and moved another one a fraction to the left.

"Leave it, McGuire. Let's have a drink before the hordes arrive." He pulled her back to the cooler and handed her a Diet Coke. "Here you go. Relax. It looks great."

The show opened at ten, and people began drifting in shortly after. It took a while for them to filter through the other exhibits and get to Kate's. Some of the exhibitors nearby had bright, attractive displays, and she worried that hers was too low-key.

By midafternoon, enough people had crowded into the small exhibit area that Kate and Venice decided to eat in shifts. In spite of the comments from a few people about the prices, Kate made a couple of sales and gave out several business cards. John's lonely cow had been the first to go, but she'd promised to print another for him. A young couple selected a black-and-white shot of a farm gate made from a wagon wheel.

"Let's eat, Kate," John said, eyeing the basket.

She danced around the table. "I don't think I can leave. They're actually buying my pictures," she said, wonder coloring her voice. "People come looking for a portrait. It's not the same as buying on the spur of the moment, just because something appeals to you."

"We'll mind the store." Venice graciously offered John the basket. "Take Kate away for a few minutes and make her eat. Just leave something for us," she warned.

Martin accepted a check for a framed print, and Venice sold three unframed prints while John and Kate shared fried chicken and potato salad behind the rocks. Kate dabbled in hers and gave most of it to John. Excitement kept her hopping up to see if anyone was buying. "I think Martin's selling another one. I'll take everyone out to dinner tonight."

John laughed at her. "Didn't you ever have a lemonade stand when you were a kid?"

"Sort of. After our first attempt, Gwen made the lemonade. I made the sign. I always wandered off on my bike and left her to deal with the customers." Kate was edging toward the exhibit area, impatient to get back. "I didn't know it was so much fun."

"Go on. You don't have to wait for me. I'm not moving until I finish my apple pie. Tell Venice I love her."

Kate ran the short distance to her show. "You can go eat now." She gave Venice a quick hug and said, "Better watch out, Martin. John's fallen in love with your woman."

"I told you you should learn to cook, Kate," Venice said. "Do you think you can keep your eye on the cash box if we both go? Maybe we should wait until John gets back."

"I'm here," John said, rounding the path. He grabbed Venice and planted a big kiss on her lips. "Martin, you're a lucky man."

"Yes, I know." Martin pulled him aside and said softly, "We saw Helmut a few minutes ago. He glared at Venice and turned the other way. We didn't want to spoil Kate's day. This is the first time she's really relaxed and had fun since all this started."

As the afternoon wore on, several more of Kate's pictures found homes. She gave one, a print of a brightly colored street clown, to a little girl whose pregnant mother had looked at the price and told the child to put it back. "It would be my pleasure," Kate said. "It makes me happy when my pictures have good homes and someone to take care of them."

The child giggled, clutching the picture to her chest.

Smiling, the woman accepted Kate's offer. She wandered off with the child and the clown.

"What a wonderful day," Kate said. She spun in the grass, arms outstretched, laughing. "'Oh world, I cannot hold thee close enough. . . .'" She let the sentence trail off as she listened. "Oh, no!"

"What is it?" John turned toward her, immediately alert.

A distant voice carried over the crowd, increasing in volume. "*And my eyes shall not spare the harlot, and I will have no pity: and she will be paid according to her ways and the abominations that are in the midst of thee.*"

"He's coming this way." He was coming for her. Somehow, he knew she was here. She started for her pictures.

"Kate, stop! Get your camera!" John grabbed her arm, spun her around. "Looks like news to me. Let's see how this will affect his fund-raising."

She hesitated for an instant, then snatched the Nikon from her bag, snapping the flash into place.

"*And I will judge thee, a woman who lives in sin and worships false prophets. I will give thee blood and fury and jealousy.*"

The crowd parted like the Red Sea before Moses.

"Get this, Kate." John moved to her side to give her a clear view of the man. "Just keep shooting. He won't hurt you."

Kate snapped two or three pictures of him with the onlookers fairly melting away.

Ezekiel stopped, surprised by the camera. Then he raised the staff and shook it, his face twisted and ugly. "*And the horde shall stone thee and dispatch them with their swords and burn thy house.*"

As if he were some alien creature to be studied, she ignored his ranting and dropped to one knee, photographing him at an angle, with his staff raised against the sky and trees above.

John stayed close beside her.

Two men in khaki with park badges on their pockets appeared and spoke to him. The prophet ignored them, focused solely on Kate. The rangers quickly gave up talking and took his arm.

"*Thus will He end thy lewdness and dreams of evil, and all women shall take warning.*" He continued to shout, staring at Kate over his shoulder as the rangers dragged him away.

The crowd closed behind them. After a brief buzz of interest, they returned to the exhibits.

"John, stay close to Kate." Venice, looking slightly disturbed, rubbed her arms. "I see darkness."

"It's over now, Venice," Martin said. "The rangers will make him leave. He's a real prophet of doom."

Kate turned to a well-dressed man who lifted one of her pictures to study it.

"I think this is the house on the farm where I grew up," he said. "Do you know where it is?"

"Yes, I took it down near Gray Court."

"That's it!" He took out his wallet. "My wife will remember it, too. She's around here—"

A sharp report shocked the park into silence, followed immediately by another. People froze in their tracks.

A hiss of air stirred Kate's hair, and a tree trunk splintered behind her. She grabbed Venice and dived for the rocks.

John pulled Martin to the ground and crouched low, scanning the woods.

"Get down! Get down!" someone yelled.

A third shot rang out. The man crouched near Kate cried out, clutching his arm. The farmhouse fell to the ground.

Kate yanked Venice's scarf from under the remaining pictures and crawled toward him.

"Thanks," he said.

More shots sounded. The crowd began running, screaming. Parents threw themselves on top of their children. Others crawled toward the safety of the rocks.

"It came from over there," a man cried, pointing toward the west from his position behind a tree.

One of the rangers ducked into the trees, following the sound. Another urged people to stay low and seek shelter.

A young man crawled over from the other side of the rocks. "I'm a doctor. Let me do it," he said, taking the gold silk from Kate.

John wriggled over the rough ground to Kate and Venice. "I can't see a damn thing. The sun's blinding me."

Martin was right behind him. No more shots sounded.

John hugged Kate tightly, then pushed her away to check. "Are you all right? Is Venice?"

Nodding, Kate checked John just as carefully. "He's a lunatic, a madman!"

"He's gone now," John said. "If he's smart, he'll ditch the robes, and they won't catch him. He'll probably blend in with all the other people running away. That sounded like a handgun. If he stays cool, he can hide it and carry it right past everyone."

After a few minutes, John crept cautiously out from the sheltering rocks. He stood and looked around. Others were beginning to surface, too. "I think it's safe now. He may be crazy, but he's not stupid. He won't hang around."

Kate stood beside him, glaring into the setting sun. By this time, anger had replaced shock. "To think of shooting with all these people around, all those children! I hope he steps on a rattler, the bastard."

The man who'd been hit leaned against a tree while the doctor tied the scarf around his arm, saying, "It just skimmed your outer arm, but you need to have it cleaned. Is no place safe nowadays?"

"At least no one was seriously hurt," Venice said. "We should be thankful he's not a marksman." Recovered from her fright, she began gathering Kate's pictures. Martin followed, holding a box for her to put them in.

Other exhibitors were returning to pack, anxious to leave the wooded park. A ranger wandered among them, asking questions, and a few minutes later, a couple of sheriff's deputies strode into the area. Several people pointed toward Kate's exhibit, and the three officials began making their way back. One of the deputies turned to the man who'd been hit.

"They'll get to us in a minute," John said. "You start, Kate, while I load the car." He hefted a box onto his shoulder and picked up the table with the other hand. "I'll be right back."

Kate and Venice hastily gathered their things until the deputies reached them. Kate introduced herself and described the shots, suggesting they call Detective Waite in Greenville. "I don't know, but I suspect it has something to do with the murder of Kelly Landrum," she said, hating to go through the whole story. She was trying to think of some plausible explanation for her involvement, when John returned.

"This is John Gerrard, the reporter who's been covering it. Maybe he has some idea why." She hoped he would catch on from her weak statement.

Venice, for once, remained silent.

"I think maybe my research turned up some unpleasant facts, and whoever killed Kelly Landrum would like for me to go away," John said, taking Kate's lead.

After a few minutes' discussion, the ranger and one of the deputies left to examine the splintered tree. The doctor and the wounded man left, and the remaining deputy took names and addresses. "Waite, you say?" He wrote down Lynne Waite's name and left them to join the others at the tree.

"Let's go," John said. "We could be here for hours if they get too curious." They gathered the remaining items and trudged back to the car.

Only Venice seemed ready to put it behind her. "Where are you taking us for dinner, Kate? You made over four hundred dollars."

"Did I really?" Kate brightened. "Well, if everyone still feels like it, let's go. Any ideas?"

"I'm in the mood for pizza," John said. "How about Mama Rosa's? Then you can have what you want—as long as it's Italian."

Venice and Martin quickly agreed.

"Yes, it sounds good." Kate knew they didn't need to report to Waite. She had no doubt the detective would track them down when she wanted them. Meanwhile, she considered the prophet. It couldn't be coincidence that he'd been at her house decorating her door and then at Caesar's Head today. And how did he know where she'd be? Her house was easy enough to find, but she couldn't picture him scanning ads for art shows to see if she was an exhibitor. But he had known.

Chapter 16

AFTER A LESS-THAN-FESTIVE DINNER, during which Venice repeatedly yawned behind her hand, Martin dropped them at Kate's. They quickly unloaded the Cadillac and said good-bye. Kate and John took the table and chairs inside and put her photographs in the Mazda—she wasn't leaving them in this house—and then she followed John in her car to the newspaper office.

"Kate, come on in. You can't stay out here in the car. I'll only be a few minutes." He hustled her into the building, nodded to the security guard, and sat her at Mike's desk, which was bare of all paper. John never understood how his fellow reporter functioned in such a sterile environment. "I have to get your film developed. I'll be right back."

"I'm fine." A yawn distorted her words.

He returned a few minutes later to find her asleep on the desk. He filed a couple of paragraphs and wrote a caption for Kate's picture of the prophet for tomorrow's paper. He left instructions for Walker to crop and place the picture for him. The layout man was good. John wanted the guy's venom to show, and he trusted Kate's ability to get the shot. Ezekiel could have a little of the publicity he'd been after.

He woke Kate. "Let's go home. It's been a long day."

While they were unloading her things at his house, John said, "Maybe it wasn't the prophet. Helmut was there today. Martin saw him. He spotted Venice and disappeared."

"Helmut! He probably didn't want to see me because he's still angry."

"Angry enough to shoot you?"

"I just don't believe it's Helmut. It doesn't feel right. How would he know we would be there?"

"Whoever broke into your house saw papers and all kinds of information on this show. He surely figured you'd be there, and it would be easy to get off a few shots from the woods. Helmut knows the area. He told us he likes to climb there on Sundays." John opened the Mazda's hatchback and took out a box of photographs. He lifted the camera bag from her shoulder and slung it over his own. "I'll carry it."

"Thanks. I may be liberated, but I'm not stupid." Ezekiel's words came back to her. "That crazy prophet could have known the same way. Maybe he's the one who broke in. He keeps talking about fire. You don't think he'd burn my house down, do you?"

"I doubt it, but I wouldn't want to take any chances. I'm glad you're with me." He kissed her forehead. "I can't see him as the murderer. But I don't know why he was up there today."

"No, it's odd," she said, dragging a box out of the car. She dropped it in the hall as soon as she got inside the door. She was tired to the bone.

"Let's have a glass of wine before we go up." John hoped it would help her relax. She'd been tense and overbright all evening. That haunted look had returned to her eyes.

She spotted the list of property owners from Lake Jocassee as soon as she entered the kitchen. She pounced on it, snatching up the papers. "I had forgotten this. Maybe there's something here."

"Do it tomorrow. You're worn out, Kate." He poured two glasses of Merlot and handed her one.

"No, I want to do it now." She traced down the names with her forefinger, gnawing on her lip as she read. *Jarmyn, Dunn, Singh, Lacher, Border, Gunterson, . . .* The list went on. She read it twice more before handing it back to John, who was leaning against the counter behind her. "I don't recognize any of them."

Something nagged at her, something she ought to know, but she was too tired to think about it. She gave up and followed John up the stairs.

Kate was hell-bent on going to the studio. "I have to finish Charlene's pictures—Rita wants them back today. And I have a lot of other stuff I have to get done."

John would have to make a fast trip to the office for his tape recorder and notes. Maybe he could get Mike's laptop and catch her at the studio. "Promise me you'll call if you go anywhere else."

"I will. I'll keep the door locked and be extra careful, but I can't hide in a closet until he's caught, John."

"I'll be there soon." He kissed her, holding her tight for a minute, and then left.

Kate stopped at the door to the warehouse and called out to James Earl. His office door stood open, and he came out immediately, saying, "Good morning, Miz McGuire. What can I do for you?"

"Nothing, thanks. I just wanted to know if anyone's been here this morning, if you've seen anyone hanging around."

"No, ma'am. I haven't seen anything at all, and I've been keeping my door open. Seems like there's been some trouble lately. The police have been here asking about the elevator. I'll keep an eye out in case anyone I don't know shows up."

"Thanks, James Earl," Kate said. "I'm going up to work in the studio. I'm keeping my door locked until John gets here, so if you want anything, knock."

"I'll ride up with you. The elevator's fine now. They put in a new cable and replaced some other parts." He pressed the button and the freight door opened immediately.

"Thanks, James Earl." She clutched the railing. Her stomach lurched with the rising elevator.

He patted her hand reassuringly.

She would hate for this kindly man to be hurt. "If anything should happen, call 911 and stay out of the way."

He mumbled something and watched as she unlocked her door. "I'll walk in with you and look around. I don't see how anyone could get in here, but I'll feel better knowing."

As soon as he was out the door, Kate locked it and turned to the file cabinet where she had left Charlene's things. She wanted to work on the picture of the girl dancing on the table. Rita would want it whether her parents did or not. She took the negatives into the darkroom with the film she had shot of Lila Stern.

She changed quickly into jeans and an old work shirt she kept in the darkroom, then mixed her chemicals. Just before she turned out the light, she decided to take the phone in with her. It took some maneuvering, and she had to put it on the floor just inside the door, but today she felt the need to be in touch. She had a lot to do, and John might call. Gwen would want her pictures, and so would the new actor. She could drop off the color film from the Sterns at Wolf when she picked up Mrs. Armstrong's proofs at the lab.

Kate doused the white light and turned on the safety light. Bathed in its red glow, she opened the container with the black-and-white film from the Sterns and wound it in the canister to develop. When the film was ready, she hung it to dry and got out the contact sheet Gwen had marked. She found the correct negatives and placed them beside the enlarger. Only when Gwen's face hung from the line and the new actor's prints were safely completed did she take out the negatives from Charlene's party, hoping the developing had been better than the printing.

A rising excitement gripped her as she fed the strip of negatives into the enlarger. She wanted to see the faces of those watching the exuberant girl. The lens quality probably wasn't good enough to do too much, but she was sure she could get something better than the drugstore prints. Before she could find the right frame, the phone rang.

It was Gwen. "Just checking. I talked to Venice a while ago. Isn't it wonderful about her and Martin! They were getting ready to go over some list of John's."

They chatted briefly while Kate, crouching by the door with the phone, looked longingly at the strip of film dangling from the enlarger.

"I'm going to look for something funereal to wear," Gwen said. "I'm getting ready to tell Thomas good-bye. He's too possessive. I feel guilty about not having canceled Atlanta yet, especially after he sent flowers Saturday. I called him at work but decided it was cowardly to do it on the phone, so I asked him to lunch instead. It seemed unfair to let him take me to dinner tonight and then tell him."

"Poor Gwen, such a hard life," Kate said, only half listening.

"I'm not exactly suffering. Adam Kinsler called this morning. He's taking me to the Abbeville Opera House to a play this weekend."

"I'm looking at his aquiline nose right now. I'm in the darkroom. I just finished his prints—and yours. I've got to go, Gwen."

"Ciao, darling."

Kate had hardly gotten to her feet when the phone rang again—the banker's wife, checking on her proofs. Kate assured the woman they would be ready tomorrow and returned to the enlarger. Charlene's face slid into the frame, a closeup showing her bright smile. Unfortunately her eyes were closed. Kate continued winding the film until she found the dancing girl. She adjusted the figure on the frame and focused it, letting the girl fill the image area. It was much better than the print had shown. She slid a sheet of eight-by-ten photo paper under the frame, rechecked the focus, and hit the timer.

When it dinged and the light went out, she put the exposed paper into the developer and then readjusted the film in the enlarger, focusing on the group watching Charlene dance. At the sound of the timer, she checked the print of Charlene and moved it to the next chemical tray, the fixer.

Immediately she turned back to the black-faced, white-eyed negative images in the frame of the enlarger. One, a blurred face near the back, was hauntingly familiar. She centered the face and enlarged it, sharpening the image as much as the negative would allow. There he was. Recognition hit her like a blow. She could see him with Charlene, jealous, possessive, angry.

Kate's heart missed a beat. Her hands shook as she worked the knobs on the ancient equipment, trying to bring the man's face into better focus, but the photographer had been concentrating on Charlene. This man was incidental, on the edge of the picture, but she recognized him, could feel the acute desire with which he watched, enthralled. But the face wasn't sharp enough for anyone else to be certain of his identity, and the photograph didn't prove anything. She just knew, and she was afraid no one would believe her. If she hadn't seen him so recently, she might not have recognized him.

She settled on the best compromise between size and clarity and burned the image into the paper, quickly dropping it into the developer. Forcing herself to slow down, she carefully scrolled through the other party images on the roll, scrutinizing each one for the same face. If she could place him at the party beyond a doubt, it would be much easier for others to identify him in the first shot. It wouldn't prove he killed her, but it might be enough to interest Detective Waite. Kate had a feeling that once Waite's sharp eye was turned in the right direction, she wouldn't miss much.

She finally picked him out in two more frames, and after settling on the best image she could get, she burned two of each. Even the skeptical Detective Burnett should be able to identify Thomas Andrews from these.

Nursing the prints through the chemical baths, she watched the images come to life on the paper. Charlene's swirling figure dominated the first one. Kate hung it to dry, admiring the way the light sparkled off her earrings, giving the girl an almost magical glow. The earrings appeared to be hammered silver with a stone in the center, maybe Mexican, certainly unusual.

Whatever else happened, Kate wanted to send this negative to the color lab and have a good picture made for the Nelsons.

As the other prints went from the stop bath into the clear rinse water, she turned on the light and examined each one. There was no doubt. She hung the prints on the line with the others and saw Gwen's Mona Lisa smile.

Gwen! Oh, please, not Gwen! Tears blurred Kate's eyes. It took two tries before she could get her trembling fingers to punch in Gwen's number.

She wasn't home. Fearing that Thomas could be there when she got the message, Kate said only for Gwen to call her or Venice, that it was an emergency.

Frantically, she called the police station, praying for Detective Waite to be there.

"Detective Waite's in court today. This is Detective Burnett."

Her heart sank.

"Please, you have to help me." She struggled to get her voice under control. "This is Kate McGuire. I know who killed Charlene Nelson and Kelly Landrum—"

"Did this information come to you in a dream, or do you have some evidence to support it?" The barely controlled sarcasm rang in her ears.

With panic clawing at her back, she did her best to explain, knowing he would never act on what she had to tell him.

"Ms. McGuire, I've never heard of this man. I can't pick him up for no reason." He wanted proof.

"Just please find Detective Waite and tell her," she begged.

Next she called John. *Where was everyone today?* "John, it's Thomas Andrews—he killed them. I'm at the studio," she told his voice mail, then hung up to call Venice, thinking what she could do. Venice's line was busy.

Her watch said 10:14, less than two hours until lunch. She thought of her savaged bed. Thomas was out of control now and wouldn't hesitate to kill Gwen, she was sure of it.

Proof. What kind of proof could she possibly come up with that would get Burnett to act? It would take his resources to find Gwen and stop Thomas.

The picture of Charlene dangled from the line in front of her. There may not be anything at Charlene's to connect her with him, but there might be something at Thomas's. If she and Kelly were meeting him in secret, both women probably went to his house.

She knew he was at work today because Gwen had talked to him. *I could be in and out in no time. I have to find some kind of evidence before he gets to Gwen.*

Knowing it was foolhardy, but unable to think of anything else, she flipped through the phone book and found his address, thankful when she recognized the street name. It was in a fairly expensive subdivision with large wooded lots. It should be easy to get in without being seen by curious neighbors. She stuffed a pair of rubber gloves from the darkroom into the pocket of her jeans. If she got caught, having them would be hard to explain.

In a last act of sanity, she scribbled Thomas's name on a note and left it on the open phone book for John. He would be here soon, but she couldn't wait.

She had to find something that would get Burnett to act and have time to find them by lunch. Gwen wouldn't fool around. Kate knew she would tell him right away—she believed that dragging things out was both cowardly and unkind.

10:19. Leaving the door unlocked for John, she grabbed her bag and ran, taking the steps two and three at a time. She couldn't wait for the elevator.

James Earl wasn't in sight as she raced out the door to her car.

John came out of his boss's office with his ears ringing. For the first time in his life, he had refused an assignment. It would have taken him ninety miles away to Columbia immediately, and he knew he couldn't leave Kate. His managing editor had called him into his office, angry and demanding an explanation, especially since the newsroom was short-staffed at the moment. But John was adamant.

Stopping at Mike's desk to pick up his new laptop, he called to check on Kate, but she didn't answer. Probably still in the dark-room, he thought. Just as he started to go to his own desk and check his messages, his phone rang. He reached across Mike's desk and grabbed it, hoping it was Kate.

"John, I've found something," Venice said, breaking in before he could say hello. "Can you come over right away?"

"What is it? Are you all right?" he asked, concerned by the anxious quaver in her voice.

"Yes. Hurry."

He found the number of James Earl's office at the Principal Players' warehouse and dialed. The old man answered quickly, and John asked if he had seen Kate.

"Yes, she's in her studio. I checked it out myself, and she locked the door behind me. No one's been here since then."

"If you see her, would you please tell her I've gone to Mrs. Ashburton's, to call me there?" He left immediately.

Martin met John at the door. "We found someone on your list. Venice will tell you." He sat down on the sofa next to Venice. Both of them were fairly buzzing with excitement.

"I recognized one, well, actually two or three of the names on the list," she announced. "But that's the only one that seemed plausible. It was Lyle Border, Margery's husband."

"Who's Lyle Border? I've never heard of him," John said, hoping this wasn't a wild-goose chase. He wished Kate would call.

"He's Thomas Andrews's stepfather," she said, as if that explained everything.

"Who's Thomas Andrews? The name sounds familiar, but I can't place him." He wanted to speed them up—he needed to get back to Kate.

"He's a sometime student at Poinsett," Martin said. "He graduated in computer science a few years ago. Now he takes business courses, working toward his MBA. I made some calls this morning to see if we could connect him with Kelly."

Venice squeezed his hand. "Go on Martin, tell him."

"He took business law at the same time Kelly Landrum did, last spring," Martin said.

"And he's been dating Gwen Gordon the last couple of weeks," Venice added, worried.

That's where he'd heard the name. Although he was interested in the connection they had uncovered, John didn't see how their information proved anything at all. He really wanted to get back to Kate. "That's great, guys. I'll try to track down a connection to Charlene. Meanwhile, I need to get to the studio. I don't want to leave Kate alone."

"Of course. Tell her we said hello," Martin said. He and Venice rose together and started toward the door with John.

Venice stopped abruptly, causing Martin to bump into her. "Oh, John! I suddenly have a very bad feeling about Kate. You find her." She shoved him toward the door and turned back. "Martin, call Detective Waite. Tell her Kate's in trouble."

Whether he believed in her talents or not, her panicky voice unnerved John. He ran for his car, yelling over his shoulder to Venice, "Call Kate!"

He raced back to the studio, praying she would be there, safe and alone. He slid to a stop at the warehouse door, spewing gravel, and leapt from the Mustang. *Where was her car?*

James Earl reached the door at the same time he did. "Mr. Gerrard? What's happened?"

"Where's Kate?" he asked, his voice tight with fear. "Her car's gone. Did you give her my message?"

The old man poked his head outside, looking for the RX-7. "I thought she was still upstairs. I never saw her leave. I was about to go tell her you called."

"Who knows where she went? Maybe she left me a message." Suddenly he stopped, struck by a horrifying thought. "If you didn't see her leave, maybe you missed someone else coming in."

"I don't see how anyone could have come in, gone upstairs, and then left. I only went to the bathroom."

"I hope you're right. Can you open her door? Bring your keys." The elevator had never seemed slower, but he knew it was faster than climbing the four long flights of stairs. When it reached her floor, John hopped out between the jaws of the freight gate before they opened fully.

The studio door wasn't locked, and he opened it in a rush, fluttering the pages of the open phone book on her desk. John looked around but found nothing.

When James Earl saw that the studio was empty, he left. "I'll go back down and see if she left me a message or if anyone's around outside."

John heard the elevator start up as he opened the darkroom door and saw the line of prints hanging from the clothesline. He took down the picture of Charlene dancing. Kate had told him about it, about wanting to have it printed by the color lab as a gift for the Nelsons. The girl filled the frame with her swirling skirt and gypsy pose. He couldn't see anything there that would have caused Kate to leave.

Carefully, he examined the other prints. These must be for the Principal Players, he thought, as Gorgeous Gwen gazed at him from one of the prints, and guessed from the posed facial shot of the man that he was the new actor. He turned to the group shots. He thought they might be from Charlene's party—Kate must have recognized one of the faces. He didn't. *Where is she? Why didn't she wait for me? She must have found something important to make her leave without telling me.*

Maybe she called Waite. He dialed the station and asked for her.

"She's in court. Hasn't been here all morning," the officer answered.

"Let me speak to Burnett, then. Is he in?"

"He's interviewing someone. Is this an emergency?"

"I hope not," John said, slamming down the phone. He looked at the pictures again. There must be someone in that group that Kate recognized. Why else would she make that many prints? They weren't good pictures, nothing he thought would interest the Nelsons. Maybe Venice would know. He grabbed a set of the pictures, punched in her number, and interrupted Martin's voice. "Did you find her?"

"No, but—"

"Stay there, I'm on my way," John said, dropping the phone as he ran for the steps. He could be down before the old elevator got back to the fourth floor.

At the door he called out, "Lock up, James Earl. If Kate comes back, don't let her out of your sight. I'm going to Venice's house." *Damn you, Kate. Where are you?*

Chapter 17

KATE DROVE SLOWLY past Thomas Andrews's house. No cars were in sight, although the garage door was closed. He could be home and have his car inside. She should have telephoned first. If he had answered, she could have hung up. If, if, if! If he hadn't started seeing Gwen, she would never have given him a thought. If he hadn't killed those girls, she wouldn't be here at all.

10:50. Get on with it, Kate! Trees and shrubs surrounded the Georgian-style brick, and a dense hedge bordered the yard on three sides. She was certain no one would see her entering, but she had to find a place to leave her car.

A couple of blocks away she saw a For Sale sign in front of a new house, the red-dirt yard still littered with construction debris. There were no cars or trucks around it; the crew was probably at another home in this new section. She pulled into the driveway. Anyone passing by would assume she was a potential buyer, looking through the house.

But how to get back to Thomas's house? She didn't look much like a jogger in her stained, baggy shirt, but at least she was wearing running shoes. Tying the ends of her shirt around her waist and snapping a rubber band around her hair—no one would jog with that mess hanging loose—she just hoped she wouldn't attract any undue notice. She locked the car, dropped the keys into her pocket, and looked around. Good. Most of the houses in this block were unfinished and unoccupied. She started off as fast as she dared without drawing attention to herself. The two blocks seemed to take forever.

11:00. At Thomas's driveway, she stopped. Her heart tripped as a car passed, but it drove on. After a quick appraisal of the neighboring homes, she took a deep breath and ran quickly along the hedge to the garage. A glance at the handle told her it was locked. She would just have to hope he hadn't come home for any reason. She would also bet he didn't have any pets. He was too perfect to tolerate anything with hair. Nevertheless, she crept carefully up two steps to the back porch and tried to peek in through a window. From the style of the curtains blocking her view, she guessed it was the kitchen. The door was securely locked. She made her way across the back of the house to a set of French doors on the other side, the wooden kind with real panes. No plastic grills over Thermopane for Thomas. At the far side of the house the lot sloped downward, exposing basement windows just above ground level.

One by one, she checked the narrow casement windows hidden by the foundation shrubbery, constantly looking over her shoulder, fully expecting to be stopped by a watchful neighbor. The house was silent, locked tight. She would have to break one of the windows. Her heart was in her throat, and she was shaking so, she could hardly get her shoe off. She had to get hold of herself and concentrate on what she was doing, forget about discovery.

The first time she hit it, the window didn't break, but it made a noise that caused her to cringe. She crouched behind the bushes, waiting, but no one appeared. This time, she hit the glass hard, and it shattered with a loud crack. A jagged shard, caught in the frame, cut her arm. Blood welled up and began to drip. Cursing, she untied her shirttail and held it against the wound. It wasn't too bad, but bleeding all over was a nuisance.

11:10. Forget it. She had to stop finding excuses and get in and out fast. Gwen could be dead within an hour. She knocked the remaining fragments of glass out of the frame and stuck her head through the small opening.

The room below her contained a workbench and what looked like computers and parts in various stages of disassembly. Nothing alarming, no bodies. She gritted her teeth and wriggled headfirst through the window, catching herself with her hands on a small table. Several small parts and printed circuit boards fell to the vinyl-covered floor, and Kate fell with them. She quickly righted herself and froze, listening intently. To her ears, the pounding in her chest sounded loud enough for the neighbors to hear, but the house was silent.

A small red light blinked above one of the computers. He must be testing something, burning it in or whatever they call it, she thought, crossing quickly to the door. Where next? A desk or Thomas's bedroom seemed the most likely places to find some trace of the dead girls.

A brief glance around the lower-level rooms yielded nothing of interest. She cautiously followed the stairs to a door at the top. Pressing her ear to the wood, she listened for a moment. Silence. She eased the door open and slipped into a long hallway. She looked into each doorway until she came to a study with a large mahogany desk facing the door. Crossing to the other side of the desk, she glanced at her watch.

11:17. Her pulse rate must be over two hundred by now, she thought, pulling out drawers and rifling through papers, pens, bank statements, and other typical home office items—nothing that would help her. She didn't bother with neatness or trying to hide her frantic search. She straightened, looking around the room. A computer sat on a small desk against the wall, but she couldn't imagine how it would help her. She hadn't touched one since she left her job as a marketing account rep with J. B. A small red light winked at her from a corner of the monitor. He must have left it on, but she didn't have time to fool with it and had no idea what to look for anyway. She didn't see anything else in the room that looked likely, and she was running out of time.

His bedroom. Surely something would show up there. If not, what would she do? Running up the stairs, she tried to think of places Gwen might go for lunch. Could she have her paged at every good restaurant in town? They could even be meeting at Gwen's. She ought to call Venice again. Maybe Gwen had gotten her message and called. *What a mess.*

She started with his dresser, stopping to look at a studio portrait of a pretty blonde woman. Judging by the hairstyle and makeup, it had been taken years ago. She bet it was his mother. She picked it up, looking for some resemblance to Thomas. A surge of intense longing shot through her, followed immediately by feelings of jealousy and betrayal. She dropped it, certain this woman was the cause of Thomas's distorted relationships. Later—if there was a later, she thought, rooting frantically through papers in his top drawer—she might consider it. Right now, her only interest was to find some evidence of Kelly or Charlene, something tangible that the police could act on.

His jewelry box contained only cuff links, tie pins, the usual paraphernalia of well-dressed men. *11:36.* She turned to the nightstand beside the bed and yanked out the top drawer, dumping the contents on the bed. Nothing. She dumped the second drawer with the same result. *Oh, Gwen. Have a flat tire, run out of gas, anything—just don't go.*

Disheartened, she pulled out the bottom drawer and emptied it onto the rug. Her breath caught. A linen handkerchief fell out, partially unfolding. A woman's bracelet and a small diamond-like stone on a slender gold chain tumbled to the floor. She raked away the stack of magazines and catalogs that had been stored so neatly, sending them in all directions, and snatched up the handkerchief. She felt the lumps before she saw them, and knew instantly that they were Charlene Nelson's silver earrings. Carefully, she uncovered them. The hammered silver curved around turquoise stones, catching the light from the window just as it had in the photograph. They looked expensive. He had probably given them to her. She folded them back in the protective linen and stuffed them into her pocket. She swiped at the other trinkets, sending them under the bed. Maybe he would think she'd taken all of them, wouldn't find them there.

Putting aside her feelings, she turned to the phone and punched in 911. The line went dead before it rang. Thomas! She ran to the window and saw the tail end of a green Jaguar at the corner of the house. As she drew back and raced across the room, a tiny red light winked at her. An alarm! How could she have been so stupid?

Panicked, she flew down the steps and ran for the basement door. She heard him at the back door. Too close! She veered off and ran full tilt for the French doors at the other end of the house. She saw the keyed dead bolt from across the room and knew she would never get out through the door. Grabbing a brass lamp, she swung it with all her might at the nearest window, smashing the framed panes. She drew back and swung again, making an opening she could get through.

Thomas's heavy footsteps pounded down the hallway and into the den. She dived through the hole, scraping her arms over the broken glass and splintered wood, and rolled to her feet on the terrace.

Without a backward glance, she fled. Rounding the corner of the hedge near the front of his lot, she heard the door bang. The seconds it had taken him to unlock the dead bolt had given her enough of a start, and she wasn't going to let him catch her now. She could hear him running across the lawn behind her. Kate flew across the ground, angled sharply to the right, and ran behind the neighbor's house, cutting across lots, dodging behind any cover she could find.

Dogs began barking in several of the houses. A fat cocker spaniel burst out of a dog door and chased her across his territory but stopped abruptly at the edge of his yard. Thank goodness for trained animals. When the dog trotted back toward the house, she realized no one was behind her and slowed, panting hard. Her heart thudded against her chest.

Taking advantage of any cover she could, Kate worked her way toward her car. She hoped Thomas hadn't seen it. He wouldn't necessarily know it had been her, but she was sure he would guess. She hadn't been subtle about her search. He hadn't been subtle about wanting to kill her, either, she thought, picturing her slashed bed. She reached the bare landscape of the homes still under construction and looked carefully around before sprinting across the scrap-littered yard like a broken-field runner. The hot black car felt wonderful to her, safe.

Kate was still shaking when she pulled up at the studio. "James Earl!"

The gray head popped out of his doorway immediately.

"Lock the door behind me. Don't let anyone in except John or the police."

He started for the door. "Mr. Gerrard's been here looking for you. He's gone to Miz Ashburton's now. I locked your studio."

"Bless you, James Earl," she said, giving him a quick kiss. Her heart was still racing, and she was shaking from the surge of adrenaline as she punched the elevator button.

She had to get those photographs and call Detective Burnett. When he saw the prints and the earrings, still tucked into her pocket, he would have to act.

Surely Thomas wouldn't go right to Gwen. If nothing else, he would want to secure his house again, she reasoned. She didn't think he would call the police. He had no reason to be suspicious of Gwen, so maybe he would forget the lunch date or cancel it.

As soon as she got inside the studio, she slung her purse onto the desk and snatched the phone, dialing Gwen's number. Still no answer. Without waiting for the answering machine, she hung up and dialed Venice's number. Venice answered before the end of the first ring. "Where are you? Are you all right?" she asked without preamble.

"Venice, I've got it. It's—"

"Dammit, Kate!" John's voice cut in. "Where the hell are you?"

"The studio. It's Thomas Andrews," Kate said, dragging the phone into the darkroom once more. "He's going to kill Gwen. Has she called there?" Kate stretched but couldn't hold the phone and reach the photographs hanging on the clothesline. Where were the ones of Thomas? Frustrated, she squinted at the pictures. "Do you have the pictures from the darkroom? I have to have them for the police," she cried.

"Yes, and do not—*do not*—move until I get there, or I'll kill you myself." His voice, harsh with fear, trailed off.

Venice's voice came back. "Kate, it's Thomas Andrews. His mother has—"

"Later, Venice. We've got to find Gwen." She squinted at the picture of Charlene, trying vainly to see the earrings. "Have you heard from her? She was meeting Thomas for lunch."

"No. I'll call some of her favorite restaurants," she said, asking no questions. "Wait for John before you go anywhere, Kate. He's been frantic with worry. And be careful!"

Kate hung up just as the studio door exploded inward. She spun around to see Thomas Andrews lunging at her, his contorted face crimson, hands outstretched.

She threw up her arms and dodged sideways, the memory of those reaching hands rushing back. She avoided the main thrust of his weight, but he knocked her off balance. She grabbed at her bag as she fell. If she could reach her keys. . . .

Thomas, off balance himself, scrambled to his feet, swiped at her with one hand. She twisted away but couldn't get up. The toe of his leather wing tip caught her keys, sending them skittering under the desk, out of reach. He loomed over her, chest heaving, and lifted his right leg, swinging the heavy leather shoe toward her. She rolled away, screaming as his foot connected with her shoulder, paralyzing her right arm.

He was too big, too fast, and she knew she would never get away from him. She had to fight—and pray for a miracle.

Holding the useless arm against her side, she got one foot under her and pushed off, plowing into his legs with all her strength. He buckled but caught himself on the desk. She clambered upright, casting about for a weapon. Her desk held a stapler and a tape dispenser, but Thomas blocked the way. A brass lamp stood at the end of the sofa, too far.

He came at her again. She dodged, but he caught her arm and slammed her into the desk. She kicked and twisted, trying to break his hold, but he held her arm in a vise grip. He drew back his fist, spittle flying from his lips. She ducked and jerked her head away. The blow glanced off her cheek, snapping her head back. Tears blurred her vision.

Thomas's arms suddenly began flailing the air as his feet flew out from under him. Kate backed up, amazed, and saw Venice's little crystal ball shoot out from under his foot. *Thank you, Ramses.* Thomas's head smacked the floor, causing him to blink and shake his head.

Panting heavily, she watched him. She knew she could never get away before he recovered. She had to disable him. She leapt, landing with both knees on his midriff. The air whooshed from his lungs, leaving him gasping helplessly.

The lamp! She rolled off him, pulled herself up on the coffee table, and dived for the lamp. She reached it just as his hand closed around her ankle. He released her just as quickly. Grabbing the lamp, she swung around to see John yank Thomas upright, smashing his fist into the snarling face.

They grappled, rolling across the floor. Suddenly Thomas was on top. She lifted the lamp as John twisted out from under the pounding fist. They moved so fast, she was afraid to use it. Both men staggered to their feet. Kate backed against the wall. John pivoted on one foot and kicked, catching Thomas's side.

Thomas faltered, giving Kate an opening. She swung the lamp with all her might, catching the top of his head. He doubled over, and John brought his knee up hard into the man's face. Thomas went down, clutching his bleeding nose, rolling across the floor in agony.

"Well done, Gerrard," Lynne Waite's cool voice said.

Kate and John whirled toward the door, where Detectives Waite and Burnett stood, guns in hand. A siren screamed in the distance.

John, still panting, grabbed Kate. "How did you know?" he asked Waite.

"The maintenance man managed a 911 call. Dill and Wolynski recognized the address and responded. They called us." Waite stepped farther into the room.

Officer Dill, who was standing in the hall just behind Burnett, nodded.

"Wolynski's downstairs," Burnett said. "He's waiting for the ambulance."

Fear for the old man slammed into Kate. "Ambulance? Is James Earl hurt?" She pushed past John toward the door.

Waite held out her hand to stop Kate. "He's woozy but coherent. Mr. Andrews here clobbered him with a rock when he opened the door, but he crawled to his phone and called for help."

"The paramedics can check out this one, too," Burnett said, crossing to Thomas, who had struggled to a sitting position. Blood dripped from his nose.

Looking at John, Burnett dipped his head in Thomas's direction. "Golden Gloves?"

"South Philly."

"Ah." The detective nodded knowingly.

"You?"

"Newark."

"Um." John nodded.

Mystified, Kate stared at the two men. She didn't know what had gone on, but she got the distinct feeling some sort of bond had been established.

Waite, in exaggerated disgust, muttered, "Men!"

They heard the siren enter the parking lot below and stop. A glimmer of flashing red light shone on the windows. Waite looked out. "Paramedics. They'll take care of him."

Grim-faced, the three police officers moved to where Thomas sat on his heels, holding his head and rocking back and forth. At a signal from Burnett, Dill pulled the quiescent man's arms behind him and slid the handcuffs over his wrists. Burnett said, "I'm arresting you for the attack on James Earl Withers." He explained his rights to Thomas, who mumbled a vague response.

He hadn't had time to meet Gwen. Kate, holding her hand against her throbbing cheek, sagged against John, fighting back tears of relief. It was over.

"Are you all right?" Waite asked, noting Kate's swelling cheek and reddened throat. At Kate's nod, she added, "You'd better sit down."

John led her to the sofa and sat beside her, keeping one arm around her, gently stroking her hand with the other.

Waite leaned against the edge of the desk. When they were settled, she said, "Now. Who wants to start?"

The whine of the elevator through the open studio door interrupted them. Venice stepped through before the gates were fully opened, Martin right behind her. "Oh, Kate," she cried. "Are you all right? I can't find Gwen, and I know something's wrong with her."

All eyes turned to Thomas Andrews, who stared back with a triumphant smirk on his bloodied, once-elegant face. "The bitch."

Chapter 18

FURY WASHED OVER KATE like a red tide. Before anyone could respond to Thomas's imprecation, she surged upward and rounded the skewed coffee table, reaching for Thomas. "You bastard! What have you done to her?"

Waite stepped quickly in front of Thomas, blocking her. "Hold it, Kate. We'll find her."

John wrapped his arms around her, pinning her against his chest, murmuring, "Cool it, Kate, cool it. Let the cops deal with him."

Burnett already had the phone in his hand. "What's her name and address?"

Kate and Venice answered together. Burnett turned his back and spoke rapidly into the phone. He hung up and said to them, "They're dispatching a car to her house right away." Forestalling the question on Kate's lips, he added, "I told them it's an emergency. They'll break in if they have to."

Waite was leaning over Thomas, who was shaking his head with his lips tightly sealed, like a child refusing to tell a secret. Disgusted, she turned back to Kate and Venice. "Tell us what happened. What does Ms. Gordon have to do with this?"

After a garbled start, Venice, holding Martin's hand, sank into a chair and said, "You tell them, Kate. I'll fill in when I need to."

Starting with her examination of the box from Rita Nelson, Kate told them about the pictures she had enlarged. "Even though it was hard to see, Thomas's face was in the picture. He looked so intense, I just knew it was him. I found him in some other shots, too."

John pointed to some eight-by-tens scattered near the door. "There. I dropped them when I came in."

Burnett stepped around Thomas and went to pick them up. While he was gathering the ones from the floor, Detective Waite brought out the ones from the darkroom. "Okay. Who's who?"

"The blonde is Gwen Gordon." Kate indicated the picture in Waite's hand and then pointed out Thomas in the group shots.

"She's been dating Thomas recently, but at lunch today, she was going to tell him she didn't want to see him anymore."

Kate turned toward Thomas. "When I saw his face in Charlene's pictures and remembered that, I understood what happened to the others." She shuddered and leaned into John's warmth. "Everyone agreed that the killer was losing control, and I was certain Gwen would be next."

Everyone there except Thomas looked at his or her watch. John said, "It's not quite one. Maybe he hasn't seen her."

Thomas gave a small snort and smiled mockingly at Kate. She dropped to her knees beside him, pleading. "Please, Thomas. Tell me if you've seen her. Where is she?"

He looked at her for a second and then spat in her face. Shocked, she jerked back. Before anyone else could move, John's fist smashed into the smug face. Thomas's head snapped and he toppled awkwardly onto his back, his cuffed hands beneath him.

"Okay, Gerrard, that's enough," Burnett said mildly, pulling John back and reaching for Thomas's supine figure. The detective yanked him into a sitting position and gave his swollen, bloody face a casual survey. "Mind your manners, Andrews," he said, dismissing the injuries. To Waite he said, "The paramedics can clean him up before they go, if the guy downstairs is okay."

As Waite relayed the message to Wolynski, John disappeared into the darkroom.

Slowly, with shaking hands, Kate untied the knot in her shirt and began wiping her face with one wrinkled tail. The other side was still bloody from her encounter with the broken glass. She concentrated fiercely on keeping her stomach contents in place. What had that supercilious bastard done to Gwen? She looked at Thomas, who was still reeling, and thought longingly of the Louisville Slugger she had seen in John's closet.

John returned and thrust a handful of wet paper towels into her hand. Keeping one, he knelt in front of her and carefully wiped her face, tucking her hair behind her ears.

Fighting back the nausea that rose in her stomach, she managed a weak smile. "Thank you."

"Are we ready to go on?" Waite asked, not unpleasantly.

"Yes. Sorry," Kate replied. "As I said, after I printed the pictures, I knew it was Thomas, and I was so afraid for Gwen." She wiped away a tear threatening to spill over. "I left a message on her answering machine, and then I called John and Venice. I couldn't find anyone, and it was getting late. I called Detective Burnett, but the pictures weren't enough for him to act on, and I knew I'd never find Gwen by myself.

"So," she continued, taking a deep breath, "I went to Thomas's house, looking for something to tie him to Kelly or Charlene. I knew it was stupid, but I thought he was at work."

Detective Waite winced and shook her head. "Where were you, Gerrard? I thought you were keeping an eye on her."

"After getting my ass chewed for refusing an assignment, I was running all over town trying to find her." He turned to Kate. "Venice told me she'd found something, so I went to check. You didn't answer, so I called James Earl. He told me you were in the studio and that no one else had come in."

Venice picked up the story. "John had given us a list of the property owners at Lake Jocassee, to see if we recognized anyone. I did—Lyle Border."

"Who's Lyle Border?" Burnett asked.

"Thomas's mother, Margery, married him about two years ago. Thomas and Margery were always very close, so I assume he would be quite familiar with the place."

Venice seemed smaller today, sitting quietly in the big chair with Martin resting on the arm beside her. That blow to the head must have taken its toll, Kate thought.

"You ladies can get a lot out of not much." Burnett shook his head and looked at Waite. "So far, except for the attack on Withers downstairs, we've got squat."

"We have more than that." Martin spoke up for the first time. "I checked with the university and found that Thomas had taken a class with Kelly Landrum last spring."

"And," Kate added, "I found the number where he works scribbled on the back of a business card in Charlene's things." She nervously fingered the earrings in her pocket. "I have something else, too."

They all turned to her. John squeezed her hand. "Go on. Tell us."

She carefully pulled the white handkerchief from her pocket and held it out to Detective Waite. "I haven't touched them. They're the earrings Charlene is wearing in the picture."

Without warning, Thomas roared and sprang from the floor, lunging at Kate, leading with his shoulder. John and Burnett intercepted him, ramming him simultaneously, and all three men went down in a tangle of limbs and expletives. Dill would have been in the fray if he could have gotten close enough. They were still sorting themselves out when the phone rang.

Waite answered. She listened for a minute and then said, "Thanks. We'll be right there." She turned slowly back to the others. "They found Ms. Gordon. She's alive, but they've taken her to Memorial Hospital."

Kate made a small choked sound, and Venice cried out, sinking back into the chair.

"Kate, Venice, is there any family we should notify?" Waite was suddenly all business, not giving either of them time to fall apart. "Give me the earrings. We aren't finished with this."

"There's only her father," Kate said. "No other family."

Waite took the handkerchief and wrote down the name Kate gave her. She frowned.

Before the detective could ask, Kate said, "Her father is Millard Gordon, the *fourth*. It was her grandfather—the *third*—who was the governor." Pictures of Gwen in various states of injury ran through her mind.

"*Those* Gordons," Waite said. "Dill, you and Wolynski get this guy cleaned up and then take him downtown. Don't let anything happen to him. Be sure you do it by the book."

"How bad is Gwen?" Kate asked from the floor, where she was fishing her keys out from under the desk. She had to get to the hospital.

The detective didn't answer.

John took Kate's arm, hauling her to her feet, and plucked the keys from her hand. "I'll drive."

Waite looked at Venice, who clung, white-faced, to Martin's arm. "Are you going to be all right?"

"Yes," she said, straightening and drawing her dignity around her like a cloak. "How badly is she hurt?"

"I won't lie to you. She's been beaten and strangled. She was unconscious when they found her." She pressed Kate's hand, holding the prints in her other hand. "I don't know how bad it is," she said, glancing at the beautiful face in the photograph.

Burnett was waiting for her at the door. Wolynski came up with the elevator and spoke briefly to the two detectives, who left at once. Kate stopped long enough to ask Wolynski about James Earl.

"He's okay. The medics put a bandage on his head and let him go home." Wolynski looked over her shoulder as he spoke, nodding to Dill. "They're waiting for us to bring this guy down."

John handed him Kate's key. "Lock up when you leave, would you? You can give the key to Venice."

"I'll bring it with me to the hospital, Kate," Venice said in a quavery voice.

"No, you won't." Martin took her arm and led her back to the chair. "You're going home to lie down first. There's nothing you can do right now, and Kate will call us. Sit down till the elevator's back. Kate, we'll get the key to you later."

Kate ran back and gave Venice a quick kiss. She had never really thought of the woman as old, but right now she looked gray and frail.

Venice's hands trembled as she patted Kate's face. "Give her my love, Kate," she said.

John and Kate took the steps, leaving Martin and Venice with the two policemen and Thomas Andrews in Kate's studio.

At the hospital, they were shown to a waiting room. Waite and Burnett were already there, talking to a man in green scrubs. Their expressions were grave. Burnett's hands were on his hips, and he was staring at the floor. Waite was biting her lip, focused on the doctor.

Oh, no, Kate thought. *Gwen.* She couldn't even think the question.

Kate ran to them and gripped the man's arm. His nametag identified him as Dr. Robbins. "How is she? Can I see her?" *What if they won't let me in?* "I'm her sister."

Burnett and Waite, with equally skeptical expressions, looked down at the small redheaded woman shoving her way into the tight group.

"You missed your calling, McGuire. You should have been a reporter," Burnett said, but he turned back to the doctor and surprised Kate by saying, "Yeah, she's the sister."

The doctor snagged a passing nurse. "This is Ms. Gordon's sister. Will you take her back?"

"Sure." The woman smiled at Kate. "Come with me. Ms. Gordon is asleep and sedated."

"Sedated? Does that mean there were no head injuries?"

"No concussion, two cracked ribs. She looks pretty bad, but the injuries are mostly superficial." The nurse looked closely at Kate. "You don't look all that good either. Your cheek is swollen and beginning to bruise, and your neck too. What have you two been doing?"

"Ran into the same door." *Cracked ribs?* Kate envisioned that heavy shoe swinging toward her. Her arm, although no longer numb, still tingled and throbbed. She hesitated when they reached the door to Gwen's room. "Will there be any permanent damage? Can you tell yet?"

"Dr. Robbins doesn't think so. Nothing was broken and the cuts should heal cleanly. It will take a while for all the marks to fade completely, but they should."

The two detectives turned the corner of the hall.

Kate pushed the door open and crossed the few feet to the figure lying in the bed. Waite stopped just inside the door and nodded to Kate. Burnett stayed out of sight.

Kate choked back a gasp and swallowed to dispel the sudden onrush of tears when she saw the once-beautiful face. She leaned over to kiss Gwen's forehead, the only visible spot that didn't look painful. Gwen never stirred.

Detective Waite stepped up to the bed beside Kate and whispered, "Gwen?"

There was no response. Kate was unable to hold back her tears. She and Waite tiptoed from the silent room.

Detective Burnett stood outside with John, who was leaning against the wall. Waite shook her head at Burnett, gesturing toward the hospital bed. "Nothing."

The nurse looked John over and then back at Kate. "Same door?"

"And they're the lucky ones." Waite looked down at her feet. Without raising her head, she said. "Jamal, you ought to see her. She's asleep. Stick your head in."

Burnett looked in. "Holy shit!" he muttered, backing out of the room. He turned to the nurse. "I hate to do it, but we need photographs. Could we do it without disturbing her? I don't want her to wake up to find a strange man snapping pictures."

"She's had a sedative, but a flash might waken her," the nurse said. "Let me call Dr. Robbins."

It was hard for Kate to remember they still had to have a trial to convict Thomas. She wanted to hang him now. "If it has to be done, could I do it? At least I wouldn't frighten her."

"Why not?" Waite looked at Burnett and shrugged. "I could tell her what we need."

"Fine," he said, taking a pager from his pocket. He glanced at the number and followed the nurse down the hall to the station.

They all watched him make a call, frown, and turn his back to them. He continued talking, gesturing angrily with one hand. The faces behind the station's countertop turned toward him.

"Uh-oh," Waite said. "Whatever it is, it isn't good."

Burnett strode down the hall toward them. "Trouble. Andrews has a lawyer, and his stepdaddy is down there already. They're screaming about abuse and false arrest and anything else they can think of. The only charge so far is assault, and they want him out now."

Waite spoke to the nurse. "Keep trying to find the doctor. We've got to talk to Gwen and try to get a statement from her."

"Can't I press charges?" Kate asked, rubbing her cheek.

"You aren't in a good position right now. I don't know how you got those earrings—and I don't want to know," Waite said, gesturing Kate to silence. "Everything we've got is strictly circumstantial right now, and he may be out on bail before we can get anything else."

"But he's killed two people and tried to kill a third!" Kate's voice rose an entire octave. "How can he get out?"

"We can't prove any of it at the moment. And you had better pray his fingerprints are on those earrings. Otherwise, it's your word against his. Did you see anything else?" Burnett asked, glowering at everyone who passed. "Where's that doctor? We've got to talk to Gordon."

John ran to the nurse's station, spoke to Gwen's nurse, and came back. "Dr. Robbins is on his way."

Kate forced herself to concentrate on Thomas's bedroom. The panic she had felt when she realized he was there overrode anything else for a minute. Then she remembered. "There was some other jewelry in the same drawer."

"Drawer?" Waite repeated. "I know you didn't do anything as stupid—or illegal—as going inside. Is that what you *imagined*, Kate? Tell me you saw all this in a vision," she said. "What jewelry?"

"I *saw*," Kate said carefully, "a gold chain with a little diamond or something that looked like one. My vision also included a silver bracelet made of heavy, twisted links. You might look under the bed."

Burnett's face lit up. "I'll try to get a search warrant."

"You might want to include his computer in it," Kate said.

He gave her a suspicious look but didn't comment.

"Ummm. Just because Thomas was a computer science major." She smiled sweetly, wishing she could duplicate Venice's "innocent" face.

"I'll do my best. We've got to get it before he's released. You stay here," Burnett told his partner. "She would probably rather talk to a woman—if she remembers." The last words were called over his shoulder as he took off down the hall, almost running into the doctor.

Waite quickly explained the situation, and the solemn young man agreed to waken Gwen. He told Waite he had been on the phone. "We just heard from her father's office. He's out of town and can't get here before morning."

"Damn!" Waite ran her fingers through her hair and scowled. "We could use some heavy hitters on our side."

"She's pretty traumatized—couldn't remember anything when they first brought her in—and this will be hard on her. Remember the injury to her throat. Speaking will be very painful. Keep it to an absolute minimum." Dr. Robbins turned to Kate. "As the only family member, you might want to try waking her."

Waite said nothing. Kate had almost forgotten her claim of being Gwen's sister. "Of course. I won't leave her."

John followed them into the room but stood back against the wall. Gwen's face was turned away, and she did nothing to acknowledge the presence of the people around her.

"Gwen?" Kate called softly, afraid to touch the battered figure.

Gwen blinked and slowly turned to face her. "Hewoh, Kate," she whispered, her raspy words further distorted by her protruding lips.

Kate wanted to scream, cry, kill Thomas Andrews. Instead she smiled and sat down in the bedside chair, placing her hand gently over Gwen's. "You're safe now."

Gwen mumbled something Kate couldn't understand.

Detective Waite spoke behind Kate. "Gwen, I'm Detective Lynne Waite. Can you just tell me who did this? I need to hear it from you."

As he often did, John listened quietly, allowing people to forget his presence, but Kate could tell by the tight, closed look on his face that he was seething inside.

A tear rolled from the corner of Gwen's eye. She squinted through swollen lids at the detective, obviously making an effort to enunciate. "I can't remember."

A collective gasp punctuated the stillness of the room. "You can't remember?" Kate asked. Waite's hand pressed her shoulder, a warning. Kate understood; she couldn't put words in Gwen's mouth. "Gwen, it's important or we wouldn't ask. Please try to at least give the detective a name."

Gwen coughed slightly and clutched her throat. Tears ran from the corners of her eyes. "Tried. Can't," she whispered.

Waite cleared her throat. Kate was sure she was trying to swallow a lump, as she herself was. The detective continued, "I'm sure it's small comfort right now, but Dr. Robbins thinks you'll heal with no lasting scars." She waited a minute, giving Gwen time to recover.

"Can you tell me the last thing you remember?" she asked.

"Tea, this morning. Then here."

They all leaned forward, straining to hear the hoarse voice. Gwen whispered, "My diary. Desk by phone. Maybe something there."

"She keeps an appointment diary in the kitchen," Kate explained. "Maybe she would have written something there." She plucked a Kleenex from the bedside stand and wiped Gwen's tears. "Hang in there, honey. By the way, Venice sends her love."

The slits that passed for Gwen's eyes closed, and they could see her body relax. She had fallen asleep again.

Waite left the room, motioning them all to follow her. Back in the hallway, she said, "I'm going to have a policewoman sit in the room with her in case she remembers. Also. . . ." She paused, ensuring their attention. "She's the only one who can send Thomas Andrews to jail right now. And I'm sure he knows it."

"He might try to come here for her?" Kate knew it but didn't want to believe it. John's firm hands gripped her shoulders.

"Yes, almost certainly. Kate, I don't know what he thinks of you at this point—you're probably high on the list but not top priority. I'm keeping someone with Venice, too, just in case. Are you staying here with Gwen?"

"Yes. I'd like to pick up some clothes and come right back."

"Thomas won't be out just yet. Go right now, and you should be all right. John, don't let her out of your sight. Then come back and stay here with the officer. I'll have someone here within the hour." She said to the doctor, "Keep an eye on her and warn your staff. We think this man's a killer. Don't take any chances. Is there a private phone I can use?"

Kate slipped back into Gwen's room to kiss her and whisper to the sleeping woman. "I'll only be gone for a few minutes to get some clothes. I won't leave you."

Kate and John hurried from the hospital to her house, where she grabbed the first clothes she came to. John drove through a fried chicken place and then on to his house. "You eat while I get into something clean. I'll bring your bag down," he said, thrusting the chicken box at her.

"Right. This stuff grows on you. Literally." She patted her hips as he ran up the stairs. Kate quickly spread the box, exposing the chicken and biscuits, and opened the potato and slaw containers. John was back by the time she poured them each a glass of tea. "My throat's so dry I can hardly talk."

"It's probably sore, too." He held her head between his hands and tilted it back, tracing the line of her throat with gentle kisses. Tears seeped beneath her lashes. He wiped them away with his thumbs and kissed her eyelids.

"Poor Gwen. It hurts me to look at her." Kate raised her hands to catch his wrists and felt the stiffness in her right shoulder, reminding her of John's role. "You've got some bruises yourself. You did good for a reporter."

"I've had worse from my sisters." He laughed and tweaked her hair. "Let's eat. I know you want to get back to the hospital."

"Surely they won't let Thomas out. They *know* he killed Charlene and Kelly and tried to kill Gwen."

"He'll probably be out in another hour. Knowing and proving are a long way apart. A judge will want some very strong evidence, especially if he's got a good lawyer." He bit into a chicken breast.

"It doesn't seem right. At least Gwen will be safe for now, but what if she doesn't ever remember? How long can the police protect her?" Kate stirred her fork around in the slaw. Every time she thought of Gwen, she wanted to cry. Or kill Thomas Andrews.

"Eat something. Given a little time and knowing where to look, the police will dig up the evidence. Speaking of evidence. . . ." He paused, searching Kate's bruised face and haunted eyes. "We'll talk about your adventures later."

"I had to do it. And it wasn't soon enough. If only I'd looked at those pictures sooner—"

"Don't start beating on yourself. If it weren't for you, they still wouldn't know it was Thomas."

She took a few bites and drank the tea. "Are you ready?" she asked. "You can eat the rest in the car. I'll drive." She put her glass in the sink and turned on the water. "And I need to call Venice."

"Leave it." He stuffed the containers into the box and stood. "Let's go. You can call Venice from the hospital, if she's not there by now."

They were at the door when the phone rang.

Waite's angry voice crackled in John's ear. "Andrews was just released."

Chapter 19

IN SPITE OF HIS UNFINISHED DINNER, John drove. He glanced at Kate. Her head rested against the seat back and her eyes were closed. In the glow of a traffic light, he could make out the faint shadow on her left cheek, Thomas's handiwork. Her collar hid the marks on her neck. His stomach tightened, thinking about it. He knew she had gotten into Thomas's house to get those earrings. Later, when things settled down, he would find out what happened, how she did it. If anything had happened to her. . . . The thought was like a kick in the gut.

Kate opened her eyes and sat up as soon as they turned into the hospital parking lot. She opened the door, grabbed her bulging bag and the chicken box, and slid from the car. She was striding across the concrete before John had fished his briefcase from the backseat. He hurriedly locked the car and ran, catching her at the entrance.

The lobby was crowded with people, some carrying flowers, some herding children, a few with blotchy faces and swollen eyes. Prime visiting hours. Kate and John waited impatiently at the bank of elevators for their turn. They squeezed onto the third one. Elevators were not her favorite place. Kate wondered what the capacity of it was. She figured there were at least a dozen people crammed into it, and given a conservative average of a hundred and fifty pounds each, that came close to a ton.

The elevator stopped at every floor, disgorging a few people at each, causing the others to shuffle their positions. Why was it the people in the back always wanted off first? Kate and John got off on four. She was sure the stairs, if she could have found them, would have been faster.

After taking a second to get her bearings, she headed for Gwen's room, John beside her. "How's Gwen?" she asked Detective Waite, who was standing in the doorway talking to a young woman in a police uniform. "Is she awake?"

"She's still asleep," Waite said. "This is Officer Bowan. She'll stay out here in the hall as long as you're going to be in the room with Gwen and promise to call her immediately if Gwen wakens."

Bowan held out her hand. "Please call me Meg. Detective Waite showed me the suspect's face in these photographs and described him. I think I would recognize him."

Kate introduced herself and John, smiling at the earnest young woman. "Believe me, I'd know him, too," she said, touching her throat.

"By the way," the detective told Kate, "we picked up Aaron Youngblood, alias Brother Ezekiel, the prophet. He says God sent him after you. Apparently God uses a ballpoint pen and writes in a neat hand—he had a piece of paper in his pocket with your address and a rough map. I suspect 'God' will turn out to be Andrews. Youngblood may eventually identify him, but no jury would put stock in anything the man says. He should probably be committed." She glanced in the door of Gwen's room. "I think we'd better get on with what we have."

Waite told Kate which pictures she wanted and consulted the nurse, who was listening from the doorway of Gwen's room.

"I think she'll sleep through it," she said and moved back to stand beside her patient.

Kate insisted on waking her first. "I won't have her waking up to a flash in her eyes. It would terrify her, and she doesn't need anything else."

The two women entered the darkened room, where the nurse waited beside Gwen. John and Officer Bowan stayed in the hall.

Kate, brushing the pale gold hair off the battered face on the pillow, said softly, "Gwen? It's Kate. I have to take some pictures for the police. Can you hear me?"

Gwen's eyes opened a fraction of an inch. "Do what you have to." Her raspy voice was barely audible. She made a little whimpering sound and went back to sleep.

Kate, unable to answer around the lump in her throat, patted Gwen's hand. She took a second to wipe a tear from her eye and remind herself that Gwen would heal, that her injuries weren't as bad as they looked.

Under Waite's direction, Kate took several shots. Then Waite had the nurse pull the sheet down. She lifted the cotton hospital gown, exposing the tightly taped ribs. Muted purple bruises leaked onto the skin around the white bandage. Kate snapped two more shots.

When they left the room, she turned to the detective. "What will happen if Gwen never remembers?"

"Jamal's at her condo with the crime-scene crew now. We'll have to find some physical evidence or maybe a witness who saw

Andrews there. With that much damage to her, he almost certainly left something. From what you've told us, he didn't know why she wanted to see him, so he wouldn't have gone prepared to hide anything, such as taking gloves or wearing anything in particular."

Kate flushed, thinking of the gloves she had taken to Thomas's house.

Waite closed her eyes and shook her head. "Just don't tell me anything I don't ask you about." She resumed her review of the steps being taken to tie Thomas to the attack on Gwen. "We have the clothes he was wearing at your studio, to see if we can match any of the stains with Gwen's blood."

After a few minutes of quiet conversation with Meg Bowan, Waite left, taking Kate's enlargements of Thomas and the roll of film she'd shot of Gwen. She stopped briefly at the nurse's station and showed them the pictures.

An orderly brought out a vinyl-covered chair for the policewoman and placed it beside the door of Gwen's room.

Kate settled in the chair beside Gwen's bed, and John moved the room's second chair next to her. She took a book from her bag while John extracted a gray laptop computer from his briefcase. He fiddled with a power cord and moved the chairs to allow the cord to relax. When he was satisfied with the arrangement, he returned to the briefcase and retrieved a black diskette.

Kate watched all the maneuvering with interest. After he got settled she said, "We didn't call Venice."

John flashed her a look from the corner of his eye. "Does *we* need a quarter?" he asked, not budging.

Muffling a laugh, she put her book down and crawled over John, careful not to disturb the computer's power cord or the notes he had clamped under his elbow on the arm of the chair. "Is that your friend's computer?"

"No, it's mine. I bought it off him this morning. He wanted a better one anyway. I think it's time I acknowledged the technological age. Next I'm getting a charger for the cell phone that will work in the car—so I can keep up with you."

She kissed him and left to find the phone and call Venice. She didn't want to discuss Gwen's injuries where Gwen might wake up and hear.

After reporting to Venice and assuring her that she didn't need to come be with Gwen, Kate got coffee from the nurses and returned to the room. She nodded to the policewoman, whom the nurses were keeping supplied with drinks and magazines.

A male nurse, identified as an RN by his name tag, hung over Gwen's bed, thermometer in hand. Kate wondered idly if *male nurse* was a sexist term, like *woman doctor* or *female police officer*. No one ever said *female nurse* or *male doctor*.

"Is she all right?" she asked, shoving both cups at John. She could hardly imagine how Gwen must feel; from the little contact she herself had had with Thomas, she was sore and stiff and her throat hurt.

"She has a little fever, nothing unexpected. We'll be checking her off and on all night. I'm going to bring in an IV and a monitor," he explained. "Dr. Robbins left instructions for liquids and something to help her relax."

Kate crawled back to her chair on the far side of the bed. She wriggled and squirmed, adjusted the thin blanket behind her, added a pillow, and finally settled in. She yawned behind her hand and found her place in the book.

"Do you want this coffee?" John asked. "Or did you bring them both for me?"

Kate turned to him, surprised. He sat with the computer balanced on his knees and a cup in each hand. She took the coffee. "I forgot. I think I'm a little tired."

"Why don't you open out your chair and try to sleep?"

"I'll read a while first." She yawned again, fishing a small aspirin container from her bag. She shook four into her hand, tossed them into her mouth, and washed them down with the coffee.

John watched as she opened the book, certain she wouldn't last long. "Let me fix your chair. Then I won't have to wake you up when you pass out."

"But I might not hear Gwen." She couldn't stop yawning.

"Gwen is being cared for. Unless the nurses make her, she probably won't wake up," he said and leaned down to place the computer and his coffee on the floor. The vinyl-covered recliner was no substitute for a bed, but he opened it for Kate and plumped the pillow. Getting up tomorrow would be tough, but he knew she wouldn't leave Gwen. He sat back in his chair and picked up the computer, watching her nod. He didn't have long to wait.

The book slid from Kate's fingers; she was asleep before she had turned the first page. John dropped the book into her bag and drew the blue cotton hospital blanket over her. He smoothed the hair off her face and kissed her gently, anger welling inside him as he studied the bruised cheek and neck, the bluish crescents under her eyes. How long had he known her? Two, three weeks? It didn't seem possible that it had been such a short time.

She made a whiffling sound and turned away from the light. John drained the coffee, then saved the two lines he had managed to write, gathered his notes, and unplugged the computer. He carried the chair into the bathroom, grateful for the handicapped accommodations that required the increased floor space. After checking Kate and Gwen once more, he turned off the room light, leaving only the small light on the headboard, and set up shop in the bathroom. The article should have been in this afternoon.

An orderly came in to set up the IV for Gwen, followed by the nurse who had called for it. John concentrated on the story, sifting through his notes, and worked steadily, occasionally interrupted by the squeaking of rubber-soled shoes on the tiled floor as the nurses and orderlies came in to check Gwen. The policewoman stuck her head in once or twice. Finally, groggy himself, he shut down the computer, turned off the light, and dozed where he was, afraid moving the chair back into the room would disturb Kate.

At the soft tap of shoes, John roused briefly and shifted uncomfortably in the chair. A nurse passed the door, head down, studying the chart in his hand. John closed his eyes and drifted off.

The soft rustling sounds of the nurse roused Kate briefly. Through half-closed eyes she saw a tall, white-haired nurse with a hypodermic needle in one hand and the tube to Gwen's IV in the other. In the dim light, struggling for coherence, she watched as the gloved hands inserted the needle into the tube. A bubble appeared in the liquid, sliding slowly downward.

A strange flutter rippled through her. Something didn't register. Weren't air bubbles supposed to be bad? Maybe even fatal? She blinked, clearing her vision, and stared at the nurse. The flash of understanding galvanized her.

Kate launched herself across Gwen's body, grabbing the tube and screaming, loosing the furies on the quiet hospital floor. Gwen screamed, a terrible rasping sound. Kate yanked the needle from her arm, praying she wouldn't cause anything worse.

The nurse yanked a gun from his pocket and turned to run. John burst from the bathroom, and the policewoman charged through the door.

"Thomas," Gwen whispered.

Thomas grabbed Kate and jerked her off the bed, shielding himself with her body. He held the gun tight against her temple. "Get away. I'll kill her!"

John and Officer Bowan skidded to a stop. Nurses crowded in the door of the room. The one in front saw Thomas and gasped.

Bowan snapped at them, "Get away from here. Call the police and clear the hall. Keep everyone in their rooms."

"Put your gun down, Officer. I mean it, I'll kill her." Thomas crouched behind Kate's small figure, hiding as much of his own body as he could. He spat the cotton wads that had padded his cheeks onto the floor. "Then back away."

Bowan carefully placed her gun on the floor in front of her. "Take it easy. No one's going to do anything." She turned to John. "Do as he says, Gerr—"

Thomas interrupted her. "Kick it under the bed. Now!" His voice cracked with panic.

Kate fought to overcome the paralysis that held her frozen. Thomas's forearm pressed against her throat, holding her upright against his chest. She could barely breathe. From the corner of her eye, she could see Gwen easing herself upward on the bed.

Bowan saw her, too. "Don't anyone do anything stupid. His finger is on the trigger, and he could shoot her accidentally if he's startled."

Kate clung to Thomas's arm, trying to loosen his crushing hold on her windpipe. Her feet barely touched the floor. She could feel the gun's barrel pressed into her temple. Anything she did might make him shoot.

"Out. Everybody out." Thomas took a step forward, shoving Kate ahead of him. "We're leaving."

Bowan backed toward the door, nudging John with her left hand. Scrabbling and shuffling sounds came from the hall, a low babble of voices. Raising her voice, she said, "We're coming out! Clear the hall!"

There was no answer, but John thought he could still hear movement in the hall. *Please don't let anyone try to be a hero.* "Get away from the door!" he cried. "He'll kill her!"

A calm voice answered. "The hall is clear. I'm the head nurse, the only one in sight, just making sure no one gets curious and comes out of his room."

John thought it was Waite, maybe disguising her voice. If so, she had gotten here awfully fast. He watched Thomas carefully, saw no sign that he had recognized her.

Bowan said, her voice raised slightly, "That's an automatic he's holding, probably a Browning nine millimeter. He can do a lot of damage with it. Do as he says, Gerrard."

So it *was* Waite, John thought, and Bowan was giving her a message. He and Bowan backed through the door. In the periphery of his vision, he saw Burnett and Waite flattened against the wall on either side of the door, guns drawn. He kept his eyes on Thomas, not wanting to give away the officers' presence. Waite gestured for John to go into the next room.

Before he could move, Thomas said, "Gerrard! You and the policewoman stand against the wall on the far side, where I can see you." He jammed the gun hard against Kate's head, pushing her to the door. "I'm squeezing the trigger. If anyone makes a move, she's dead."

"If you shoot her, you won't have a hostage," John said, struggling to keep the panic out of his own voice as Thomas appeared in the doorway with Kate.

In an instant, while he was still sheltered in the doorway, Thomas shifted. "Maybe not. But you won't be the one to stop me."

As soon as the pressure left her temple, Kate knew what Thomas was going to do. She hit his gun hand with all her strength just as he pulled the trigger, knocking his hand sideways. At the same time, Waite shoved Kate to the floor, out of the way. John slammed into the wall as Burnett caught Thomas's arm with both hands and twisted. Waite, her gun aimed at his head, reached out with her left hand and wrenched the Browning away from Thomas.

Kate, her heart wedged in her throat, scrambled across the floor to John, who was holding his left arm with his hand. Blood ran through his fingers. She wrapped her trembling arms around his midriff and held him as tightly as she could. "Help him! Someone get out here!"

"I'll be all right, Kate," he said against her hair. "It's really not bad. I'll be lucky to get a war wound I can show off." His head snapped up. "What the—"

Kate spun toward the group on the other side of the hall to see Gwen's battered form weaving in the doorway, holding Bowan's revolver in both hands. Waite kept her attention on Thomas as Burnett gently removed the gun from Gwen's hand. She swayed.

Burnett slipped the gun into his pocket and caught her. "Back to bed, ma'am. It's all over now."

"No," she protested through swollen lips. "Don't shut me out. I need to know what's happening."

Nurses began peeping around the doors of the patients' rooms. Four more officers in blue uniforms rounded the corner and halted in surprise at the crowded hallway. Waite nodded at Officer Bowan. "You do the honors, Officer. Three counts of murder, two of attempted murder."

Bowan whipped out her handcuffs and began reciting his rights.

"Three?" John asked over Kate's head.

"Yes, we finally got the warrant. Found a stolen car in his garage, an old Ford. Someone murdered an old man for it. The Meals-on-Wheels lady found his body a week ago. I suppose he needed something he could get around in without having someone spot that fancy Jaguar. And what was he doing in Gwen's room, Kate?"

From the doorway of Gwen's room, where Burnett had pulled up a chair for her, Gwen said, "I remember what happened now. When

I saw him standing by my bed, it all came back. I almost didn't recognize him with the white hair and fat nose and cheeks."

"I was too sleepy to recognize him at first," Kate said. "The swollen nose helped his disguise. But he injected an air bubble into Gwen's IV. I hope I didn't hurt you, Gwen." She pulled John across to Gwen. She couldn't bear to let go of him, even for a moment, but she needed to hold Gwen, too.

"Fat cheeks?" Burnett asked.

"Yes, he had cotton wads in his mouth," Gwen rasped, running on adrenaline. "He spat them out when Kate jumped across the bed and pulled the IV out of my arm," Alert now, she held tightly to Kate. "It was worth a little pain. You saved my life."

Waite reached up and touched Thomas's stiff, whitened hair, sniffed her fingers. "Shoe polish. And that's makeup covering the bruises on his face."

"How did you get here so quickly?" John asked the detectives, his bloody arm snaking around Kate's shoulders. A nurse tried ineffectively to pry him loose and check the neat furrow the bullet had plowed in his arm.

"We were already on the way. Someone found an orderly in the bushes with a big knot on his head, wearing only his underwear. He had gone out to smoke. I guess it really *was* hazardous to his health." She curled her lip at Thomas. "We were just wrapping up the search at Thomas's house when they notified us. We knew it had to be him."

Just then Venice came bustling around the corner by the nurse's station, a sleepy-eyed Martin and a nurse trailing behind her. "Don't tell me I can't come in here, young lady. My friends are in trouble, and I'm going to be with them."

"But, ma'am," the nurse said helplessly, throwing up her hands.

"Kate," John called as a doctor pulled him aside to examine his arm. "Would you get my computer and notes from the bathroom? I need to get on this right away."

Chapter 20

KATE HUNG UP THE PHONE and turned to Gwen and Venice. "John said Thomas was sentenced to life without parole. His mental state probably saved him from the death penalty."

The three women breathed a collective sigh of relief. They had gathered at Gwen's condominium, expecting John's call. He was at the courthouse covering the sentencing phase of the trial and had promised to let them know as soon as the judge pronounced the sentence. The women had had enough of the courtroom during the earlier part of the trial.

"He said Charlene's father was there. Maybe they can get on with their lives now," Kate said. "Isn't it wonderful that Rita got a scholarship to business school? It's strange that it happened out of the blue like that."

"Yes, isn't it." Venice tossed a quick, knowing look at Gwen. "Sometimes I think there really are guardian angels."

"I'm just glad it's over," Gwen said, changing the subject. "But I feel so sorry for Thomas's mother. She'll carry the guilt forever."

"It wasn't her fault. If he had been a more stable person, her marriage wouldn't have seemed such a betrayal to him." Kate took a sip of her coffee and stood, setting the cup on the mantel.

Gwen wandered over to the window and absently rubbed her side. Her ribs had healed, but she still had an occasional twinge.

"At least the trial was quick. I was afraid it would drag on for months." Kate moved restlessly around the room, touching a glass egg, straightening a book.

"There was so much evidence," Venice said. "Gwen's testimony and the scene at the hospital. The information in his computer about elevators. I don't see how there could have been any doubt." She carefully touched a napkin to her lips. "And there was the attack in your studio, Kate."

"Yes. And I never thanked you for the crystal ball, Venice. Ramses was right. It was definitely important—Thomas fell on it." She shuddered at the memory. "It may have saved my life."

"We all had a lot of close calls. If your breaking into Thomas's house hadn't triggered his alarm, I would certainly be dead." Gwen paled, touched her throat. "He was choking me when the buzzer went off in his pocket. It must have been strictly an alarm, because he grabbed it right away. As soon as he looked at it, he panicked and ran."

"Thank goodness he was so paranoid." Venice patted her hair. "Such an elaborate alarm he had rigged up. Ah, well, it's over," she said, dismissing Thomas. "Let's plan my party."

Kate ducked out of the cold December rain and rang Gwen's doorbell. She tilted the tray of hors d'oeuvres in her hand, letting the collected water run off the plastic wrapping. "Here they are," she said when Gwen opened the door. "John made them last night."

"Great. I'll put them on the coffee table." Gwen gave her a quick peck on the cheek and took the tray. "Where's John?"

"On his way from work," she said, collapsing the umbrella and dropping it into the lacquered stand by the door. "He was going to stop for a shower, and then he'll be here." She shrugged out of her coat and hung it in the closet, revealing a sleek green slip of a dress, the one Venice had admired. A glittering row of rhinestones outlined the thin straps and ran across the top.

In the living room, Kate greeted Martin and Venice. "Hi. Ready for the big day?"

"I've been ready for years," Martin said, smiling fondly at Venice. "You look stunning, Kate." He sounded mildly surprised.

"Yes, the transformation is amazing," Venice said. "You should do it more often. Wait until John sees you."

Much to her annoyance, Kate felt herself blushing. "I thought jeans would be inappropriate for your rehearsal party, Venice. Is everything ready for tomorrow?"

"Yes. I could have done it weeks ago, but I wanted to wait until Gwen had recovered. I admire her for going about her business while her face was healing, but I didn't want her to get all the attention at my wedding." She turned to Gwen. "I may have made a mistake, my dear. You're more beautiful than ever now and will still get lots of attention."

"You're sweet to say so, but I'll never have the warm glow you do." Gwen glanced quickly in the mirror.

Her face had healed, but they all knew the wounds inside would take much longer.

Kate had felt Gwen's withdrawal but didn't know how to help her. She had hoped planning this party for Venice and Martin would bring her out. Maybe when John got here they would get a real smile from her.

The bell rang again. Kate stayed in the living room near the fireplace and let Gwen get the door. She wanted John to come to her, maybe be a little surprised. He had never seen her like this. She had worked hard at her makeup and hair tonight, knew the dress was flattering. She deliberately turned her back to the door, gazing into the fire. Meryl Streep's mysterious, intriguing appearance in *The French Lieutenant's Woman* hovered in the back of her mind.

It had all the effect she had hoped for. John followed Gwen into the room and stopped dead, staring across the room at Kate.

She turned slowly to face him, smiling softly, caught in the golden glow of firelight.

When he could breathe again, he let out a long, low whistle. "Are you the same redheaded witch I know and love?"

Kate's mysterious smile broadened into her usual wide grin. "Yes, I am," she said as John kissed her.

After a moment he turned to Venice. "Now I get to kiss the bride." He gave her a loud, smacking kiss. "Martin, you're a lucky man. I know that's fried chicken I tasted."

"Hmmm. You're right." He patted his stomach and laughed.

They all began talking at once. Gwen disappeared into the kitchen. Kate was about to go after her when she heard a cork pop and stopped.

Gwen returned with a tray of champagne flutes and a bottle of Dom Perignon. Her smile was nearly as big as Kate's. "Let's have a private toast before everyone else gets here." She raised her glass. "Be happy, my friends."

Kate drank and then lifted her glass again. "To life."

CHECK ELLIS VIDLER'S WEB SITE AT

www.ellisvidler.com

WOULD YOU LIKE TO WRITE A REVIEW
OF A SILVER DAGGER MYSTERY?

VISIT OUR WEB SITE FOR DETAILS

www.silverdaggermysteries.com

ALL SILVER DAGGER MYSTERIES ARE AVAILABLE
IN BOTH TRADE PAPER AND HARDCOVER
AT YOUR LOCAL BOOKSTORE
OR DIRECTLY FROM THE PUBLISHER
P.O. Box 1261 • Johnson City, TN 37605
1-800-992-2691

WE'RE BLOWING THE LID OFF THESE MYSTERIES COMING SOON:

HOME IS WHERE THE MURDER IS by Carolyn Rogers	When injury forces San Antonio police-woman Rachael Grant to return home, she learns the family guest ranch, Tumbleweeds, has been sold. Her inept cousin is accused of killing the new owner, and Rachael finds herself searching for the real murderer as well as the real meaning of home.

Entangling the countryside in a confusing mass of lies and deceit, an insidious governmental conspiracy creeps across South Carolina's Lowcountry like rancorous kudzu, leaving death and a betrayal of justice along its path.	JUSTICE BETRAYED by Daniel Bailey

DEATH OF A DUNWOODY MATRON by Patricia Sprinkle	When Yvonne Delacourt, one of Dunwoody's most beautiful people, is found murdered, part-time sleuth Sheila Travis finds out there are more people who despised Yvonne than there are names on the country club waiting list. But all it takes is one with a reason—and a secret—worth killing for.